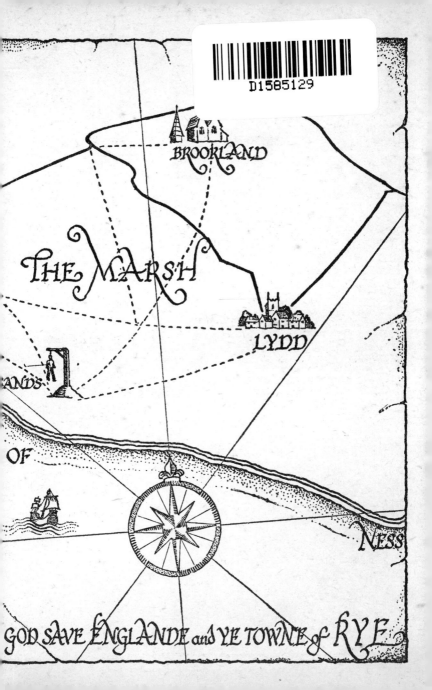

THE GAY DOLPHIN ADVENTURE

THE
GAY DOLPHIN
ADVENTURE

By
MALCOLM SAVILLE

ILLUSTRATED BY
BERTRAM PRANCE

LONDON
GEORGE NEWNES LIMITED
TOWER HOUSE, SOUTHAMPTON STREET
STRAND, W.C.2

MADE AND PRINTED IN GREAT BRITAIN BY
WYMAN & SONS LIMITED, LONDON, READING AND FAKENHAM

FOR
MY WIFE

FOREWORD

IN the western corner of Kent there stretches for some twenty miles in length by three to eight in depth the lonely and mysterious Romney Marsh—land which once was covered by the sea and now is below its level, dotted with sheep and intersected by deep, dark dikes.

On the Kent-Sussex border, at the very edge of the Marsh, the ancient town of Rye clings in a huddle of grey walls and red roofs to a rocky pyramid rising abruptly from the windy levels. You can go to Rye, as Jon and Penny did, to explore for yourself its cobbled streets and narrow winding courts and alleys. You will not find the *Gay Dolphin*, nor Trader's Street, but there is a street from the end of which you can look out over Camber Castle to the sea. And two miles away to the west, on another but very different kind of hill, Rye's forgotten sister port of Winchelsea drowses in the sun and you can go there, too, and perhaps find the old windmill in which Jon hid.

The country in which this story is set is real, but the people are not and have no reference to any living person. Hastings, Rye and Winchelsea are three of the seven Cinque Ports that in the Middle Ages were responsible for the sea defence of England and were the cradle of the British Navy. The other ports are New Romney, Hythe, Dover and Sandwich.

M. S.

CONTENTS

CHAPTER		PAGE
	FOREWORD	6
I.	FRIDAY : JON AND PENNY	9
II.	SATURDAY : MR. GRANDON	37
III.	SATURDAY : nt 8 APRIL 7	53
IV.	SUNDAY : THE MILL	76
V.	MONDAY : BEACH VIEW	100
VI.	TUESDAY : ALLIES	118
VII.	TUESDAY NIGHT : TRADER'S PASSAGE . .	142
VIII.	WEDNESDAY : ROMAN'S ISLE . . .	158
IX.	WEDNESDAY : PENNY AND THE TWINS IN TROUBLE	173
X.	WEDNESDAY : JON AND DAVID TO THE RESCUE	200
XI.	WEDNESDAY : NOAH'S ARK	213
XII.	THURSDAY—15–6–10	238

CHAPTER I

FRIDAY: JON AND PENNY

THE morning sunlight, slanting down through the murky roof and through the smoke and steam of Charing Cross Station, settled in silvery pools round the bookstalls and barriers. Sometimes the scurrying passengers were caught in the beams and picked out, as actors are on the stage by the spot-lights.

Just by the entrance of the main departure platform a particularly broad beam caught and then held two hatless heads—one red and the other yellow. The red-head was a girl of about fifteen with wide-set grey eyes and a tip-tilted, freckled nose. She was wearing a blue blazer over a green jersey and a grey kilted skirt and carrying a shabby raincoat over her arm as she looked up at her taller companion and argued with him.

Her name was Penelope Warrender, but she was always called Penny. Sometimes Jonathan, her cousin, called her "Newpenny" because of the colour of her hair, and now he was grinning down at her in the superior way which always infuriated her.

"What are you going to do, you idiot?" Penny was storming at him. "It's no use standing there grinning when you've left the tickets behind. And you haven't got enough money to buy any more. You know you haven't, Jon. . . . I bet you haven't any. I bet you all I've got, which is only two shillings and twopence. Here we are stranded in this beastly station and the car will be waiting at Hastings for us like your mother said, and she'll be waiting for us at Rye all in vain, and all you can do is to stand there and grin. . . . If you'd got any sense at all you'd go now and ask a policeman or someone to lend you the money."

Her cousin hunched up the knapsack on his back and ran

his fingers through his tousled hair. He was four inches taller than Penny and just sixteen. Never, under any circumstances, could Jon look tidy. Always his wrists seemed longer than his sleeves and his trousers too short. His tie, when he remembered to put it on, was often adrift from his collar and his rather heavy glasses inclined to hide the intelligence of his eyes.

" I did not say I'd left the tickets at home," he explained carefully. " I said that I wouldn't much mind if I had because I could spend a very pleasant hour or so here inspecting these engines. I haven't got many Southerns. . . . Why don't you listen, you silly girl ? "

" You're nothing but a lout," Penny raved. " All I can say is that it must be pretty grim at your school if they're all like you. . . . Where *are* the tickets, anyway ? Give them to me and I'll take proper care of them. . . . Well, just give me mine. I'm entitled to it, aren't I ? I'll get a seat for myself and you can go and talk to the engine-drivers and unscrew the engines or whatever it is you do when you play your little baby railway games. . . ."

But even while she was still talking Jon felt in his pocket, produced two green tickets, heaved up his cousin's suit-case and joined the queue passing through the barrier. Penny gasped with fury and followed him ; but it was just like her to catch him up on the platform, laugh at him cheekily and take a share of the weight of the suit-case.

" We've absolutely got to get a carriage to ourselves, Jon," she said. " We can't start off an adventure like this with anybody else. When we find an empty one I'll pretend to have whooping cough if you like, and you can keep everyone at bay from the window. That generally works, doesn't it ? Or would you rather be the whooper ? I don't care really, but I'm pretty good. I did it last term once on the way to a match. . . . Look ! Here's an empty one. . . . No, it isn't. That's no good. Two kids and their grandmother just come in from the corridor. . . . Come on, Jon ! Do buck up. I can't think why everyone wants to travel to-day . . ." and she chatted on while Jon pursued his leisurely way up the platform. He seemed to take one long stride to each two of Penny's excitable hops and skips, for she had already soon forgotten the suit-case in her eagerness.

Jon was quite used to her breathless, impetuous ways, for although they were cousins they lived together in the holidays. Penny's parents were in India, and she had not seen them for many years, and Mrs. Warrender, her aunt, was almost nearer to her than her own mother. And she had worshipped her uncle, who had been killed in the war.

But clever as Jon was—and exams were no bother to him, for he romped through everything at school—he was not quite clever enough to realize that " little Newpenny," whom he looked upon as a rather amusing kid sister, would have walked through fire for him.

The suit-case was heavy, so he put it down for a moment to rest, while Penny dodged round the refreshment trolley and hurried ahead. Then, rather absentmindedly, he bought two buns, sat on the case, and watched her red head bobbing along by the side of the train. He knew there was no real need for him to hurry. Penny would get what she wanted if it was to be got ! Just for a second, as he sat there eating his bun in all the bustle of the busy station, he had that horrid choky feeling that still came to him when he thought of his father. Come to think of it, *he* had always made a great fuss of Penny. " Red-headed baggage," Captain Warrender used to call her, and his wife always agreed that the description fitted her as well as any other.

Suddenly a yell disturbed his musings :

" Hi, Jon ! Buck up ! I've got one ! " And there she was almost as far as the engine and waving wildly. He got up, wedged the remainder of one bun into his mouth, crammed the other into his pocket, lifted the suit-case and started off up the platform.

There were not many minutes to go now before the train left and the big engine was hissing gently just under the signals. Jon had his eyes fixed on it and did not notice the porter until he had collided with him. He apologized and then looked in astonishment at the woman whose luggage the porter was carrying. She was the sort of person that deserved a second glance if only because of her extraordinary appearance. She was short and very broad and rather inclined to waddle. A bright orange scarf was most unbecomingly draped round her greyish hair, which was cut short like that of a man. As she turned to speak to the porter, Jon, groping again for the suit-case which he had dropped, saw that she wore heavy horn-rimmed glasses, with lenses so thick that it was difficult to see her eyes.

" Come along, my man," she was saying. " Never mind that star-gazing lad. He should look where he's going. You hurry on and get me a corner. . . . And don't drop those bags . . ." and she turned her enormous back on Jon and waddled after the porter.

Jon, still fascinated by the crude check design of the strange woman's costume, was slow to follow until he realized that Penny, hopping first on one leg and then on the other and grimacing horribly, was urging him to greater speed as the porter approached the compartment she was guarding. Jon saw the danger and spurted, but he was still ten yards away when Penny jumped in and slammed the door. The porter reached the compartment, looked in, put down the bags and was just about to open the door when Penny let the window down, put out her head and was seized with an awful fit of coughing. The porter was almost blown backwards by the blast, but he rallied and put his hand to the door again.

Penny, now scarlet in the face, shook her head at him, but before she could speak the large woman arrived, with Jon only just behind her.

" Come along !   Come along ! " she boomed.   " Open the door, man !   Open the door.   This will do as well as anything else, I suppose. . . . What's the matter with you, child ?   Let me in, please."

Penny gasped piteously and fought for breath.

" Oh, Jon, dear. . . . There you are at last. . . . Tell the lady, Jon, . . . I think we ought to tell her. . . ."

" Nah then, missy," said the porter, opening the door, " you go an' corf in the corridor and let me get the lidy's baggage in."

Penny moved reluctantly aside, glaring fiercely at Jon as she did so.   The porter put four suit-cases on the rack, while the woman fumbled in a great black bag and presented him with sixpence.   Then she heaved herself into the carriage and flopped down in the seat opposite Penny.

" And what is it that you ought to tell me, my dear ? " she asked as her bag slid off her lap to the floor.

Penny picked it up for her, and, to Jon's admiration, gazed at the woman with wide, innocent eyes.

"Well," she said, "I've *had* whooping cough, and we thought . . ."

"Oh, we did, did we? I've had it, too, my dear, so you needn't worry. . . . Now, my boy, come in if you're coming, and don't fiddle about there in the doorway."

Jon flushed with annoyance and squeezed past the big woman's knees and dumped his knapsack on the rack in the far corner.

Penny looked at him reproachfully. Was it possible that he was sulking a little? Then he caught her eye and winked, so *that* was all right.

"Are you coming over here, Jon?" she asked hopefully.

"No, thanks," he said tersely. "I shall be busy on this side for a bit, and I want you to stay over there and write down the numbers of any engines you see. Got the pencil I gave you? And the paper?"

Penny nodded rather wistfully. She couldn't see any sense in looking for the numbers of engines and marking them off in the little book which Jon treasured so carefully. But boys sometimes were peculiar, and everybody seemed to agree that Jon was clever, just as everybody said that she was a scatterbrain, so she supposed that both statements were true. And, come to think of it, she had helped Jon with all sorts of crazes—stamps, frogs and newts, and once she had gallantly hidden a horrible fear of white mice for his sake; so this engine-number business was comparatively harmless.

"I wonder if I've got time to get ours," Jon was saying as he leaned across her to the window. "Pity you were in such a hurry, 'cos I was going to have a word with the driver. . . . No! I'll have to check up at the other end now. We're just off!"

"I'll be glad if you'd just get off my feet, young man," said the large woman as the train started, but she did not sound cross, and when Jon apologized she smiled at him.

Penny, who had disliked her just as soon as she had seen her coming up the platform, watched her fiddling about with her bag and her books and her papers and her cigarettes, and thought what fun she and Jon would have had if only they could have been alone.

Then, "Get ready, Penny," Jon called from the other window. "Don't miss any."

Penny sighed. She knew she had lost the pencil which he had given her. She was always losing things. She was that sort of girl, as Mrs. Warrender had often told her. Things disappeared out of her locker and out of her desk at school. Her clothes vanished during the night while she slept. Letters which she put in a safe place to answer were spirited away. Hair-ribbons and hair slides were stolen, and life, if she had permitted it, could easily be one long and desperate hunt for the things which detached themselves from Penny. She remembered Jon giving her a pencil stump and sheet from his notebook in the Underground, but she could not remember what she had done with them. Perhaps she could pretend she saw the numbers and call them out to him ? It couldn't possibly matter whether they were real numbers or not. After all, a train was just something that took you somewhere and an engine was just the thing that pulled the train, and it was interesting to see that on this line there seemed to be a number of trains without engines which must be very boring for Jon.

Penny liked people better than things, and although she had before now cheerfully admitted to Jon that engines sometimes carried drivers and stokers who looked very friendly and jolly in their greasy blue dungarees, lots of other people looked jolly, too, and there seemed no need to write them down in books.

She looked out of the window. The train was gliding swiftly now above the squalid roof-tops of the South London slums, which for a minute were hidden by a green electric train overtaking them. She fumbled again in the pocket of her blazer and looked up to catch the large woman's eye. She was not sure, but she thought the stranger winked at her. It was difficult to be certain, because her glasses were so thick, but just then a big engine hurtled by on her side and Jon called, " Did you get her, Penny ? Schools' class, wasn't she ? "

" Oh, I'm so sorry, Jon, but I didn't quite . . ." she began when the strange woman surprisingly interrupted and said :

" Lancing. Number 904. . . . And here's a pencil, my dear. I always have stacks of pencils "—and she dived into the untidy black bag and produced a handful.

Jon turned from the other window in amazement. " I

say," he said, " thanks awfully. That was jolly quick of you. Are you keen on engines ? "

" Not a bit," was the answer. " But I'm quick to see things," and there was quite a friendly note in her voice as she smiled at them both.

When the train had left the edge of London behind and was roaring through the suburbs she asked Jon to get one of her cases from the rack and then produced some chocolate.

" Share it between you," she said. " I'd rather smoke," and she fumbled in the bag again for a cigarette. After this it was difficult for them not to be friendly when she spoke to them, and Jon was trying to guess what she was and where she was going when she gave herself away by looking suddenly at Penny and saying abruptly :

" I'd like to sketch you, my child. Can you stay still for a few minutes like that ? Look out of the window."

Penny flushed as the woman groped in the bag again and brought out one of the pencils and an old envelope and began to draw with quick, firm strokes.

Jon crossed to her side and saw Penny coming to life on a scrap of paper.

" Why, you're an artist ! " he blurted out in admiration, and the woman laughed.

" I always enjoy being told so," she said, giving the envelope to him. " Perhaps you would like to keep this of your sister ? If you don't want it, I dare say someone else will one day. . . . But is she your sister ? You're not much alike."

Penny reached over and snatched the envelope from her cousin just as he was explaining : " No. We're cousins, but Penny's people are in India, so she lives with us in the hols. . . . What do you think of yourself, Penny ? Funny little thing, aren't you ? "

" Ballinger is my name," the woman said. " Yes, of course you can have it. Send it to your parents and tell them I'd like to paint you one day."

It was just about then that the train ran through Ton-bridge, and Jon was kept busy spotting engines. When he had noted down seven and Penny had found him one and the train had lurched over the points and turned south in the direction of the sea, Miss Ballinger looked up from her paper and said, " Are you off to Hastings for your summer holiday ? Late to start in September, isn't it ? "

Both of them had forgotten their first dislike of her by
now, for although she was certainly very odd to look at and
had rather peculiar manners, she was proving to be both
friendly and interesting, and Penny, in particular, always
responded quickly to people who were interested in her.
So although Jon put his notebook in his pocket and opened
his mouth to answer Penny spoke first.

" We're not really going on a holiday at all, Miss Ballinger.
This is all rather an adventure for us, though I expect Jon
is too grown-up to admit it. You see, we're going to our
new home, and we've never even seen it before. And it's
very thrilling and romantic—it's all rather like a story, I
think—going to a place that you've only imagined and never
seen. It may be quite different when we get there, but I
know what I'm expecting, and I feel almost sick inside when
I think I may be disappointed. . . . Everyone I've told
about it says that Rye is wonderful. Do *you* know it . . . ? "

" Know it ? " she said. " Of course I know it. And
Winchelsea, too. I've got a little place down on Winchelsea
beach. You'd both better come over and see me one day.
How long are you staying in Rye ? "

" We go back to school on the twenty-second," Jon said.
" But we'll have a fortnight. I wonder if you know the
Gay Dolphin? It's a little hotel in Trader's Street, and
that's where we're going to live. . . ."

Here there was a crash as Miss Ballinger's bag fell once
again to the floor. As Penny stooped to pick it up for her
she glimpsed an extraordinary expression on the elder
woman's face. It had come and gone in a flash, and she
only noticed it because it made her feel, just for a second,
that she was looking at someone quite different. When
she placed the bag back on the big slippery lap, Jon was
still talking, and Miss Ballinger looked friendly and interested, and nothing more. Penny almost rubbed her eyes
in astonishment.

" My mother's been down there for three weeks getting
the place ready, and now we're going down to help a bit
before she opens properly," Jon was saying. " You see, it
wasn't very easy for her with Penny and me at school when
Dad was killed, and then—it's rather like a book, as Penny
says—an old uncle of Mother's who had lived in Rye all his
life died. He owned the *Gay Dolphin*, and he left it to her."

" I've stayed there before now," Miss Ballinger nodded.
" I know it well. I've sketched it many a time from Trader's
Street. Well, young man, if your mother wants guests, I'll
come. I remember that the place was not very well run.
When does she re-open ? Do you know ? "

Jon produced his wallet and took a neatly-folded letter
from it. Before he spoke again Penny looked out of the
window. They had passed Tunbridge Wells now and were
rushing through the lovely Sussex Weald. Her eyes pricked
as she thought that it was rather beastly for her darling aunt
to have to start a hotel now because of the war and everything.
But the place sounded so thrilling that it was sure to be
fun even if it was a different sort of life for her. Besides,
Jon and she might be able to help in lots of ways in the
holidays.

Jon was talking again.

" I've got a long letter from Mother here. Perhaps you'd
like to hear what she says about it all ? "

Miss Ballinger nodded. " Indeed, I would. I love Rye,
and I know you'll love the *Dolphin* as much as I do."

Jon smiled and went on. " There's nothing about the
place on the first page except that she says she has kept on
the manager, which is a big help ; but of course we shall
have to help her to make a real success of it. I believe
Americans come to Rye a lot, and we hope some will stay at
the *Gay Dolphin*. And will you tell your friends about it,
too, Miss Ballinger ? It's decent of you to say you'll
come, but what about your cottage ? You won't want
to stay with us if you've got somewhere else to live, will
you ? "

" Oh, yes, I will. My bungalow—it's not a cottage—
was the only place in Winchelsea I could get and, as I told
you, I like the *Dolphin*, and I'll like it better still if it's got a
new owner. . . . Does your mother say when she's going
to open ? But you can ask her to put my name down, anyhow. Read me what she says about Rye, for I say it's a
magic little town that casts a spell over everyone who comes
in under the old gateways and climbs its cobbled streets."

Penny looked up in surprise. Miss Ballinger's voice
changed as she spoke the last words quite softly.

" Yes," replied Jon. " Mother says that, too. She says
we'll never want to go away again, for Rye is like home at

once. . . . Here it is. . . . She tells us about Winchelsea,
too. ' I can hardly believe that two such places as these
ancient ports really exist,' she says, ' and because I want
you both to see them for the first time in the best way I
want you to come to Hastings, and Vasson, my nice porter,
will bring the old car over to meet you there. . . . Our *Gay
Dolphin* is great fun, and I know you'll both love it ! Your
rooms are ready and Jon's is in the front with a little window
looking two ways—one out into the street in front and the
other down the street, right over the very edge of the town
across the flat marsh to the sea.' What does she mean by
the marsh, Miss Ballinger ? " he added as he turned the
page.

" It's the flat land reclaimed from the sea that stretches
from Rye on it's hill to the sand dunes. I'll tell you more
about it presently if there's time, but we're getting on fast
now. It's really the western edge of Romney Marsh. . . .
I'd like to hear what else your mother says."

Jon smiled and went on. A station flashed backwards and
Penny was just able to read Robertsbridge when she heard
her name.

" Penny's room is at the back," Jon was reading again and
she wondered why on earth he didn't skip this part. It was
nothing to do with anyone but them.

" . . . at the back. A tiny room, darling, and not really
big enough for you to be untidy in but with a window which
looks into a funny little walled garden. . . ."

Jon skipped another page and Penny thought, " He's
skipping the wrong things, the idiot. Why did he read that
out about me being untidy ? "

He went on : " This is the bit I was looking for, Miss
Ballinger. Sorry about that little bit about the rooms.
Here it is. She says . . . ' I'm sure there are secret passages
and ghosts here and one of the maids told me that this was
one of the Inns used by the Marsh smugglers in olden days.
She said that the window in Jon's room was built to jutt out
over the street so that a lantern placed there could be seen
away down at the little harbour at the mouth of the muddy
river two miles away, where the boats would be waiting with
contraband from France, to be exchanged for wool from the
Marsh sheep. This is a strange old house, but I know that I
can make it really lovely, although Uncle Charles certainly

left it in a muddle. And this reminds me that the old man
has left me a lot of ancient documents and letters that look
as if they won't be deciphered until Jon has had the wit to
translate them. So you can see that there'll be plenty for
you both to do, with secret papers and new places to
explore.' "

He looked up from the page.

" Do you think she's right, Miss Ballinger ? It sounds
grand doesn't it ? "

" It certainly does. I should like to see those old documents she mentions. I'm interested in things like that. . . .
Does she say when she'll be ready for visitors ? "

Jon skipped the last pages.

" No, she doesn't say that. There's a bit here about the
new manager. She doesn't say a lot really about him, but I
don't think she likes him. . . . But we shall soon know for
ourselves. Where are we ? "

Another station flashed backwards as he spoke.

" Battle," said Miss Ballinger. " Not far now. I haven't
got time to tell you all the stories I've heard about Romney
Marsh and Rye, but as your mother says, it's not so very
long ago that smugglers, or Owlers as they were called,
ruled the Marsh. Honest people—but some say there were
no honest people left, as all made their fortunes by carrying
and smuggling wool from the famous Marsh sheep—dared
not put their heads out of doors at nights. If you've read
your Kipling——"

" Oh, of course," Penny interrupted, " I remember now !
Puck of Pook's Hill and *The Smuggler's Song*, which says
' Watch the wall, my darling, while the Gentlemen go by ! ' "

Jon looked suitably impressed by this display of learning
as Miss Ballinger nodded and went on :

" That's it. Kipling loved Sussex. He lived not far
from here. . . . But Rye's on the edge of the Marsh, as I
say, and you can explore it for yourselves. There's nothing
else like it. I've tried to paint it a score of times and I can
never get it. Marsh folk have a saying, I'm told, that the
world is divided into six parts—Europe, Asia, America,
Africa, Australia and Romney Marsh, and it's true that it
might be a different country. But Rye hardly belongs to
the Marsh. Once it was a great port and the ships of the
British Navy were built there with timber from the great

when we got here. She was friendly enough nearly all the way, but didn't seem to want us to come out of the station with her. . . . Oh, well! Why worry? Here we are, and I hope the car is waiting."

But it wasn't. There were only three cars waiting in the sun-drenched station yard and they were obviously taxis. Jon got out his mother's letter again and read, " it's a pre-war green four-seater Morris, and the driver's name is Fred Vasson. He's nice. You'll both like him."

" What did I tell you, Jon? He's gone. He couldn't wait. He didn't know about you and engine drivers. What a pity ! "

" All right. You said all that before several times. You go and ask any of those chaps if they're Fred Vasson and I'll go and telephone mother, and see if he's left."

Penny looked at him in admiration.

" The great brain at work," she said, as she sauntered over to the waiting taxis. She asked the two older drivers if they were Fred Vasson and they shook their heads; but the third driver, who was much younger, said he was sorry he wasn't ! Penny tossed her red curls and eyed him coldly before going back to find Jon. He was waiting for her at the door of a telephone kiosk.

" Have you got a sixpence ? " he called as soon as she came in sight. " There seems to be a hole in my pocket. I can feel it in the lining, but I can't get at it, unless I cut it open."

Penny squeezed into the box with him and shut the door and grudgingly produced one of her own rare sixpences. Jon got out his mother's letter again to find the number. Just as Mrs. Warrender answered the telephone Jon felt Penny nudge him violently in the back and hiss, " Jon, Jon ! Look quickly ! " but there was not room for him to turn, and he had to strain to hear his mother's voice.

" —Sensible of you to 'phone, darlings," she was saying. " You are at Hastings station, are you ? . . . Fred's on his way now, but the car wouldn't start. He should be there in ten minutes. . . . Are you both all right ? . . . Longing to see you, Jon. . . . My love to Penny. 'Bye."

Before he could replace the receiver, Penny forced the door open and dragged him outside.

" Did you see her ? " she gasped. " Quick, Jon ! I want to know where they're going."

" Who do you mean ? " Jon protested. " What's all the excitement ? "

" Miss Ballinger, you idiot ! She came out of the Refreshment place there, with such a peculiar-looking man. There they are ! Look ! They're getting a taxi."

Jon was just in time to see their travelling companion's broad back filling the taxi door and a small, slight man with a black hat getting in after her. Then he turned to his cousin.

" Well, what about it ? " he asked. " Why shouldn't she go into the Refreshment place and why shouldn't she get into a taxi ? You're always getting excited about something, aren't you, you silly little girl ! "

Penny ignored the last remark.

" The only thing which was peculiar about her was the man with her . . ." she began, and Jon interrupted.

" Gosh ! What a sentence ! Don't they teach you English at your school ? " He was beginning to get a little of his own back.

" You know what I mean, Jon. Don't be such a beastly prig. I'm trying to tell you about the peculiar man. He wore a most sinister black hat—the sort of hat that nobody who isn't sinister doesn't wear." Jon raised his eyes in horror at this further misuse of the English tongue, but Penny, who often spoke like this when excited, pretended not to notice.

" ——Anyway, he had very black sloping eyebrows, if you know what I mean, and a very small sloping black moustache thing on his lip. . . . I tell you what I think he is, Jon. . . . I think he's in a band somewhere and I don't think he's English either. . . . I tell you another thing, Jon. I think that if he hadn't been carrying her bags he'd have been waving his arms about. That's the sort of man he was," she finished triumphantly.

" I don't see that it matters," Jon persisted. " What did she look like, anyway ? "

Penny looked puzzled. " Come to think of it," she said, " she looked different, too. I can't quite explain. . . . Anyway, what does Auntie say and where's the car ? "

" Just coming," Jon said. " Here ! lean against this wall. It's beautifully hot."

So they leaned against the station wall in the sunshine.

Faintly there came to them the smell of hot tar and oil and fainter still the smell of the sea.

" Funny," said Jon after a little, " but seaside towns always smell different, don't they ? I like it."

" I like smells, too," Penny agreed. " And here comes a green car and it looks old enough to be ours. . . . I say, Jon, if that's Fred Vasson, I like him."

The car swept round the station approach and pulled up opposite them.

" You'll be Master Jonathan and Miss Penelope ? " asked the driver, in a slow drawl, as he got out. His eyes were very blue and, as he touched his old felt hat, they noticed that his hair was fair. It was difficult to judge his age, because his brown face was a mass of wrinkles which ran all together as he smiled.

" You'll have been worried maybe," he went on, " and I'm right sorry I be late, but start she wouldn't, and I'm not much of a hand at they engines. But we be all right now, and I'll soon have you home. Be you both getting in back ? "

" No," said Penny decidedly. " I'm coming in the front with you, Mr. Vasson, and Jon can sit behind with the luggage. You see I don't want to miss seeing *anything*."

So Jon made himself as comfortable as he could, but before very long he was leaning forward with his elbows on the back of Penny's seat looking for the sea. Fred showed them the ruins of the ancient castle on the cliff top ; then they crawled up the narrow street of the old fishing village which snuggled between two hills, with railed pavements high above their heads.

" Reckon tides 'ud cum right up street in old days," Fred explained. " Sometimes now when wind's south-west and tides are high we get trouble round these parts."

The car climbed fast now up through streets of drab houses and then turned east into a broad, tree-shaded road. On their right now and far below them was the sea. It was a lovely road and Autumn was already touching with a tender hand the woods through which they rushed. Soon they passed near a church with a high square tower standing lonely on the gorse-crowned down.

" Fairlight," Fred said. " And 'tis a landmark they say for all sailors beating up the Channel. But if it's churches you fancy, you'll be seeing something better afore long."

Even Penny was quiet when they came at last to Winchelsea and Fred drove slowly down the wide street that skirted the churchyard and the ruin of the once mighty church.

" Miss Ballinger said that once the sea came right up to the walls of Winchelsea, didn't she ? I can't see where," said Jon. " This place might be anywhere for it doesn't look as if it had ever been a port and I can't even see the sea."

Fred stopped, jumped out and opened the door.

" I was to stop here and take you to the look-out, Madam said."

They walked a few steps down the road and realized that the hill upon which the old town was built fell away abruptly a few yards where the road turned sharp left under the arch of a magnificent mediæval gateway, with round watch towers. Tucked under the edge of the hill was a little roofed look-out, with a seat to which Vasson led them. Jon whistled in surprise at the view spread out before them. Directly below them the side of the old cliff dropped almost sheer to the flat, grassy levels below. The road, like a step cut in the side of the cliff, ran steeply downhill to their left.

Penny clutched Jon's arm.

" Why, Jon ! " she whispered. " It's like she said. I can see what she means and what Auntie meant too when she said it was magic. This funny little town, all forgotten and deserted by the sea. . . . Look how flat it is down there. And look at the sheep everywhere."

Jon nodded.

" Yes, you can imagine the sea coming right to the bottom of the cliff," He turned to Fred. " What keeps the sea back now ? I suppose those roofs over there are on the beach, but it is all so flat that it looks as if the sea could easily come rolling over again."

Vasson looked at the boy soberly.

" So it could," he said, " and it's been near it more'n once. I mind a time when I was but a lad when the bank broke over yonder. . . ."

" What bank ? " Penny interrupted.

The man pointed to the right.

" Those cliffs you see way up yonder are called Cliff End and right there these flat marshes begin. Pett Level 'tis called here. The great bank of shingle to keep the sea back

starts at Cliff End and runs right along to the mouth of the
river below Rye yonder."

Jon and Penny followed his moving finger.

" Them liddle houses and shacks and the like," he went
on, " they be called Winchelsea Beach, and folks come there
in hundreds in summer. Houses be put up behind t' bank,
o' course."

" What's that bit of yellow land sticking out into the sea
like a finger ? " asked Penny, looking further east.

" The Ness," Vasson answered. " Dungeness. Look
hard and see if you can spot the lighthouse at the end. 'Tis
black and white."

Jon couldn't see it even after he had polished his glasses,
but Penny picked it out after much eye-straining. Next
Fred showed them a squat little ruin, with a round keep
standing forlorn in the middle of the marsh ; this, he told
them, was the remains of another castle called Camber.
And last he showed them Rye itself, standing compact on its
pyramid of rock, with the westering sun glowing on its
huddled roofs. A river wound round the base of the little
town and made its way to the sea, and the light was so clear
and clean that Penny nearly stooped for a pebble to toss
into its streets.

" Now you can see why these two towns were important
ports," Jon said. " When the sea came up to them they
would be like forts on islands. Just how far did the sea come,
I wonder ? "

Fred lifted his hand again and pointed.

" There's the old cliff," he said. " Runs right along there
from back o' Rye to back o' Winchelsea here. There's a
way to walk under old cliffs all the way."

Penny jammed her hands into her blazer pockets and
flicked back her curls.

" Come on," she said. " Let's go. I want to get inside
Rye and see what it's like. I want to get home."

And at these last words Jon quite unexpectedly squeezed
her arm as they walked back to the car.

They drove slowly under the old gateway.

" Strand Gate 'tis called," Fred told them, and " Of course,
it is," said Penny. " It couldn't be anything else. It faces
the strand."

At the bottom of the hill they turned off the road that led

to the beach, crossed a canal, and tore along a wide road as straight as a ruler. Just as it seemed that they were coming close to the ruin of Camber the road swung away, and Rye was before them and getting bigger every minute. They crossed the muddy-banked tidal river and just had time to see the black, tarred drying sheds in which the fishermen hang their nets, and a few boats drawn up out of the water, before finding themselves in the heart of the town.

The streets were narrow, and some that led steeply upwards were cobbled, with houses leaning precariously over the pavements. Neither Jon nor Penny had ever seen a little town like this before. Fred was concentrating on his driving and did not even attempt to answer their questions as he twisted and turned and finally crawled up a street which led up to the great church which they had seen crowning Rye from the Winchelsea look-out.

Then, " Nearly home now," he grunted and turning two more sharp corners pulled up suddenly at the end of a wider street in which grass tinged the cobble stones.

" Maybe you'd like to walk home from here," he grinned. " There she is ! Swinging up for you in the sunshine," and he pointed ahead to the end of the road.

Down below in the streets of the town all had been noise and bustle, but here Jon and Penny were in a strange world. The houses on each side were crowded together, but were all different—little white houses with black doors were squeezed between bigger houses whose fronts were criss-crossed with beams. Some of the front doors were up two steps and some were below the level of the pavement. Brass gleamed behind the windows, scarlet geraniums flamed in window-boxes and, right at the very end of the street on the right, a gaily-painted sign hung over the pavement.

" Oh, Jon ! " Penny whispered, " I believe that's it. That's the *Dolphin*, I'm sure."

Jon smiled down at her.

" I believe it is. Let's go."

Their shoes rang out on the pavement as they walked together in the sunshine towards their new home. A face peered at them from behind a curtain; they heard the loud buzz of a bee busy in a window-box, and a black cat came delicately down two steps and pushed its head against Penny's legs. As she stooped to stroke it, Jon said :

" Look, Penny. This street is rather like that in Winchelsea. It seems to stop at the end, and as we are on the top of a hill I expect there's a cliff there, too. We should be able to see the marshes and the sea when we get there."

" Now look at the wicked old Dolphin," Penny interrupted. " Look at the look in his eye, Jon. No wonder they call him gay."

And so they came home. Fred Vasson, having lighted his cigarette, passed them slowly and turned the car sharp into an archway under the hanging sign, and while they were looking up at this Mrs. Warrender came out to greet them. When she had disengaged herself from Penny and given Jon a hug she slipped an arm through each of theirs and led them a few steps to the end of the street, which was guarded by an old wall.

" Look at this first," she said, " and then you can explore the *Dolphin* later. Did Fred tell you something about Rye and Winchelsea as you came along ? . . . He doesn't talk very much, but he's a splendid person and a great help to me. I think you'll like him. . . . There ! Look ! Here we are at the very edge of the cliff, and from Jon's window, as I think I said, you can look out to sea. Across the river and away to the east is Romney Marsh, and to the right a little behind us is Winchelsea on her hill. . . . Look below, and there's the river you crossed when you arrived and some men building a fishing-boat—at least that's what Fred told me they were doing. . . ."

As Jon had said, it was like Winchelsea in a way, for both towns stood on their rocky hills and faced the sea which had long since deserted them. But here the cliff face was rocky and glowed with colour.

Penny leaned over the wall and grabbed a cluster of tiny pink flowerets waving among the delicate green, feathery leaves of a bush.

" It's tamarisk," Mrs. Warrender explained. " I believe you see it only at seaside places. I love it."

" There's a way down here," Jon said, pointing to some shallow steps that led down by the side of the houses on their right.

" It's called Trader's Passage—after the Freetraders or smugglers, I expect—and you can get down to the road and river that way, but it's hard work coming up. . . . Now let's go in and you can see your rooms and explore and we'll have some tea. . . . I suppose you had some sandwiches ? Were they nice ? "

" Very thirst-making, darling," Penny said. " I'm quite parched. . . . But Jon's had a lovely day, Auntie. You ask him ! He spoke to one engine-driver and has got lots of numbers as well," and she slipped out of reach of her cousin's avenging hand as they turned out of the sunshine into the shadow of the archway. On the left was a door marked " Hotel Only," and opposite another door, newly painted white, with " Private " on it.

" This is us," said Mrs. Warrender, pushing open the latter. " Not all our rooms are this side—you see, the two parts of the building are joined by this bridge over our heads—but you must always use this door and keep out of the way of the guests. We open on Monday, but I did want you down here first, and we're practically ready now, thanks to Fred, and, I suppose, to Mr. Grandon."

" Who's Mr. Grandon ? " asked Jon as they stepped into a dark little hall.

" Oh, he's the manager. I'll tell you about him later. He's out now. . . . Come and see your rooms."

Penny soon lost count of the corners they turned, the corridors they walked and the stairs they went up and down before they reached Jon's room. He didn't say much when he saw it. Just " Thank you, Mother. It's grand ! " But they both knew how thrilled he was.

The window, as Mrs. Warrender had tried to explain in her letter, jutted over the pavement, so that it was possible to see up the street, over the edge of the cliff to the mouth of the river and the sea and right out over the grassy levels across the Marsh.

There were shelves round the walls for his books, which had yet to be unpacked from the two heavy corded boxes at the foot of the bed, a dressing-table with lots of drawers and a small desk in the window.

" I think, if you don't mind," he said, " I'll move things round a bit and put the bed right in the window. I'd like to sleep there so that if I lift my head at night I'll be able to see the lighthouse flashing."

" Arrange it as you like, Jon," his mother said. " I knew

you'd have your own ideas. . . . Now come and see Penny's rabbit hutch."

So they all squeezed along another narrow passage and up a short but narrow twisty staircase.

"You're in a different part of the house now, but I was so sure Penny would like this little room that I had to keep it for her. Here we are! Mind your head, Jon. The doorway is low."

Penny gasped with excitement. It was certainly a tiny room, but it was gay with chintz, and there were flowers on the window-ledge by the fluttering curtains and on the little dressing-table with its dainty frill. And on the bed-spread by the pillow was the sad-looking and now very thin white teddy bear, who had gone to bed regularly with Penny until not so very long ago. Suddenly her eyes filled with tears and she dared not trust herself to speak. They were so decent to her! They were such darlings! Only Auntie and Jon understood what it was like to have a real mother and father so far away that, except for snaps and letters, they weren't real at all. And now this lovely little room!

Just for a few seconds Penny felt much older than she really was, and she pushed rudely past Jon, who was in her way, and put her head out of the window so that they shouldn't see how she was feeling. After a little the mist cleared from her eyes and she saw that she was looking down into the little walled garden and on the other side of the wall were the shallow steps of Trader's Passage. At the bottom of the garden, which sloped down the hill, was the side of another house, and on the right another wall, which she guessed correctly divided the garden from the yard with its big garage.

"What a sweet little garden," she said as she felt Mrs. Warrender's hand on her shoulder. "But nothing much grows in it, does it?"

"I've had roses, Penny, and some of them are here on your dressing-table, and those are gillyflowers growing in the wall."

"Is that old tree growing *through* the wall, Auntie? I suppose it was big when they built the wall and the people who lived here wouldn't have it cut down as its roots were here, so they had to build round it."

Jon leaned over her other shoulder.

" I've seen one or two like that before," he said. " That s a withy tree—a sort of willow."

Penny was now feeling better, so she turned back into the room, sighed rapturously and looked up into Jon's friendly face.

" Isn't he *wonderful*, Auntie ? It's his mighty brain. He knows everything."

Mrs. Warrender separated them.

" You can come up and unpack after tea. Your trunks arrived safely, you see, and you'll have plenty to do getting tidy. Now we'll have tea in the lounge and you can see whether you like it, and what the hotel part of the house is like."

They went downstairs again, and Fred, now very smart in a dark-green uniform, brought them tea and toast as they sat round a smouldering but sweet-smelling log-fire.

" We never lets 'un out, miss," he smiled as he saw Penny's inquiring glance. " In winter we bank it up the chimney, but now we just about keep 'un going with oak logs. There's always fire on this hearth."

The large chairs were very soft and comfortable, and Penny was tired after the journey and all the excitement of their home-coming. She heard Jon telling his mother something about last term and then must have dozed a little until she heard her name.

" Penny, darling," Mrs. Warrender was saying, " I was telling Jon that I've got another surprise for you to-morrow, but I may want your help, too, in getting everything ready for Monday. And that reminds me to tell you both about Mr. Grandon. I want you to remember that he is my manager and that he is really running the *Dolphin* for me. I want you to be polite to him—and none of your amusing little games with him, please, Penny ! But there's no need to have anything much to do with him. Remember that he has got his work to do and that our side of the house is nothing to do with him."

Jon lighted a spill for his mother's cigarette.

" Don't you like him, Mother ? You don't sound as if you do. Why are you telling us to be so careful about him ? "

Mrs. Warrender laughed.

" Oh ! I don't know, darlings. I don't really like him

and yet he's very efficient. I don't think he's English some-how, but old Uncle Charles must have thought a lot of him because he left a letter with him for me which recommended him very strongly. . . . Anyway, whether we like him or not, I can't do without him. You see, running a place like this is not just a game, and when the first guests come it will be very different for us all. . . . It's going to be an odd sort of life for you two dears, I'm afraid. . . . I do hope you won't mind it too much. . . . After all, the war did some odd things to most of us, but perhaps you're really neither of you old enough to understand all that. . . ."

Jon, feeling very uncomfortable, mumbled something, but Penny, although the tears stung her eyes again, managed a choky sort of laugh.

"Don't you worry about us, darling, 'cos we shall love it —or I shall, anyway, although I expect it will be dull for Jon, because I shouldn't think that this place has even got a railway station."

"Well, let's see this Mr. Grandon, anyway," said Jon. "Can't you ring for him or something?"

His mother looked shocked.

"Of course I can't," she said. "I wouldn't dare. Any-way, he's out and won't be back until late to-night. . . . What would you like to do now? Go and unpack and then meet for supper at eight in our own sitting-room?"

Jon got up and stretched.

"What about all those papers, Mother—the papers that your old Uncle Charles left and that you said I could go through?"

"Oh, yes! Those are part of my surprise, but we'll look at them to-morrow."

So Jon went upstairs to unpack his books and move his furniture round. Penny, who always postponed action of that kind if she could, wandered out into the street again.

The shadows were lengthening now as she leaned against the low wall and looked down over the gently swaying tamarisks to the road and river below. The tide was running out and she could see a few seagulls wheeling above some rubbish on the muddy banks and some blue-jerseyed fisher-men, looking rather like toy models, leaning against the rails of the bridge. Up here she was above the world, and as she gazed first out over the darkening marsh and then up their little cobbled street past the wicked-looking Dolphin, she could almost imagine that she was living in a different time.

Perhaps, as darkness fell over the land and the shutters went up in Trader's Street, so cloaked, masked and mounted figures would come trotting silently along secret paths over the Marsh. The " gentlemen " were riding by ! And then a yellow light would gleam in the little window of the *Dolphin* over the pavment and the signal would be answered thrice over where the river ran dark and silent to the sea. Perhaps next would come the ring of heavy steps over the cobbles and a flood of light as the Redcoats flung open the door of the inn and the lantern in the little room above would be dimmed.

Then the window really did open and Jon pushed out his tousled head.

" What's the matter with you, duckie ? " he called rudely. " You look as if you've gone crackers. What are you gaping at ? "

By way of answer Penny extended her tongue as far as possible in his direction and ran in.

At supper she was her usual cheerful self, but she was ready for bed when her aunt suggested it.

Upstairs in her little room she felt too sleepy to do anything much about tidying up, although Mrs. Warrender had looked rather disapprovingly at the muddle when she came to say good night.

After she had turned out the light Penny drew back the flowered curtains and pushed the window open wider. She shivered as a gust of salty wind from the marshes and the sea shook the leaves of the withy tree in the garden below, and then she jumped into bed.

She seemed to go to sleep at once, and it was odd that she should wake so suddenly. She switched on the bedside light, and saw that she had only been asleep for two hours. She sat up in surprise. Everything was quiet. No board creaked. The wind hadn't risen, and only by straining her ears could she catch the faint and drowsy murmur of the sea. Then she remembered ! With all the excitement to-day she had forgotten to write in her diary. Penny had to put up with a lot of teasing both at home and at school about her diary, but a daily entry was one of the few rules she set

B

PENNY LOOKED DOWN INTO THE LOUNGE. BUSY AT THE TELEPHONE
WAS THE MAN SHE HAD SEEN AT THE STATION

herself. For years now not a day had passed without the writing of a few lines in this precious book. What she wrote was very private, but much of it found its way at last across the seas to her father and mother in India.

She remembered now that she had not risked packing her diary, but had put it in the satchel in which their sandwiches and a few other treasures had been carried.

But what had she done with the satchel?

She jumped out and then realized that her dressing-gown was in the trunk, still unopened at the foot of her bed. Not worth opening that now! She grovelled about under the bed just in case she had dropped the haversack there, but soon satisfied herself that it was not in the room.

She sat down again and tried to concentrate, and this time succeeded. In her aunt's sitting-room, of course! She remembered now slipping it off and dropping it on the floor behind the chair. It was a nuisance, but she would have to go and get it because she knew she wouldn't sleep again now until she'd written something about this wonderful and exciting day.

She slipped her skirt on over her pyjamas, struggled into her jersey and then opened the door. She remembered that she must go down the little twisting staircase, but once down she lost her sense of direction and did not know which way to turn. She was fairly certain that she ought to go down again, but it was dark and the corridor twisted abruptly, and although she found two more stairways going down she couldn't remember coming up either of them!

She wished she had a torch or could find a switch on the wall. The hotel seemed empty and was very quiet and she felt her heart thudding as she wondered how she was going to find her way back to her room. Then she had an awful feeling that she was going in the wrong direction, turned back and came at last to her own little staircase again. At least she hoped it was her staircase. She had just decided to leave the diary until the morning when she distinctly heard a sound somewhere below her.

Her heart thumped louder than ever and she felt the palms of her hands grow damp. The sound came again! A sort of quiet hiss or whir. Then she realized it was the sound of a telephone dial, and at the same time she noticed the faint colour of reflected light at the end of the corridor.

She crept along with her hands on the wall, turned sharp left, nearly stumbled over a low step and found herself on a landing looking down another staircase into the lounge.

In the far corner, by a shaded light, was the figure of a strange man, with his back to her, busy at the telephone.

He was speaking now with his hand half over the mouth-piece, but he was forced to raise his voice, and Penny came down three steps as she heard him say :

". . . Yes, yes. The children have arrived, but never fear. . . . It is no matter. . . . Yes, I will find the papers, and if I cannot bring them to you I will copy those that will give us a clue. . . . Sunday I will meet you. . . . Yes. The old mill at six and I will bring the papers if I can . . ."

Then Penny shifted her weight and the stair creaked. The man whipped round and she put her hand to her mouth as she recognized him.

It was the man with the little black moustache whom she had seen with Miss Ballinger at Hastings station.

CHAPTER II

SATURDAY: MR. GRANDON

PENNY was dreaming. It was a hateful dream : she was struggling along a dark, twisting corridor while behind her pounded a black horse on which was mounted a masked rider. Nearer and nearer he came until she could hear the horse breathing. An odd sort of breathing it was, too. More of a gurgling than a breathing. She struggled and put up a hand to push back the horse's head. His head was hard and she had to push with all her strength.

Then she woke to find herself twisted round on her pillow and pushing until her fingers hurt against the head of the bed. She turned on her back and looked towards the window, for she could still hear that weird gurgling. Then she realized that it was pouring with rain and that the gutters round the corners and gables of the house were gurgling and singing. The curtains were parted, and from her pillow she could see a grey, dull sky through the open window and rain-drops splashing on the corner of her dressing-table.

She jumped out of bed and closed the window. Her watch said half-past six, so she got back to bed and snuggled down for another sleep. But now she was very wide awake, and as she put her arms behind her red head and gazed gravely at the ceiling the adventure of the night came back to her.

She recalled every word spoken by the man at the telephone —the man who must surely be Mr. Grandon, her aunt's manager ! The man who knew Miss Ballinger. The man who was to meet somebody at the old mill on Sunday at six and was sure that he could find the papers and had told some other mysterious person that they, " the children," had arrived.

She remembered how the stair had creaked ; how she had fled back into the sheltering darkness as he had turned to look at her ; how she had wished that Jon had been with her as she blundered round the corners of the long corridor and, more by luck than anything else, had found her own little staircase and the welcome light that shone like a beacon from her open door.

She remembered, too, how she had scrambled into bed with a fast-thumping heart and how, though she had strained her ears, there had been no other sound but the sighing of the wind in the roof-tops.

Well, it was all true. It had really happened and she had enjoyed an adventure that Jon had missed within a few hours of their arrival at their new home. She had always believed that the *Gay Dolphin* would be the sort of place for adventures.

She stretched luxuriously and wiggled her toes. How mad Jon would be when she told him what he had missed ! She could tell him at breakfast. But on second thoughts why not tell him now ? This was news which would not wait, and if it really *was* Mr. Grandon perhaps it would be wiser to talk it over with Jon before mentioning it to her aunt. Jon was a lazy brute in the mornings, as she well knew, so it would be rather fun to wake him and rout him out !

So she got up again and rummaged about in her suitcase which she had been too lazy to unpack properly the night before. There wasn't time to do it now, but she really would have to put her things away after breakfast or else Mrs. Warrender would be peevish ! She tossed a few things on to the floor and found her shorts at the bottom of the case. Then she washed her face and scrubbed her teeth, put on her green sweater and slipped out into the passage and down the little staircase. It was light enough now for her to see where she was going and although she remembered the way down the big staircase to the lounge she realized that she had no idea of how to find Jon's room or her aunt's sitting-room either. She tried two more staircases, but wherever she went she was confronted by closed, silent doors, and somehow she hadn't the courage to start opening them and looking into rooms which ought to be empty but perhaps were not !

She knew it was no use whistling or calling for Jon down the corridors. He wouldn't hear if she blew a trumpet through each keyhole ! While she was still wondering what was the best thing to do she heard someone whistling softly downstairs, so she ran to the top of the big staircase and looked down into the lounge. Fred Vasson, in a green baize apron, was just plugging in a big electric cleaner, and turned with a start when she called softly :

" Good morning, Mr. Vasson. How are you this morning ? "

" Good morning, miss. You be up early on a wet morning. Maybe you couldn't sleep well in a strange bed ? "

Penny came down the stairs slowly. Just for a moment she felt tempted to say something to him about last night's adventure, but then decided against it. This was all for Jon. And perhaps it would sound rather silly to ask Fred if he knew where her cousin's room was, so she contented herself with just being friendly. This was one of the things she was particularly good at. She sat on the edge of one of the big chairs and swung her legs and it was while Fred was telling her how the sign of the *Gay Dolphin* outside had just been painted by an artist who lived further up the street, that she had her bright idea and realized how she might be able to wake Jon.

" I say, Mr. Vasson, do you think you could lend me a mac ? Any old mac would do. You see, I haven't had time to unpack yet and I want to go out for a bit."

" But it's pouring down, miss ! And it's early, too, and there won't be anything to see in this weather."

" Just any old mac would do, Mr. Vasson. Just to save me going upstairs again. I love rain. I've always loved the rain. You ask Mrs. Warrender some time and she'll tell you how I've always liked going out in the rain—and most particularly before breakfast ! "

He looked doubtfully at her shoes and then went over to a cupboard under the stairs.

" Some gent must a' left this some time," he said as he produced a grubby-looking raincoat. " It'll be a bit on the roomy side for you, but it'll keep the rain out for a liddle," and he opened the door for her.

For a moment she stood in the shelter of the arch looking at the rain, and then ran out into the street. Jon's window was just above her and, as she had hoped, the narrow pane which faced out to sea was open. She looked round for something to throw in, but the rain water was rushing down the gutters and there were big puddles over the cobblestones and not a pebble or handful of gravel anywhere.

She stood under the window and whistled and called his name, but, as she had expected, this had no result. Rather disconsolately she wandered over to the wall and looked down to the river. The rain was slanting fiercely in from the south-west, and the sea and Winchelsea on its hill were hidden. Perhaps, after all, she would have to ask Fred the way to Jon's room. Then she noticed the weeds growing at the foot of the wall. Pulling up a big wet handful, she shook the rain from her curls and quite unnecessarily tip-toed over to the still open window and glanced up the street. There was no one in sight so, putting the tip of her tongue between her teeth as she always did when concentrating, she leaned back and tossed up the clod. Even as the wet earth sailed through the air she remembered with glee that Jon had said that he was going to move his bed under the window.

For a long, long moment there was a silence and then came a sort of splosh, followed by a strangled cry. Again there was a silence until Penny, unable to bear the suspense any longer, giggled, and this brought her cousin's face to the window.

At the sight of him the giggle changed to a laugh. He was struggling to put on his spectacles and one side of his face was covered in mud, which was running down into his mouth. He wiped the mud off with his pyjama sleeve and, when his glasses were safely on his nose, spluttered :

" Oh, it was you, was it ? I might have known if I'd had time to think. That was just the silly sort of trick that our fags play on each other in their first term, and I see now it's the sort of game that silly little schoolgirls play on each other ! Have you tried pulling a chair away just as some-body is going to sit down ? You ought to try that. It would make you giggle. You great baby ! Why don't you go in and keep dry or p'raps you haven't noticed it's raining. Next thing will be that you'll catch cold and spoil our holidays."

Penny was furious. She had a temper to match the colour of her hair and it always made her angry when Jon reminded her that there was a difference of a year in their ages. She was just about to return his abuse when she remembered why she wanted him.

" Be quiet, you idiot," she hissed. " Buck up and come down. I've got something vital and urgent and secret to tell you, and I didn't know where your room was. Get up, Jon. It's urgent ! Really it is ! "

" Oh, go back to bed yourself," he growled. " It's too dark and too wet and too early to get up, and I'm going to sleep again. Don't be such an ass, Penny."

" *Please*, Jon," she pleaded. " I really meant it. I've had an adventure in the night and I want you to know all about it, but you must be quick and I must see you secretly. . . . Jon ! Are you listening ? Listen ! Get up right away and then, when you're ready, open your door and leave it open and listen for me. I can't find anybody or anything in this house because all the doors are always shut. Will you, Jon ? Please do," and without realizing it she had put her head on one side and smiled up at him so good-humouredly that he nodded, and shut the window.

She wandered back into the yard, and saw Fred disappearing through a narrow door just past the hotel entrance. She followed him into a dark little room with a long table under the window.

" Do you live here, Mr. Vasson ? " she asked as she slipped her shoulders out of the dripping mac.

He smiled his slow, friendly smile. " I work here sometimes. Odd jobs come to me ! . . . Have you been far ? You're not too wet I hope ? "

Penny shook her head, but did not satisfy his curiosity.

" No, not far, thanks. Just had a look at the rain. I'd like to come and see you here sometimes. May I ? I like this little room ! "

" Ye'll allus be welcome," he replied gravely as Penny slipped out and went into the hotel again. There was nobody about, and as Jon ought to have had time to have washed himself by now, she crossed the lounge and started up the polished stairs. When she was half-way up she turned back and realized that her shoes were so wet that they were dirtying the wood that Fred had probably just been polishing. Better to carry her shoes ! She sat down on the stairs with a sigh and had just got both shoes off when a soft voice from above her said :

" Good morning, young lady. You, I think, must be Miss Penny ? It would seem that since your arrival you spend most of your time on the stairs. . . . Very singular, Miss Penny! Very odd!"

Penny was so surprised that she jumped up, slightly abashed for once and looking rather foolish. One shoe dropped down the stairs with an awful clatter as she said:

"Oh, good morning. . . . I just got my shoes a bit wet. . . . It's rather a wet morning, isn't it? . . . How do you do? How did you know my name?"

It was, of course, Miss Ballinger's friend and the man who had been at the telephone last night. She felt certain that it must be Mr. Grandon, but she did want to make sure before she saw Jon. And so, standing half-way up the stairs, with one shoe off and her hair shining with the wet and her heart thumping with the excitement of the encounter, she asked him who he was.

He smiled at that. Rather a slinky sort of smile under his little black line of a moustache.

"I am Mr. Grandon, and happy to make your acquaintance. . . . I hope we shall be friends," he added with a foreign little bow.

So she had been right all the time, and there was some connection or understanding between Mr. Grandon and Miss Ballinger! She was nearly mistress of herself again as she ran up the stairs, carrying one shoe but forgetting the other. On the landing she flashed him one of her special smiles.

"I don't see why not," she said as she brushed past him.

"Miss Penny," he called softly, "Miss Penny, I hope I did not disturb you when I was at the telephone last night?"

For a moment she was dumbfounded. Then—"I don't know what you mean," she gasped, and ran down the crooked corridor. As soon as she had turned the first corner she leaned against the wall and wondered once again where she was. This house really was absurd! She was beginning to feel rather like poor Alice, wandering down corridors and not being able to open the doors. And there was another story, too, where a Princess went up lots of winding stairs to meet an old fairy godmother but could never find the same way up again. Then she heard a muffled, unmusical humming which she recognized as Jon's, so she padded on down the corridor still carrying one shoe, and when she turned

another corner it was to see her cousin's untidy head peering
round an open door.

" So there you are," he said. " Have you gone mad or
something ? Or been walking in your sleep ? You look as
if you're doing Lady Macbeth now. Do you *have* to walk
round in your socks and carry one shoe ? "

She pushed him into the room and shut the door. She
closed it carefully and quietly, instead of slamming it as
usual, and then stood with her back to it and looked round.

" I say, Jon, I'm sorry about that clod, but you did look
funny. It was a jolly good shot really ! You know I'm not
much good at throwing, but I got it in first time. . . . I say,
it has made a mess of the pillow, hasn't it ? What will you
say if Auntie asks how you did it ? I'll explain that you
suddenly went like that Nebu . . . Nebu-something-or-other-
King in the Bible who went out and ate grass."

But Jon didn't laugh. He just looked cross and went
over to the basin and squeezed out some paste on to his
tooth-brush. Penny tried again. It wasn't quite as easy
to tell him as she had expected.

" You have made your room nice, Jon. I like the bed
under the window like that."

" I though you did," he said grimly. " Come on, Penny !
If you've really got something to tell me, do buck up and
get on with it."

In a flash she was between him and the basin. She reached
up and grabbed the collar of his open shirt and shook him
so that the tooth-brush fell to the floor.

" Don't be so beastly, horribly superior," she flamed at
him, with her eyes unexpectedly moist. " Don't be so
grown-up. How can we have any fun or adventures here if
you start off by being such a beastly prig ? Don't I always
tell you everything ? . . . Sometimes, Jon, I absolutely loathe
you," and with this she pushed him back so hard that he
sat on the bed gazing up at her in surprise.

Then, slowly he grinned and patted the bed beside him.

" All right, little Newpenny ! Come and tell me all
about it."

Penny fumbled in vain for a handkerchief, picked up a
grubby specimen of Jon's off the dressing-table, trumpeted
loudly and sat down demurely beside him. After a slow
start—for she found it difficult to explain how she had felt

when she was lost in the dark corridor—she poured out her story, while he listened impatiently. Once or twice he tried to interrupt, but she brushed him aside.

"Let me finish, Jon, and we'll have a pow-wow afterwards. We've got to stick together on this and that's why I wanted to tell you all about it before we met at breakfast. . . . Well, there I was standing on the stairs . . . absolutely *transfixed with terror*, Jon . . . and listening to him telling somebody that *we'd* arrived. . . ."

"What do you mean? *We* had arrived. . . ."

"I'm telling you, aren't I? Give me a chance . . ." and she made the best of her opportunity to keep him listening.

". . . and it's all very mysterious and horrid, Jon," she finished. "Don't you remember that Auntie told us last night that she didn't really like him and now we know for certain that he's something to do with that funny old Miss Ballinger. . . ."

"We don't really know that, Penny. We can't be sure."

"Of course we know. Didn't he come to meet her at the station and didn't she try to get rid of us in the railway carriage, so that we shouldn't see him meeting her?"

Jon nodded.

"If you're right, I suppose that would be because after we'd told her that we belonged to the *Dolphin* she realized that we should soon know him. . . . But why, Penny? It doesn't make sense."

"Oh, I don't know why! That's what we've got to find out, isn't it? That's going to be our big job. Why, Jon, our adventure started before we got here."

"Well, Penny, you can't be sure that he was talking to that rum old Miss Ballinger on the telephone, can you?"

"No, I can't be sure, but I jolly well bet that it was her. . . . Those papers he mentioned, Jon! He said he'd find them and meet her at the old mill to-morrow. . . . It's just like a story! Anyway, I hate that Grandon man. He made me lose my shoe coming up all quiet and slinky like that and I think he's vile."

"I'm looking forward to seeing him close. I couldn't really see him at the station. Just a black hat. You have all the fun, Penny. . . . Oh, gosh! That sounds like a gong and I suppose we'd better go down to breakfast. What happened to my toothbrush?"

" It's here," said Penny. " I've just trodden on it. Your beastly paste is all over my sock and when I walk it will come off on the carpet. Scrape it off with the handle of the brush, Jon. You ought to be more careful in your nice new room."

So, while she stretched out her foot, he chivalrously removed the sticky paste and then tried to comb his unruly hair into some sort of a parting.

" What are we going to do ? " Penny asked as she sat on the bed and watched him.

" We'll talk about it again after breakfast. Meanwhile, don't say anything to Mother, because I'm going to tell her that I'd like to meet this mysterious Mr. Grandon, and maybe we've got all the wrong ideas."

Penny snorted. " Not on your life ! Do you think I dreamed it all last night ? "

Jon turned round. " I never thought of that," he said. " I'm always telling you that you eat too fast and you excelled yourself at supper ! What are you going to do about your shoe and where have you left the other ? Are you going up to put on another pair ? "

" No, I'm not. I'm sick of those stairs. The other shoe is down in the lounge somewhere. We'll go down that way and cross over the yard. Come on."

" We'll have to get used to going the other way to our rooms by Monday," Jon said as he shut the door behind him. " I really think you'd better put the one shoe on, Penny. Don't fly into a rage, but you look a bit of an ass carrying it ! "

Downstairs, in the lounge, Fred Vasson was now polishing the brass. After Jon had answered his " Good morning," Penny said :

" You don't happen to have seen a shoe about, do you, Mr. Vasson ? It happened to fall downstairs just now and at the time I didn't bother to come back for it. . . . I was in rather a hurry," she finished lamely as she saw Fred's expression of astonishment.

" A shoe ? " he muttered.

" Yes, like this. Only the other side of course," and she extended the shod foot for inspection.

Fred slowly shook his head. He had been much impressed by Penny's winning ways from the moment she had elected to sit next to him in the car, but this peculiar behaviour shocked him. He was fairly certain that young ladies did not come down to breakfast wearing only one shoe after going for a crazy walk in the rain.

"No, miss," he said solemnly. "No, miss. I haven't seen a shoe and I've been all over the floor, as you well know, miss. Was it *after* your walk it fell off, did you say ? "

Jon grinned and Penny flushed and peered vaguely about under one or two chairs. Then the door opened and Mrs. Warrender came in, followed by Mr. Grandon, who was carrying Penny's shoe rather in the way in which the Prince's herald must have carried Cinderella's glass slipper.

"There you are, children! Where on earth have you been ? I was just coming up to your rooms to find you. I want to introduce you to Mr. Grandon, who is going to do all the hard work of running the *Dolphin* for me."

Mr. Grandon bowed his little bow again and, with a flash of white teeth, shook hands with them both after carefully transferring Penny's shoe to his left hand. As he took Penny's hand she looked him straight in the eye and was not certain, but thought she detected a suspicion of a wink in his. Anyway, he made no mention of a previous meeting.

"I was about to send the maid up to your room with this shoe, Miss Penny," he smiled. "Doubtless you left it on the mat when you came in from your walk. Allow me!" and before she realized what was happening, he was on one knee and lacing up her shoe. She mumbled her thanks, and then followed her aunt and Jon across the yard and into their own sitting-room.

Penny settled down to her breakfast as quietly as she could, hoping that the episode of the shoe would not be referred to again. But it was.

"I don't quite know what you've been up to, darling," her aunt said as she passed her a cup of coffee, "but I have an idea that it's something you shouldn't. Mr. Grandon came over here with your shoe in his hand—at least, he said that he thought it must be your shoe—and said that he would like to meet you both. It seemed to me to be a little peculiar for him to have your shoe, but of course I just told him that you were like that! "

Penny reddened and took a hasty gulp of coffee, but before she could answer Jon looked up and said :

"Oh, you know what Penny is, Mother. She was just having a bit of a rag with me and happened to drop her shoe. Your Mr. Grandon is very polite, isn't he? What do you want us to do to-day? Can we help you indoors as it's so wet? We haven't learnt our way about the house yet."

His mother flashed a quick glance at Penny and then smiled. She was really very understanding.

"That's something you had better learn to do, I agree," she said. "Hurry up with your breakfast, and then I've got a surprise for you. I kept it specially for to-day. Jon! We shall have to fix a ' Private ' notice on your door because you are really in the guest's part of the house, but I just had to let you have that room. Penny's doesn't matter, because nobody will ever find their way up there!"

"I can't find my own way," Penny grinned. "Come on, Jon. Do buck up. I've finished. . . . Oh, well! If you're going to have another piece of toast I might as well, too. . . . If I don't eat with you I know you'll only get anxious and start bolting your food. . . . Oh, Auntie! There's my satchel! Will you excuse me, please, just for a moment to see if my diary is there. . . . Oh, yes, here it is. Do you know, I was so excited yesterday that it wasn't till I was in bed that I remembered that I'd forgotten to write in it, so I. . . . Ow! Jon, you are a clumsy beast. You kicked me. . . . Oh, well, here it is now, so that's all right and I'd better take the satchel up to my room and put it in a safe place, hadn't I?"

When at last they had finished, Mrs. Warrender said :

"I suppose you've unpacked and put your clothes away, Penny?"

"Not exactly, darling. I haven't really had time. I thought I'd do it better in daylight."

Mrs. Warrender sighed. "She doesn't improve, does she, Jon? I think you had better meet us in the lounge in half an hour. Once I've got Penny straightened up I'll show you my surprise. Come along, my lass."

Penny turned at the door, glanced at Jon and put her finger to her lips.

It was three-quarters of an hour before she appeared, and Jon was, by this time, very bored and trying to amuse himself with the radio set in the lounge.

" Well, what do you think of your new home ? " Mrs. Warrender smiled from the door.

Penny ran over and flung her arms round her.

" Do you mean this room is ours, darling ?   Our very own to do what we like in ? "

" That's what I thought !   There's not much furniture, as you see, but that is a very valuable table and I should think it must have been built up here, for they could never have got it up the stairs in one piece.   And you can have those three chairs and there's plenty of room in the two cupboards, and I suppose there's no reason why Jon shouldn't build some bookshelves if he's careful not to spoil the woodwork. . . . There's something odd about this room, Jon, and I don't quite know what it is.   It seems strange that such a nice room should have been built in this way under the roof. That fireplace is really old and has been used a lot, and as soon as I found the room I wondered why it should have been used at all for living in."

" Perhaps it was a hiding place ? " Jon said.

" A secret room ? " said Penny.

Mrs. Warrender dusted the table top and then sat on it.

" But it isn't really secret, is it ?   I mean anybody could find that little door outside Penny's room.   It isn't really hidden. . . . No, I believe that there is some sort of a mystery about this room and it is one of the reasons why I've given it to you both.   It is your own room and you can do what you like here.   You can have a fire if you like and if you want to be up here at night you can go out into the town presently and see if you can buy an old oil lamp and hang it from one of the beams.   Or better still, ask Fred if he can find one hidden away somewhere.   Fred can generally find anything.   But you must carry your own coal and oil and you must promise me to keep it clean yourselves, because I have told Mr. Grandon that none of the staff are to come past Penny's landing. . . . You've got your key and, so far as I know, that's the only key in existence, so I shan't be able to come up here again unless I'm invited."

" You will be, darling," Penny promised.   " But you'll be the only one. . . . I think this is the most wonderful thing that ever happened to me, don't you, Jon ? "

But Jon had just seen a big, black tin box in a corner over

by the fireplace and although he was really just as excited as Penny, all he said now was, " What's that box, Mother ? Did you know it was there ? "

" Of course. I nearly forgot to tell you. See if you can lift it on the table here, Jon. . . . Help him, Penny. Good ! " She rummaged in her bag and produced another key while the children stood by expectantly. " Here's the key to the box, Jon, and take care of that, too. The box is full of the old papers, books and things which were left for us, with the house, by dear old Uncle Charles. The solicitor, Mr. Harding, told me that Uncle thought that you, Jon, might like to sort out all the other papers and things for me. What *are* you grimacing about, Penny ? Have you got a pain ? "

Poor Penny, who had been trying to catch Jon's attention with a very meaning wink at the mention of the papers, tried to turn it into a laugh.

" No thanks. Not a pain really. Just a bit of stitch, p'raps."

" I did tell you, didn't I ? " Mrs. Warrender went on, " that everybody here says that the *Dolphin* was one of the Inns most used by smugglers in the old days. I suppose that was because of its position and because there was a quick way down to the river by the steps at the end of the street there."

" Yes," Penny nodded. " We did know that. You told us, and so did somebody else in the train. . . . What did you say, Jon ? Don't grunt like that. It sounds beastly ! "

Mrs. Warrender looked down at her shining nails and went on with a little laugh.

" I'm going to tell you a secret and it's to be kept a secret, too, although I don't see how there can be anything in it really ! Mr. Harding, who is rather musty but rather an old darling, told me, with lots of hums and haws, that for as long as he can remember, it has been said in Rye that smugglers' treasure was hidden in the *Gay Dolphin* or somewhere near it. . . . Don't look so solemn, Penny ! I'm sure it's only an old story. . . . Anyway, Uncle Charles must have known all about these rumours and Mr. Harding hinted that he bought the *Dolphin* in the first place because he believed that he would find the treasure himself. But he never did find it and it is just possible—just a crazy idea, I think—that

" Jon," she said, "why do you think Auntie said that about the treasure ? You know—that bit just as she was going out, about it being a help to her if we did find it. . . . She didn't sound very happy, did she ? . . . Jon ! I *hate* it when she isn't happy. I *hate* it now, because I tell you she is jolly worried really, and I'll tell you something that we've never said before."

She twisted round from the window and faced him, still on her knees. The light was behind her so that he couldn't see her face but he did have the sense to realize that she wasn't quite such a kid as he had thought when she went on :

" She's lonely, Jon, that's what it is. It's easy for us to have fun, but she hasn't got your father any more." She gulped. " We're all she's got to help her really, and we're not here all the time, although I wouldn't mind staying away from school next term. . . . And she thought of this lovely place for us, and although she half-pretended that all this about the treasure was really a joke, I believe that she'd be jolly pleased if we could find it."

Jon nodded soberly from the table on which he was now sitting.

" Yes, Penny. I think she would, too. I think she's more worried than she tells us."

" Well, we've got to help, then. There's only us, Jon. Let's *swear* to find this treasure. You're the one to do it. You're always passing exams. but I'll run about for you and fetch things just as long as we can help Auntie."

He looked at her without speaking. This was a very different Penny from the harum-scarum scatterbrain who threw clods of muddy weeds through his window while he was still in bed.

" But we don't know that there is any treasure," he said cautiously, at last. " It would be awful to let everybody think we were going to find it and then flop ! "

Penny flamed at him. " *Tell* everybody ! Of course we shan't breathe a word to anybody, you idiot. Not even to Auntie, until we've found it. Least of all to her ! Can't you see it's something we can do for her ? We've got this lovely place of our own and we'll work and plan here and just go on having our holiday in the ordinary way and not tell her a word of what we're doing. . . . And all the time, Jon, we'll be ferreting out things and following up clues and shadowing people, and she will never guess how we're working for her until we find it and give it to her to stop her worrying. *That's* what I mean ! "

" That's all very well, Penny, but you're talking like a book and not even talking sense. We haven't got any clues."

She jumped up and rubbed her legs which were sore with kneeling.

" You are so *dull*, Jon ! I bet you've got a box full of clues. Have you forgotten the box already ? . . . Jon, I believe Auntie really thinks there is something and I *know* she hopes there is. Wouldn't it be wonderful if we could find this treasure for her ? I don't see why there shouldn't be a clue in this room. It's the sort of place that's made for clues. . . . I bet this room was used by smugglers and I expect mine was, too, 'cos it's just underneath. . . . Come and look at the window and see if you can make out these letters. Maybe they are a clue. Maybe we can start looking for the treasure right away after you've read this. I can't do it. The letters are funny and I think the first word is God. Come and look."

Jon laughed and got off the table.

" Sorry if I was a wet blanket, Newpenny ! Of course we'll search and we'll go right through the box in a minute. . . . And don't you worry about running about for me, although I don't think that you really meant it ! We're in this together. . . . Now let's look at your discovery," and he knelt down beside her on the floor and because he was looking at the glass he did not see her blush scarlet with pleasure at his words.

" Look," she said, as her grubby finger rubbed away some of the dirt. " There are words here and they go across to the next pane, but I can't understand all the letters. . . . If you'll read them out, I'll write them down if you've got a pencil and paper."

Jon found a pencil but was still searching for a scrap of paper when Penny said : " Don't worry about it. Read out the letters and I'll do them in the dust on the floor with my finger."

So Jon started. As Penny had already discovered, the letters were difficult to read. But by putting his own finger over each as he deciphered it, they got the message at last.

" God Save England and ye Towne of Rye," Penny read out triumphantly. " That's it. It's not much of a clue for us, is it ? We must ask somebody here if it used to be a watchword or something. . . . It might have been a password, though, mightn't it ? Perhaps someone was kept prisoner in this room ? P'raps there were bars across the window once. . . ."

" Doesn't help us now, anyway," Jon said. " But it is interesting. It's been scratched on with a diamond. Nothing else is hard enough to mark glass like this. Maybe it was done by a prisoner ? . . . Now, I've got an idea, Penny. It's raining hard again. . . . Let's spend the rest of the day up here. Let's get a lamp and hang it from this beam and I'll fetch some wood for a fire and perhaps Mother would let us have some grub and then we'll lock the door and go through the box."

Penny agreed that this was a good plan, so Jon locked the door behind them and they went downstairs to see what they could find. So that no time need be wasted, Penny went by herself to find her aunt and beg for provisions.

" And I'd better borrow a broom and a dustpan and some dusters first of all," she said to Jon's amazement. " We must get the place clean and tidy before we start. Lend me the key and I'll get on with that right away, while you find Fred and see if you can borrow an oil lamp. And don't forget the fire. We must have a fire."

Jon handed over the heavy key and Penny skipped off towards the kitchens. He was at the door of the lounge when she came back for a moment.

" If Fred won't do it for you," she said, " you'd better let me know. He'll find anything for me I'm sure. He likes little Penny ! "

This was more like the Penny he knew so well and he was still grinning when he found Fred Vasson in his den off the yard. Fred was busy with something in a vice, but when John told him that his mother had said that he might know where there was a hanging oil lamp, he stopped his work and said :

" Now that be very unaccountable, fur I kin put me hand upon the very thing. . . . Used to hang over door to lounge before they had electric. . . . There, Master Jon. . . . Will that do ? " and from under the bench he produced an old copper lamp with a reflector and a glass chimney and a chain to hang it by.

Then he showed Jon the oil tank and the wood shed where the kindling and logs were kept and Jon filled a sack with the latter and toiled up the narrow stairs with it on his shoulders. When he was halfway up he realized that Fred had not asked him any questions. He was beginning to understand why his mother thought such a lot of Fred. The sack was difficult to manœuvre up the narrow stairs past Penny's room. She was before him—he could hear her singing something quite unrecognizable and banging about with a broom. Suddenly she stopped and he called :

" Open the door, Penny. I'm nearly stuck with this beastly thing."

She heard him and ran over to help him up the last few stairs.

" It's all right," she said. " I found Auntie and she says we can do what we like and she told that funny old cook to let us have what we wanted for an indoor picnic and the old dear didn't seem too pleased about it when I told her some of the things I thought we should need. . . . I told her we would like a kettle and a saucepan and some coffee and some cocoa because I like cocoa better although you say it's a sissy drink, and some milk, and I thought we could cook some sausages too, but I hadn't quite got the nerve to ask for a frying pan ! Maybe you'd better do that ! I think she'll like you. I expect she likes boys best."

She paused for breath and looked fixedly at his feet.

" What's the matter with 'em ? " Jon asked as he dropped the sack. " Gosh, but it's dirty in here. It was fresher before you started work on it."

" What have you got on your feet, Jon ? " Penny asked.

" It may seem an odd habit to you, but I wear shoes," he explained patiently.

" Have you got rubber soles ? " Penny persisted.

Jon stood on one leg to see.

" No, I haven't. Have you gone silly ? I know *you* don't wear shoes before breakfast if you can help it, but I can't see why you're interested in what I wear."

Penny put down her broom.

" Come over here and tell me if you see what I see." She

led him over towards the fire, but stopped a yard from the
bare hearthstone.

"Look!" she said. "That's not your shoe and it's
certainly not mine, and I know jolly well Auntie didn't stand
over there this morning, and I'd bet anything that she didn't
wear rubber soles anyway. . . . Now, can you see it?" and
she pointed to the floor, which, as yet untouched by her
broom, was covered with a thin film of dust. In one place,
about a yard from the wall, was the mark of a rubber sole.
It was quite clearly defined and there was no mistaking it for
anything else.

Jon shook his head. "It's not Mother's," he said
decidedly. "She doesn't wear rubber soles. She hates
them. I suppose it's one of the maids or somebody who
came up to clean."

"But it's not been cleaned," Penny said quickly. "I'm
cleaning it now and didn't Auntie say she'd kept it secret?"

"Somebody must have brought that box up here for her,"
Jon continued. "I expect it was that solicitor chap.
Mother could hardly have carried it up those stairs. P'raps
Fred did it for her?"

"P'raps he did," Penny agreed. "But I'll look at his
shoes when I get the chance. . . . I don't know, Jon, but it
looks *new* to me."

Her cousin knelt down and looked at the footprint more
closely.

"You're right, Penny. It must be fairly new because
there's hardly any fresh dust over it."

"Somebody's been up here before we came," Penny persisted. "And I'm sure it's all very sinister, Jon. Auntie
said this was our secret place and that everybody had been
told not to interfere with us."

Jon laughed. "Mother said that there was only one key,
didn't she? Meanwhile, you'd better fix on a plan for
looking at everybody's shoes! I'll leave that to you,
Penny. You're best at shoes."

"Well, you can laugh, but I still bet it's sinister," she
said as she swept all round the footprint. "I shall remember that pattern anyway."

So while Penny swept and polished, Jon laid and lit the
fire, so that the flames were soon flying up the wide chimney
and the glowing embers falling to the stone hearth from the

high iron bars. Then he went down again for the lamp and a hook while Penny fetched the kettle and saucepan and a basket covered with a white cloth.

" She smiled at me ! " she said as she staggered up the stairs. " Cookie did, I mean, so I guess it's going to be all right. She also said that it wasn't a very nice day for a picnic, and I just smiled and I expect she thinks we're mad. . . . Let's eat it now, Jon, and then get right on with the box and go right on with it until we find something. . . . I met Auntie, by the way, and she said we've got to wash up all these things ourselves. It's rather a bore, but p'raps we could save up the dirties for several days and do them all together on Saturday nights."

" It's Saturday to-day," Jon said.

" Then that's no good. Let's make it Fridays. . . . Oh, Jon. Look what Cookie has given us, even if she does think we're mad. Treacle tart, thick with treacle—all brown and crumbly, and this is ham and here are two meat pies. . . . Put the kettle on, Jon, and I'll make the cocoa. . . ."

Jon made a few more journeys while she was laying one end of the big table. He brought up some notebooks and a pile of his own books, besides a big pitcher of water and some glasses which Penny had forgotten. On the last trip he met Mr. Grandon, who smiled at him curiously, while Jon tried to look as if it was quite a normal thing for him to carry a jug full of water in one hand and two glasses in the other down the hotel corridor at this time. Not until they had passed did Jon wonder whether there was any way in which he could examine the soles of the manager's shoes without making him suspicious !

The meal was great fun and they soon forgot the mood of a few hours ago when Mrs. Warrender had left them. The rain had stopped now and the sun shone fitfully over the roof tops and through their narrow window, making strange, wavy shadows on the floor-boards. The logs in the fire spluttered and crackled and their scent and the pleasant warmth of the flames helped to make the old room a friendly place.

" We want a few pictures on the walls," Jon said with his mouth full of pie.

" Yes, I know," Penny agreed. " Engines ! They'd look lovely, wouldn't they ? If you put any up, I'll take 'em down again. . . . Buck up, Jon. I can't stand this waiting much longer. The excitement is awful. Like Christmas morning, only worse, 'cos this isn't a present and it might be an absolutely awful surprise. . . . Yes, thanks, I will have some tart. . . . No, thanks. I'll cut it myself. I'd rather. I don't like all the crust. . . . ! "

At last they pushed the remains of the meal to the far end of the table, rolled back the cloth and lifted up the black box again well into the light.

" We've got to have plenty of room to spread things out," Jon said as he put the key in the lock ; and " Oh, Jiminy," Penny shuddered, " p'raps it's a skull and some mouldering bones ! "

The lock clicked and the lid swung open easily enough, but there were no bones—just some bundles of papers and a few old books and some rolls which looked as if they might be maps.

" Are there any leather bags, Jon ? Bags full of jewels or gold pieces ? Are you sure ? Put your hand in and scrabble round at the bottom of the stupid old box ! "

Jon pushed her back. " We've got to do this properly, Penny. Don't be an ass. Sit down and let's look at everything in turn."

But it was not easy to do this, for some of the bundles were letters and old bills, and the old-fashioned writing was too difficult for either of them to read. After some hesitation, Jon put these on one side, meaning to come back to them if they could not find something more exciting. They picked out two of the books next and banged so much dust out of them that Penny sneezed violently.

" This one is all about smuggling," she said as she wiped her eyes. " Look, Jon. The date in it is 1870 and it's got some marvellous pictures of awful-looking men being hung up—all right, then—*hanged up* in chains. . . . It wasn't much fun being a smuggler if you were caught was it ? I wonder whether the smuggler who scratched that on the window was hiding from the soldiers. . . . We'll read this book one day, Jon. . . . It will make me feel a bit sick, I expect, but I'll just have to read it. What's yours ? "

" It's a History of the Cinque Ports. I can't think why books like these were left in this box. There must be a reason, Penny."

" What are those Ports ? "

" Cinque Ports, little Newpenny! Cinque is French for five!
Rye is one, and so is Winchelsea, and so is old Hastings.
Somebody told me that, but I forget who.   There are other
ports, too. . . . It will say in this book. . . . Here are the
others—New Romney, Hythe, Dover and Sandwich."

" Well, that's just silly," said Penny.   " That makes
seven, not five."

" We haven't got time to bother about that now, but I'll
keep this book out and read it later."

There was another big, flat book next and in this was
pasted a number of newspaper cuttings.   They looked at a
few of these and found that they all referred to smuggling
and smugglers on Romney Marsh.   There were also some
descriptions, cut from old magazines, of the capture of a
gang of smugglers and of their trial in the old Court-house
in Rye.   Another article, cut out and pasted in the book,
told the story, illustrated by quaint, old-fashioned engravings,
of the Battle of Brookland.

" Brookland ?   Brookland ? " Jon puzzled.   " It's a motor-
racing track.   Or it used to be. . . . And yet somebody was
telling us something about a place with that name."

" I know," Penny said.   " It was Miss Ballinger, in the
train.   When she was telling us about the Marsh. . . .
Never mind that now, Jon.   It's only a place.   What's
next in the box ?   I think it's all jolly dull so far. . . .
What's that big roll ? "

The roll was easily the most exciting discovery so far.
Penny held one end while Jon unrolled it from the other
and held it down.   They saw at once that it was a rather
primitive, sketchy map and, when they had turned it round
and got it the right way up, Jon realized that it was an attempt
to show part of the Marsh near Rye and the coast beyond
it to the west.

" Look, Penny!   That's Rye, because he's drawn it on
its hill . . . and there's something drawn on the sea just
by Rye. . . . What is it ?   A bird ? "

Penny jumped with excitement and let go her end of the
map, which rolled up as if it was on a spring.

" Of course it's not a bird ! " she shouted as she held
down her end again.   " It's us, Jon !   It's the Dolphin.
At least it's meant to be a Dolphin, I think, and it's got a
silly grin on its face, so I s'pose that means it's gay."

Jon looked admiringly.

" P'raps you're right," he said. " It might be ! But why should the man who drew this map suggest the *Dolphin* ? "

" Because of the treasure, silly ! I bet this map is the clue, and I bet it's in the *Dolphin* somewhere—the treasure, I mean ! "

" There's nothing written on it or drawn on it that looks like treasure though. . . . Let's look at some of the other things. Winchelsea is shown, look, and he's drawn a little hill or volcano down by the sea, there. . . . And that's a windmill, there—and here's another at the back of Rye, and it looks as if it's in the middle of a wood, which is stupid. . . ."

Here Penny let go of her end of the map again.

" Jon ! " she said hoarsely. " Jon ! Don't you see, we've got it ! He said ' the old mill ' on the telephone. There you are ! There it is ! "

" Well, here are two," Jon agreed, " and we don't know which one, and they may both have fallen down now, for all we know, and there may be dozens more we know nothing about. . . . There's something here which might be a mill. . . . Gosh ! It's that place again—Brookland. It isn't a windmill though ! It looks more like a barn with something sticking up by the side of it, like a Chinese pagoda. . . ."

The more they studied the map the more exciting it became, and they both began talking at once and interrupting each other until Jon pushed Penny's hand away and let the map roll up.

" Wait a bit ! " he laughed. " We'll never discover anything this way. Let's empty the box first and just be certain that there's nothing else as important, then we'll put everything else back and really study the map ! "

Penny agreed reluctantly, and they went back to the box.

" There's a whacking great book at the bottom here," Jon said after they had lifted out some more magazines and two smaller books about Rye. " This is what made the box so heavy," and he tipped the box on to its side so that the book fell forward. Something small also tinkled against the box and fell to the floor, and Penny groped about for a moment before she found a small key. When she got up from her knees Jon was gazing in rather a puzzled way at the big brass-bound book before him on the table.

"LOOK!" WHISPERED JON, STARING AT THE ENVELOPE. "IT'S
ADDRESSED TO ME! DO YOU THINK IT'S A TRICK?"

"It's a Bible," he said. "What they call a Family Bible, I think. It's locked. Is that the key?"

Penny flung it on the table.

"I s'pose so. Let's get on with the map, Jon! I get scripture at school, and if yours is a decent school you ought to have it, too. To-morrow's Sunday, and we don't want to start it now, do we? Put it back with the other things and let's do the map properly."

But Jon was playing with the key, and even while she was talking he felt the lock click back and the heavy clasp opened.

"Buck up, Jon," Penny urged. "Put it back in the bottom of the box."

He didn't answer or move, so she looked at him and spoke again more sharply. The Bible was open before him on the table and he was staring stupidly at a large white envelope which he held in his hand.

"Look!" he whispered. "It's addressed to me! But it can't be. Do you think it's a trick?"

Penny shook her red head in bewilderment. The envelope was addressed clearly enough—"Jonathan Peter Warrender, The *Gay Dolphin*, Rye, Sussex." Just that and nothing more. He turned the envelope over, but there was no other message or writing on the back.

"It must be a joke, Penny. It was in the front of the Bible. . . . I just opened the cover and there it was staring at me."

"If you open it maybe you'll find out how it got there," said Penny, practical for once!

But Jon kept on turning it over between his fingers. "I think I ought to show it to mother," he said. "Do you think she knew it was there? P'raps it's a joke?"

Penny hopped from one foot to the other.

"Don't be so beastly infuriating, Jon! Open it! It's addressed to you, isn't it? It must be for you and for nobody else. Open it before I go mad. . . . I told you that Bible meant something!"

He laughed instead of disputing the last remark.

"Come on then! Let's see if we can solve the mystery. It's getting dark again in here. Come over to the window."

He pulled over a chair and Penny pushed him into it and leaned over him with her chin on his shoulder. The envelope contained many sheets of thin paper covered closely with neat writing. This is what they read together in the little hidden room under the crooked roof of the *Gay Dolphin*, while the rain lashed at the window-panes and the wood ashes in the old fireplace trickled through on to the stone hearth :

> " The *Gay Dolphin*,
> " Rye, Sussex.

" MY DEAR GREAT-NEPHEW JONATHAN,

" It will seem very strange for you to receive so long a letter in so unusual a way from an old man you have never seen. But if you are as sensible and steady as I hear, you will soon realize, I hope, why this comes to you in this way. I understand that you were fourteen years of age when your father gave his life for his country, so I think you are old enough to know that life is going to be very difficult for your mother in the future. Your mother is my only niece, and for a number of reasons it is many years since we met. But your mother has never been too busy to remember a lonely old man, and almost since you were a baby she has found the time, several times a year, to write me happy, friendly letters, that have told me about you and of her own plans and hopes. And this, my boy, is a gift which is very rare—a gift in which the young make the old feel that they are not forgotten.

" Your mother wrote to me when your father was killed. I wished very much to do something to help her—and indeed to help you and your cousin through her—but the only thing which I had was the *Gay Dolphin*, and that I have sadly mismanaged for many years because my main interest in life has been the study of the past and of my own beloved town of Rye in particular. I decided, therefore, to ask your mother to take over the management of the *Gay Dolphin* for me and that you should all come and make this place your home. A few days after I had made this decision and before I had told your mother of it, several important things happened. Firstly, I was taken ill, which was not surprising, considering my age; and secondly, I was persuaded that an operation would save me much pain and probably prolong my life. This letter is being written to you, together with a few others, before I go into hospital, and the fact that you read it now will tell you that at least I have been saved much pain. You will know by now, too, that I have left your mother the

C

Gay Dolphin and all that is in it. I want you all to make it your home, not only because it was my home or because you have Sussex blood in your veins, but because I believe that somewhere within its walls there may be treasure trove which will help to make your mother's life much easier.

" You may well be wondering why I should tell all this to a boy so young, but it is because you *are* a boy and because I do not want your mother to be worried about treasure that may not exist that I pass on to you this faint chance and these clues that have now come to me at the end of my life. . . ."

Here Penny, who had been breathing more and more heavily as her eyes flew down each page, and whose hair had been tickling Jon's ear until he had given himself a crick in the neck, interrupted with a wild cry—" Stop ! Stop, Jon, you beast ! You're going too fast. Don't dare turn over another page. I'm only at the top now. . . "—and then, when she reached the last words, " Oh, the darling. The precious old darling ! "

" Who ? " asked Jon. " And stop breathing down my neck. Who's your old darling now ? "

" Not you ! This wonderful old Uncle Charles of Auntie's. You ought to be jolly proud that he's written a letter like this to you. . . . Go on ! Turn over ! What are you waiting for ? "

Jon sighed and turned to the next neatly written page.

" If you know anything about this part of England," the letter continued, " you will have heard that the Marsh and all this coast as far as Cliff End has for centuries been much used by smugglers, and the people of the Cinque Ports—there are several books about the Ports left for you to read—are the descendants of those who made the first wooden ships for the British Navy. The men of the Ports have always been wild, and independent. Time and time again these towns have been attacked and plundered from the sea, and when our ships were not fighting for our King they were generally engaged in a little piracy on their own account. So you will see, Jonathan, that Rye has a history thrilling enough to stir the blood of any proper boy, for her streets have echoed to the cries of sailors home from the seas, of pirates returning with rich booty and of bloody fights with the French, who many a time swept in with fire and sword. And not so very long ago Trader's Street echoed to the tramp of the King's Men as they searched for the lace and brandy brought in from France in exchange for wool from our Romney sheep that crossed the English Channel in the dark.

" The *Gay Dolphin* is almost as old as Rye itself. I am not sure how old it is, but there is no doubt that it was much used by smugglers and I am now fairly confident that it contains some secret which I have never discovered. There have always been rumours that some fugitives from the Battle of Brookland found their way to Rye and that, as they were hotly pursued, they hid some booty in a place which has yet to be discovered. Three of these fugitives were caught and hanged, the story goes, but two escaped. Rye rumour says that all five sought shelter in the *Dolphin*, but this has never been proved, although I believe that the inn would be obvious sanctuary for them.

" I want you to understand that although I have always known of these rumours and old tales of hidden treasure, I only thought of them as stories until yesterday, when the clues attached to this letter were brought to me at a time of my life when they are of little use to me. I believe the parchment to be genuine and can say little more to you now than that. They were brought to me by the son of an old servant who had just died. This old man, who served me for many years here in the *Dolphin*, now claims that he is a direct descendant of one of the men who escaped capture after the Battle of Brookland and sends me the clue without any other message, beyond one of affection and remembrance for a kindness which I once did for him.

" Here then, my dear boy, is something for you to do— something which, at your age, I would have given anything to tackle. There may be no treasure, but if there is and you can find it for your mother, you will have done a lot to help her. Do not be too disappointed if you find nothing, and do not expect too much. If the clue is genuine other people may be after it, so I suggest that you be on your guard and be careful to keep the secret. And do not worry your mother with all this unless you have to do so.

" I have a little more to tell you. I have put this letter in the Bible for a reason which may soon be plain to you ; and the contents of the box should help you in your search, for I have collected together many papers and letters which refer to smuggling in this district. The map, I think, deserves a lot of study. It was found in a bricked-up cupboard in the lounge here, many years ago, and it seems to show tracks which would be used by smugglers on the Marsh and on the levels to the west of Rye. You will see that the artist who drew the map seemed to think that the *Dolphin* was the centre of Rye, and certainly all the tracks marked lead through our ancient town.

"And so, my dear boy, I wish you well and all good fortune in your search. Remember always, whatever happens, how your father would expect you to behave and what your mother hopes for you. But it is because I believe that you will remember these things that I have decided so suddenly to pass these papers to you instead of to my old friend Mr. Harding, who would not believe in treasure if he saw it before his eyes. All that I have told your mother of this is that I want you to have the box.

"I am sorry that we have never met.

"Your affectionate Great-Uncle,

"Charles."

Jon held the last page still and gazed out of the window as Penny slipped down on her knees beside his chair and read the final sentences. Then she was quiet, too, and when he looked round it was to see tears on her cheeks. He didn't feel very cheerful himself and had the sense to wait in silence till she said, in a very little voice :

"The clue, Jon ? Where's the clue ? "

It was pinned to the last page of the letter and was but a dirty piece of parchment with a few letters and figures drawn on it :

"I was right, you see, Jon ! I was always sure there was a treasure . . . and I'll tell you another thing, if you haven't thought of it. . . . This scrap of paper is what Mr. Grandon

wants. . . . This is what he's looking for. . . . These are
the mysterious papers. You'll see that old Uncle Charles is
right. Other people are after this. . . ."

She whirled round, with her back to the window and with
her elbows on his knees and her chin on her clenched fists
went on, "You *promised* we'd be in this together, didn't
you, Jon ? Just the two of us. You'll share everything,
won't you, until we find it. You *swear*, Jon, don't you ? "

He rumpled her red head.

" Of course I do. I can't do this by myself, Newpenny.
Get up ! You're hurting my knees ! "

They went back to the table and looked at the muddle.

" I'm jolly thirsty," Jon said. " Will you go down and
get some tea and I'll put the kettle on here and tidy up a
bit, and then we'll settle down to this clue."

When the dirty tea-things had been pushed up the table
to join those still remaining from lunch, Jon took out the
parchment again ; but the longer they looked at it the less
sense it made. Penny suggested that " nt " might be a
place marked on the map, but they could not find any
separate letters or figures there when they searched.

" The date is clear enough, anyway," Jon said at last.
" I wonder if it refers to a letter in one of those bundles in
the box ? "

" It isn't clear at all," Penny argued. " It might be the
8th of April 1857, 1867, 1877 or 1907 or 1927 or 1937, or
it might be April 7th with just an 8 in front to make it more
difficult. And I don't see how one of those letters could be
anything to do with it because Uncle Charles said that he'd
collected those from all over the place. . . . Anyway, there's
no connection between the clue and the letter that I can see."

Jon nodded gloomily. " And this ' nt ' beats me. It
might be somebody's initials. P'raps the man who sent
Uncle the clue ? He didn't say anything about it, did he ?
Let's look at his letter again,"

While he was skipping through the pages Penny said :

" It *is* agreed that we don't tell Auntie, isn't it ? You
won't, will you, Jon ? It will spoil it if we breathe a word
until we hand over the treasure."

" I believe I've got a brain-wave, Penny. It might be.
. . . Look ! Uncle said he put my letter in the Bible for
' a reason that may be plain to you.' Do you think that

' nt ' could mean New Testament ? P'raps that's as far as he got with the clue himself, but it might mean that he put the letter inside the Bible just to start us off ? "

Penny looked at him admiringly.

" Of course you're right, Jon. This is a real treasure hunt, isn't it ? Find the New Testament—but I can't think what April 8th has got to do with it. I didn't think that the Bible had dates like that ! Only the Ides of March, but I b'lieve that's something else."

Jon undid the clasp of the great Bible again and opened it on the table.

" Find the page where it starts off Matthew, Mark, Luke and John," Penny said brightly, " and all the rest of the books come after with Revelation at the end, which is easy to remember."

" You've given me another brain-wave, Penny. Let's see what the eighth book is ? Here it is. Second of Corinthians. . . . But what does April mean ? By the way, the Ides of March come in Shakespeare's Julius Cæsar."

" So they do ! He had to beware of them. How silly of me. . . . Listen, Jon ! When they give out a text they give the chapter after the name of the book, and then the number of the verse, don't they ? Just suppose that in some way April is a clue to the chapter in Corinthians ? "

Jon turned over the big pages. " There are thirteen chapters. Let's look at the beginning of each one to see if it says anything about spring or the time of the year."

They couldn't find anything which made sense, although one chapter began with the words, " *Would that ye could bear with me in a little foolishness*," and another with " *This is the third time I am coming to you.*"

" We shall have to read it all, Jon ! I'm sure that's the only way. Come on. You read the first chapter and I'll read the next."

" Wait a sec, Penny. We said just now that it might have something to do with the time of the year. April is the fourth month, isn't it ? Let's try Chapter Four. . . ."

" And verse 7," Penny broke in excitedly. " That's it, of course."

And when they read the first words of this verse they felt sure they were right : " *But we have this treasure in earthen vessels* " !

" We've got it ! We've got it ! " Penny chanted, and in her excitement flung her arms round Jon and hugged him.

" What's come over you ? " her cousin said, coldly disengaging himself. " I think we've solved the meaning of the clue, but we're not much nearer finding the treasure. ' Earthen vessels ' might mean an old vase."

" Or a teapot ! " Penny said cheekily, dodging round the table out of his reach.

" . . . Or a flower pot ? "

" . . . Or just a hole in the ground p'raps ? "

Jon began picking up the maps, the books and the papers and putting them back in the box.

" I've got a headache," he said. " Let's go out even if it is still raining. I'd like some fresh air and we can talk as we go. . . . We've done jolly well, Penny, and we'll find these earthen vessels somehow, but I don't like the sound of them because they may well be buried somewhere. . . . Pack those crocks up while I lock the box."

" What are you going to do with the clue ? " Penny asked as she piled up the dirty plates on the tray with a fearful clatter. " Shall I sew it in your shirt ? "

" No, thanks ! I'm locking everything in the box except the clue and that I'll keep in my wallet. . . . See me put it in, Penny ! Now, I'll carry that tray and you take the key and be sure to lock the door after us. The fire's out so that's safe enough."

They spent a little while in the scullery keeping their promise that they would do their own washing up and then made friends with two of the maids in the kitchen. Jon, who could be very affable when he liked, flattered the old cook who responded well to treatment. Then they went over to find Mrs. Warrender.

" Have you been up there all day ? " she asked when they found her. " How have you got on and do you like the place ? "

" It's wonderful, darling," Penny replied. " We shall practically live there while we're at home. I hope you don't mind."

" I mind very much ! There's no proper fresh air up there, and you'd better go out now for an hour. It's stopped raining and should be a lovely evening. Go and explore the town and I'll have some supper ready for you when you come back."

This was what Jon really wanted anyway, so they went for their macs.

" What we want here," Penny said as they went out into

" I'd like to see it working, anyway," said Jon. " But let's get back now and find Fred and ask him if there's another windmill round here. It's getting dark and cold and I want my supper."

So they walked back down the hill and watched the lights of Rye come up in the hundreds of tiny, crowded windows. The mist from the Marsh came up to meet them now, and covered all the green levels and the sweeping river too ; but miles away, where they remembered the sea was thundering on the shingle beach of Dungeness, the lonely lighthouse winked its warnings as the dusk deepened.

Their steps echoed on the cobbles under the old Land Gate as they walked up to the church. Penny slipped her arm through Jon's and for once he didn't ask her what she was doing.

" I know it's Miss Ballinger he's going to meet to-morrow," she said, " and we shall jolly well have to trail him to find out."

" If there's another mill," Jon said, " we shall have to go to one each. I only hope there aren't three. I've been thinking about earthen vessels, but it doesn't make sense, does it ? This is going to be a real puzzle, but I think we've got to find out first what this man Grandon has to do with it."

" I'm tired of calling him Mr. Grandon," Penny replied as they swung round into Trader's Street. " I'm sure he's a villain really and I know jolly well we shall have to expose him to somebody in the end. . . . After all, Jon, we know he's after something which really belongs to Auntie and I hate him. When we're talking about him I'm going to call him ' Slinky.' It suits him better. He's slimy. . . . Miss Penny, indeed ! "

" Look at that," Jon interrupted. " They've got our *Dolphin* sign floodlit. Doesn't it look fine ? " and when they reached the hotel Fred Vasson was standing on a step-ladder adjusting one of the new lamps.

" Ready for Monday," he grinned down at them. " Reckon we've got to look smart next week. Reckon we've got to give the Missus a good start."

" When you come down, Fred—I say ! I do hope you don't mind me calling you Fred and not Mr. Vasson," Penny said. " We want to ask you some things about Rye. Can we come and see you in your little den after supper ? "

" You'll both be welcome if your mother doesn't mind,"
he said. " Bring some mugs and I'll make you some cocoa."

So after supper with Mrs. Warrender, who only asked
them casually about their walk and refrained from any other
awkward questions, they rushed off to Fred.

He had drawn a pair of old red curtains across the window
and when the door was shut the heat from a hanging oil lamp
and a stove was almost overpowering. Penny was glad she
had changed into a frock and Jon took off his pullover at
once. Fred had cleared part of a bench for them to sit on
and while he watched the milk in the saucepan he began to
talk to them about Rye. They could hardly keep pace with
his stories and he did not seem to mind how many questions
they asked just as long as they were about this part of the
country.

" What does ' God Save England and the Towne of Rye '
mean, Fred ? " Penny asked.

" It means just that, lass. Ryers have allus thought
themselves a bit separate like and Ryers would know that it
was one of their own who said or wrote those words. Rye
didn't allus go quite the same way as the rest of England ! "

Then he told them that Owlers were the Marshmen who
ran the wool from the Romney Marsh sheep to boats which
would run it tax free out of England to France.

He told them also a little about the great battle fought in
the past between the smugglers and the Excise men. Jon
was just about to ask him if a pagoda could be found in the
marsh near Brookland when Penny broke in to say—

" We've got jolly interested in windmills since we came
here, Fred, and we found one up on the hill at the back
there. Does it work ? "

" Yes, miss. Her works all right. She's worked for many
a long year ! "

" Are there any more near here ? " Jon put in at the
crucial moment.

" Not in Rye, but there's a rare old ruin of a place at
Winchelsea in field not far from churchyard. Most people
about here call that the old mill, but 'tis said, I'm told, that
all would be built about the same time. . . . Now pass me
your mugs and I'll tell you about the battle of Brookland . . ."
and as he turned to the stove Jon looked at Penny and
mouthed silently, " Told you so. Just our luck."

"Oh, gosh!" Jon muttered to himself as he tore the note into small pieces and threw them into the wastepaper basket thoughtfully provided by his mother. "Oh, gosh! I had a feeling she'd be up to something. She's probably sitting outside his bedroom door waiting for him to come out."

Then he washed and dressed as quickly as he could and went downstairs. Penny was not in the lounge and neither was Fred, so he went out into the yard. His mother's front door was locked; he lifted the flap of the letter box and bent down in the hope of seeing through into the hall. Just at that moment the door shifted slightly under his hand and began to open inwards, and he heard Penny say softly and sweetly:

"Good morning, Mr. Grandon. I just happened to be passing in the hall and heard you try the door. It's a much nicer morning, isn't it? I'm so glad. . . ."

"Don't be an idiot, Penny," Jon interrupted. "Open the door properly and let me in."

"Jon!" she gasped. "I thought it was Slinky. I thought it *must* be Slinky. . . . I hoped it was anyway," she added in a burst of candour.

Jon squeezed past her and shut the door behind him.

"What are you supposed to be doing anyway? Suppose I had been Grandon? What would you have done?"

"I should have engaged you in conversation," Penny said coldly. "And what are *you* doing here, might I ask?"

"You might well ask! I found your silly note and came right away to find you, although why I wasted my time I don't know."

"You said that before," Penny said brightly. "But what note do you mean?"

Jon sat on the stairs and pulled her down beside him.

"Do you mean to tell me that you didn't write a note and put it under my door this morning saying that you were going to find Slinky and talk to him? Did you or didn't you?"

Penny nodded brightly. "Oh! That note, Jon! Of course I did, but I'd forgotten just for a moment that I'd written to you. . . . I say, Jon! Do you know that I don't really know where he is? He's got a room somewhere here and I thought I'd wait for him to come out, but I do hate all the closed doors in the house. I'm afraid to open any of them. I suppose I was thinking about him so much that

when I saw the letter box waggle I was sure it must be him.
. . . I thought it would be best to sit on the stairs here and
listen. If I'd heard him open a door somewhere I should
have found him."

"And what were you going to ask him so specially ? "

"Oh, I don't know. I'd have thought of something!
But you do agree that we've got to watch him all the time,
don't you ? "

"Well, don't let him catch us sitting here," Jon said.
"Whenever he meets us it seems as if we're doing something
silly—you with one shoe on and me carrying a great jug of
water, for instance. Let's go outside in the sun and talk about
it till breakfast. There's no sense in making him suspicious.
. . . But I would like to know if he wears rubber soles ? "

"I suppose I could ask Fred that," Penny said as they got
up from the stairs. "But I don't really like letting him out
of my sight."

The first person they saw when they got out into the yard
was Mr. Grandon, talking to Fred at the door of his little
room. Both men looked up and smiled when they saw the
children, and Penny muttered, "You see, Jon ? He escaped
somehow in all these passages. He *is* slinky. He's always
where he's not expected. . . . Oh, Mr. Grandon," she
called suddenly and sweetly, "whatever are you standing
on ? Is it a little mouse or something ? "

Mr. Grandon looked at her in surprise and then down at
his neat, shining black shoes. But he didn't lift his feet!
All he said was, "Standing on, Miss Penny? Nothing, I
thank you, except my own two feet. Did you imagine that
you saw a mouse ? A shadow perhaps. . . . You must take
care not to see too many things in your new home, Miss
Penny. . . . I mean, of course, too many things that are not
really there."

Penny flushed with humiliation and mumbled something
as she followed Jon out into the street.

"Very smart, indeed ! " was her cousin's comment as she
joined him. "Very clever ! Now, of course, he's quite
sure that we're both mad. He knows you are and he will
guess that I am just because I have to walk around with you
sometimes ! Look here, Penny, if we're going to get any
sense out of this puzzle, you must promise to do what I say
and not dash off and do so many stupid things on your own ! "

"I don't see that that was stupid! He might easily have lifted up his shoe and then we could have seen whether he had rubber soles!"

"Oh, Mr. Grandon," Jon mimicked, "there's a naughty little mouse by your foot. Please lift up your shoe!"

In spite of her fury Penny had to laugh and admit that she had been rather stupid, and as they leaned over their favourite wall and looked at the gently swaying tamarisks she said, "I'm sorry, Jon. I'll try to do as you say, really I will. I know you're much cleverer than I am, but I hoped to find out something this morning and surprise you."

Halfway through breakfast Mrs. Warrender said, "You'll both be ready for me at a quarter to eleven, won't you?"

"Ready, darling?" Penny asked innocently. "What for? We're always ready for you."

"Church," said her Aunt. "And not in those clothes either."

Penny looked shocked. "You don't mean that I'll have to wear a *hat*, do you, Auntie? I never wear a hat now, you know. I don't think I can get mine on."

Jon sniggered at this last remark, but was quickly quelled as his mother turned on him.

"And Jon, too. In your blue suit, please Jon. And a decent collar for once. What were you saying about a hat, Penny? Nonsense! What do you do at school? You have to wear a hat when you go to church, don't you? Of course you do. . . . You'd better wear your green frock and don't forget your gloves. I'd like to see you looking respectable just for one hour in the week!"

Penny was looking very worried.

"But Auntie, darling. I don't think we can *both* go this morning. Do you mind if one stays at home on guard? Perhaps the one who stays could go to Evensong, if that's what you think we ought to do!"

"What do you mean—on guard?"

"It's just a game, Mother. She doesn't mean anything really. We'll be ready for you."

When they were alone again Penny, forgetting all her previous promises of collaboration, turned on Jon furiously.

"Why didn't you stick up for me?" she demanded. "If you'd had said you'd got some work to do this morning and would go to church this evening, you could have stayed at home and watched *him* and Auntie would have excused you."

"What would be the sense of that," Jon explained patiently. "First of all, we've got to go to church because mother likes us to do so, and, secondly, we've both got to watch those windmills to-night, haven't we ? "

Penny beat her forehead with her hand. "Oh-what-an-ass-I-am," she chanted. "Oh, how clever you are, Jonathan Warrender. . . . But I've got to wear a hat. Isn't it ghastly . . . ? Jon, I've just had an awful thought. Have you got the clue safe ? "

He opened his pocket-book and glanced inside.

"Yes ! It's there. Let's go to our room and have another look at the map. We've got some time yet before we need change."

He felt in his jacket pocket. "The key ! " he gasped. "I haven't got it. . . . I left it under my pillow. . . ."

They dashed up together, but the key was still where Jon had left it when he had seen Penny's note pushed under his door.

"It's such a jolly big key," Jon said as they climbed Penny's stair, "that it's awkward to carry around. It's heavy, but I'll have to do it."

"I'll make you a sort of pouch in Handwork next term," Penny offered. "Would you like your initials on it ? "

Jon shuddered as he put the key in the lock and pulled the heavy door towards them.

"Don't you dare," he said. "Now I've got to find the key of the tin box, but I know I've got that somewhere. . . ."

When the box was opened they spread the map over the table again. After a while Jon said, "You know, Penny, we can't do anything practical until to-night. It's not really any good trying to follow Slinky as you call him. We don't really know where his room is, except that it's this side of the house, and we can't very well sit outside his office while he's in it or follow him into the kitchens. But we shall both have to go to a mill to-night, and we shall have to go separately and hide so that we can see who it is that Slinky meets and listen to what he has to say. Let's not worry about the map or these papers any more until we know for certain what he's after ! He doesn't realize how much we know and he might easily give something away to-night. And if I keep the clue safe in my pocket he can't see that, so that even if he is after the treasure he hasn't got as far as we have. You do see that, don't you, Penny ? "

His cousin nodded. " I s'pose so. I do so hate hanging about though and doing nothing, and I'm afraid that if we let him out of our sight we shall miss something important."

" I know how you feel, but I'm sure I'm right. We're a step ahead of him and he doesn't know what we've got. What worries me is ' earthen vessels.' We shall have to put our heads together over that one, Penny, but the answer may be in this box. I'm not looking forward to it, but I was thinking this morning that we shall have to go through all these papers and letters and probably read the books as well."

Before Penny could answer there was a step outside and the sound of a knock on the door. Jon dropped his pocket-book and slammed down the lid of the box. Then he ran over and called, " Who's there ? What do you want ? "

His mother's voice answered :

" I'm not coming in, Jon. I only wanted to make sure that you were up here. Is Penny there, too ? You've only got a quarter of an hour to get dressed and I think it's too bad of you both . . ." and as they looked at each other in guilty silence they heard her steps go down the stairs. Then they rushed at the box and crammed everything into it except Jon's pocket-book. Jon tried the lid after he had locked it, just to make sure and then pocketed the key. Then they were just as careful in locking the door of the room before they rushed downstairs to change.

Penny was down first and was sent back to put on clean shoes and fetch her gloves.

" Why you should behave like a baby just when you are asked to look clean and tidy and wear your nicest clothes I can't imagine, Penny ? You know perfectly well how I expect you to look when you come out with me to church. . . . Please hurry."

On the stairs she met Jon coming down and stopped him after one glance. " Stoop down a bit, Jon, and I'll fix your tie. It's under your ear now, and you'll only be sent back again. Wait for me. I've got to change my shoes. Oh, gosh ! Look at yours, too. They're filthy ! You'd better go back and change yours as well."

It was fortunate that the *Gay Dolphin* was near the church but it was a silent and breathless trio that hurried into the big porch just as the two golden cherubs by the unusual clock overhead struck the first stroke of eleven. Jon ran ran his fingers round the inside of his collar and Penny felt that her face was as red as her hair as they slipped into a pew just as the choir entered.

The first thing Jon noticed when he had wiped the steam from his glasses was an enormous pendulum swinging in the central tower very near to the pulpit. This was extraordinarily interesting, and during the Psalms he began to work out some mathematical problems connected with the swing, and for a time he forgot all about the treasure and Mr. Grandon. Not so Penny, who was on the other side of Mrs. Warrender and was trying to find " earthen vessels " in the Epistles and Gospels of her Prayer Book !

By the time the sermon began Jon was feeling much cooler. He slipped his hand into his pocket and felt the cold iron of the key. Thank goodness, he had remembered to bring that with him. And the clue, too ! Or had he brought the clue ? He started and felt the outside of his coat for the familiar outline of the pocket-book in his inside pocket. Then he breathed a sigh of relief and sat back as Mrs. Warrender nudged him warningly. That had been a shock, because, oddly enough, he had no recollection of picking up the pocket-book after his mother had called them.

For a moment or two he struggled to follow the arguments of the preacher, but his eyes kept returning to the swinging pendulum. The more closely he watched it the drowsier he became, for although the church was so large it was warm and stuffy inside, and he had wakened early this morning. His wandering thoughts returned to the clue. Who could help to decipher " earthen vessels " ? Then another thought struck him. He had felt for his pocket-book just now, but had not looked to see if the clue was safe inside ! He had no recollection of taking it off the table and putting it back into his pocket-book. Or had he ever taken it out ? He couldn't remember ! He shifted uncomfortably on the hard seat and slipped his hand into his pocket. He felt, rather than saw, his mother glance towards him, so he kept the hand there until he could slide it out quietly with the book. Slowly, gently and unobtrusively he opened the

He's been up here while we've been at church. I knew he
would. I told you the moment we were out of the way.
I'm positive I'm right. This smell is the beastly stuff he
puts on his black, greasy hair. I smelled it on the landing
yesterday and again when he stuck his head under my nose
when he put on my shoe ! "

" But how could he get in ? " Jon said. " Even if you're
right, how could he get through the door ? I locked it and
took the key to church with me and it's never been out of
my pocket."

" He's got another key, of course," Penny said triumphantly.
" He must have."

Jon looked worried. " I must ask mother if she knows
of another key. I believe she told us there was only one.
. . . Now let's turn this box out once more and then we
must rush down to lunch."

They took everything out of the deed box but there was
no sign of the parchment.

" It's gone, I'm afraid," Jon said despondently. " I suppose I must have dropped it. I know I had it in my bedroom
this morning, and I know I had it when we came up here
after breakfast."

" That's it," Penny agreed. " You've dropped it and
Slinky was watching to see us go out and then he came up
here and unlocked the door with his key and now he's got
the clue. . . . But I tell you one thing, Jon. He doesn't
know as much scripture as we do, and maybe he will never
find ' earthen vessels.' "

" Well, if he's got it we've not so much start as I thought.
We shall have to buck up and solve the riddle. I think
we'd better come up here again after lunch and go through
these other papers. . . . Come on."

Lunch was a happier meal than they had expected, mainly
because Penny began it well by apologising to her aunt.

" How are you getting on upstairs ? " Mrs. Warrender
asked presently. " Have you found anything interesting yet ? "

" Yes, we have," Jon said. " But you don't mind us
keeping it a secret for a while, do you ? But there are one
or two things we wanted to ask you, Mother. . . . Did you
by any chance go up to our room while we were getting
ready for church ? You know—between when you called
us and the time we were ready ? "

" Of course I didn't," Mrs. Warrender replied. " I told you I wasn't coming up without an invitation, and I only came then because it was getting late, and I didn't want to send Mr. Grandon or Fred or one of the maids."

" What about Mr. Grandon ? Would he come up, do you think ? " Penny asked suddenly.

" I'm sure he wouldn't. He knows the room is there of course, but he knows, too, that it is yours, because I told him so before you came. And he has told the maids too. Why do you think he would be interested to go up there ? "

" Oh, I don't know," Penny said vaguely. " I just thought he seemed a busy sort of little man. He *is* busy, you know, Auntie ! He's always popping up somewhere, isn't he ? "

Mrs. Warrender looked at her niece suspiciously, but before she could answer Jon asked whether she knew if there might be a duplicate key to the little door somewhere.

" Of course there might be, but I have never seen it. Fred knows about the room, too, and you can ask him if there is a spare anywhere. I believe I asked him once, but I can't be sure. I shouldn't worry about it if I were you, and don't spend all your time up in that stuffy old room. Are you going out this afternoon ? "

Jon smiled across the table.

" There's lots if things we'd like to tell you, Mother, but we'd rather wait until we're certain. You don't mind, do you ? . . . And we'll swear we'll go out later, and if we want tea we'll have it upstairs, if you don't mind."

" I don't mind," Mrs. Warrender replied, " but don't take everything too seriously, will you ? I want you to have lots of fun before you go back to school and I didn't mean you to spend all your time upstairs among those musty old papers. I never did suppose that you would find anything that was important, but I thought you would have some fun searching. . . . See you to-night for supper, then."

They spent two hours upstairs, but got very tired of searching long before Jon flung the last bundle of papers back into the box and slammed down the lid.

" I'm sick of this, Penny ! My head aches with reading and I can't make much of most of these stupid old letters. If the kettle's ready, let's have some tea before we go. How have you got on with those books ? "

Penny went over to the fireplace and kicked the smouldering logs into a blaze.

" They're terrible, Jon. . . . Hangings and trials and torturings are all jolly exciting, but I don't think they tell us anything we want to know. . . . I think we shall have to ask Fred to tell us some more of his yarns. He never finished that one about the battle of Brookland because you interrupted him, but I've found something about it in one of those books. It says that many of the smugglers escaped the King's Men in the battle and hid their booty which was being brought inland. It says it was landed at that place marked on the map. . . . Here it is, Camber. Let's find it again."

They munched some buns while they examined the map, and then Jon said it was time for them to go.

" Look here, Penny," he said, " I'm sorry we've got to split up, but I'm sure it's the best thing. I'll start now, because I'd better go to Winchelsea. It's further away, for one thing, and we don't even know whether I shall be able to get anywhere near the mill when I get there. Fred said it wasn't far from the church, and this map certainly marks it at the back of the town. You don't mind me going there, do you ? "

" I hate it," Penny replied. " I want to come, too, and anyway I don't like the old mill we looked at last night. I don't think Slinky would want to meet anyone there. Let's risk it and go together to Winchelsea."

But although she tried all her wiles, Jon stuck to his point and maintained that one of them must go to each mill to be sure that Slinky did not escape them.

" Keep out of sight, Penny, and although you won't be able to hide near enough to hear what is said, you will be able to see who is coming to meet him."

" We know that already, Jon. It's Miss Ballinger—and why bother if I shan't be able to hear what they say ? . . . Oh, very well ! I'll go ! Don't get into such a state. I'll go ! I'll go ! But I won't stay after half-past six."

" Plenty of other things we shall be able to do together," Jon grinned. " There's no need for you to start until about a quarter past five and, whatever happens, don't let yourself be seen. Are you going to wear any shoes ? "

He dodged the book she threw at him, and then they

locked everything into the box again, made the fire safe, packed up all the tea things, locked the door behind them and crept down the stairs. Jon nearly dropped the tray when they met Mrs. Warrender in the corridor, but she only said, " Going out now ? " and when they assented nodded, " Good hunting then ! " just as if she knew what they were going to do.

" I don't really know the best way," Jon said, as they went out together. " I believe buses go along the road we came with Fred, but there must be a short cut across the marsh to Winchelsea. Come and start me on my way, Newpenny. You've still got plenty of time and we'll see if we can find a footpath when we get the other side of the bridge. I suppose the map didn't show a path, did it ? "

Penny shook her head. " I should think it showed a million ! It's practically all dotted lines, and I'm never sure whether they mean paths or birds' tracks in the snow ! "

They went together down the steps of Trader's Passage, past the boat-builders, over the bridge and then stepped out on to the long, straight road that led first towards Camber, and then back towards Winchelsea.

" There must be a quick way across," Jon persisted as he looked towards the little town. " It looks a straight walk from here. I could just hop over this black fence. . . ."

" And fall in that ditch," Penny interrupted with relish. " It's all ditches as far as you can see. I should walk along the road, Jon. It's much safer and better for you too. You know you don't get enough exercise ! Good-bye. I'm going back now. Where shall we meet ? I don't think we'd better go upstairs again to-night somehow. . . . I think Auntie would be rather peevish if we disappear again."

" Well, don't write me another note, whatever happens,' Jon said. " We'll meet somehow. I agree that we shall have to be with Mother after supper, but p'raps we could slip upstairs just before we go to bed."

" Or *after* we go to bed. That would be more fun," Penny laughed as she blew a kiss to him and turned back towards Rye.

Jon kept to the road for a little longer. Although the levels looked very tempting in the lovely light of the late afternoon sun, and although hundreds of sheep were grazing placidly between the dark dikes, it was true that there were no clearly defined tracks. He had almost reached the turn in the road and was thinking of asking the next car for a lift when he noticed a plank bridging the dike just below the level of the road to his right, and decided that this might be the short cut for which he was looking.

For a time all went well. There did seem to be a faintly marked path which was certainly used by sheep and the feel of this was pleasant after the hard road. As he crossed another dike he looked back towards Rye and was surprised to notice that it now seemed very far away. Winchelsea seemed equally remote, and as he stood there above the dark water he had the feeling that he was utterly and suddenly alone. He had left even the sheep behind and for the first time since he had left the road the larks were silent. Then came a gentle breeze from the south and swayed the heavy heads of the bullrushes in the water ; but because the marsh was lower than the road he could see neither the ruins of Camber nor the line of the sea—only the twin towns on their hills glowing in a golden haze from the setting sun.

He stepped off the bridge and faced Winchelsea again, but from this moment it seemed that he was bewitched, for the track vanished and he found himself on an island surrounded by dikes too wide to jump and too deep to wade. The only way out was the way he had come, and so he was forced to hurry back towards the road. When he got to know this country better he realized how dangerous it was to leave the roads, which are built above the marsh, and that most of the tracks on the levels are made by sheep and generally lead only to another more tempting pasture. By the time he reached the hill which leads up to the Strand Gate of Winchelsea he was very tired, hot and out of breath. He was also very anxious, because it was after half-past five and he had yet to find the old mill.

The citizens of Winchelsea were enjoying the Sunday evening sunshine as he toiled under the gateway. He glanced over to the look-out from which they had looked over the levels for the first time on Friday, and noticed a little group standing round a seated figure. He was wondering whom he had better ask about the windmill when, with a shock, he realized that the shape of the figure was familiar. and as it was seated on a camp stool and facing an easel, he had no doubt that the artist was Miss Ballinger. Fortunately, she did not appear to see him, so he hurried past, hoping most fervently that she would not call him back.

This was certainly rather puzzling because it did not now seem that she was the person Slinky was going to meet—unless, of course, the windmill was very near and she could reach it easily.

He walked quickly up the street, hoping that he would not meet Slinky. At the door of the inn he asked a man if there was an old mill nearby.

" Somebody told me there was," he went on, " and I'm looking for an owl's nest as a matter of fact."

The man accepted this very reasonable explanation and confirmed that there was a ruin in a field at the back of the town not more than five minutes away.

" And a liddle old owl or two there be there, I'll be bound," he added confidentially.

Jon followed the directions and soon found that the town finished as abruptly to the north as it did to the south, although on this side the slope of the hill was more gradual. He went through a gate into an elm-fringed field, climbed a stile and found himself looking over flat country which stretched away into the blue distance of the Sussex Weald. The field before him fell away sharply in one place, and at the topmost ridge of the hill stood the gaunt, black ruin of a mighty windmill. There were no sails on this mill, and from where he was standing the sky showed through the timbers of the roof. This was certainly an old mill, if not *the* old mill, but it did not seem as if he would have much chance of hiding near enough to it to overhear any conversation that might take place outside. This gave him an idea. Suppose the meeting was *inside* the mill and not outside. Or, better still, was there a chance for him to get there first and hide inside in a place where he could hear all that was happening if Slinky met his companion just outside ?

Then he noticed two things. The first was that the sun had disappeared ; heavy clouds were coming up from the sea, and that without sunshine the old mill looked particularly mysterious and lonely. The second thing scared him at first, for it seemed to be a black hat, without a head inside it, moving slowly along towards the mill just on the level of the ground ! Jon adjusted his glasses and looked again.

It was certainly a black hat, and it was undoubtedly moving too smoothly to be blown along by the wind. He ducked down behind the hedge and tried to think things out. A black hat suggested Slinky at once and the old mill suggested the same person, but the poor man could hardly have shrunk to the size of a doll !

Then he had his big idea !

It must be Slinky who was walking along a ditch or a sunken path or road that was not visible from where he was crouching. After a little the black hat disappeared altogether, so Jon got up and ran along his side of the hedge in the direction from which the hat had moved.

His guess was a good one, for after a minute's running he came to a sunken road, climbed the gate, and very cautiously made his way towards the mill. The road had obviously been used by the wagons which had brought the grain to the miller and later returned for the baker's flour. Luckily the track twisted and turned more than once, but Jon moved very carefully and was certain he made no sound as he made his way cautiously round each corner. After a little he noticed a still burning cigarette stump, so, very carefully and slowly, he climbed up the steep bank and by holding on with both hands to a little hawthorn bush he raised his head until he could see over the edge. He was astonished to find himself so near to the mill, though not so surprised to see Slinky leaning against it and lighting another cigarette. Jon held his breath, praying that his quarry would not look down as he threw his match away. Then he realized with a shock that unless he did something definite at once it was more than likely that he would be found by Slinky's visitor, who must be due at any moment.

Jon was quite certain that this meeting was going to be very interesting. He had to think quickly, and as a thorn from the branch he was grasping was now hurting him badly, he let go and slid, as quietly as he could, down the bank into the lane. He lay still for a moment, but there was no sound from above except that made by the rising wind as it whistled through the creaking skeleton of the mill.

He went forward a few steps and noticed a little track running sideways up the bank, and realized that it must have been by this way that Slinky had reached the mill.

He had been facing in the direction of Winchelsea, Jon remembered, so if he was both quick and quiet he ought to be able to run across the open space just ahead where the lane finished and hide on the opposite side of the mill. Even as he dashed from the shelter of the lane that had proved to be such a good friend, he wondered if he could hide under the ruin, for he now saw that it was built above the level of the ground and supported on great stone blocks. There ought to be room for him to wriggle underneath, although it didn't look very inviting ! As he ran across the open he was buffeted by the full force of the wind, and realized that he was on one of the most exposed places for many miles around, but he reached the shelter of the mill, dropped to his knees and peered underneath. Against the light on the other side he could see Slinky's thin black trouser-legs flapping in the breeze. Then, bravely overcoming his aversion, he began to crawl over the filthy rubbish that had collected here through the years.

It was not at all pleasant ; and he had only covered two or three yards before he realized that he would not be able to see Slinky's visitor, nor would he be able to overhear their conversation because of the noise made by the wind as it whistled under the ruin and tore through the broken woodwork above him. As he backed out on hands and knees he decided that all he could do now was to creep round the mill in the hope that he could hide near enough to Slinky and his visitor to hear their conversation. There would almost certainly be a door into the mill somewhere, but he could not remember whether Mr. Grandon had been standing by it when he had watched him over the bank just now. He began to edge his way round very cautiously and felt the great ruin groan and sway under his hand as it was struck by the full force of the wind. Then he came to a doorway and to some broken steps which led up to another hole in the wooden walls above his head. He guessed that there was a " first floor " to the mill and that this would make an ideal hiding-place for him.

Suddenly the rain lashed across the field, and he knew that Slinky would be looking for shelter. He looked quickly again at the rotting steps above him and decided that he had no choice. The last four steps had gone long ago, so he had to jump for the handrail and pull himself up. He

JON FOUND HE COULD HEAR EVERY WORD THAT WAS BEING SPOKEN BELOW

was careful to put his weight on the sides of the steps and not in the centre, where they would be weakest, and although he felt one of them give under his feet he managed to get his hands on to the edge of the floor and pull himself to safety. Even as he scrambled up he heard voices and the sound of running footsteps. He had only just been in time.

When he got off his knees he saw that he was in a round room with a great wooden shaft running through both floor and ceiling. There were so many cracks and splits in the wooden walls that the place was quite light, and Jon noticed at once a big trap-door with a ring in the floor. He examined this carefully, but it fitted closely, and it was obviously much too heavy to lift. He put his ear down in the dust, but could hear nothing, and then moved over to the great shaft. This, of course, could not fit the floor so closely, and there was a crack about half an inch all round, but he tried in vain to see through this. Then he lay down full length, and with his head against the massive oak shaft and his ear to the crack, found, to his excitement, that he could hear every word which was being spoken below.

" Lucky for me that the rain came just then," he thought, " as otherwise they would have stayed outside."

A woman's voice was speaking.

" Well, don't let's spend any more time in this foul place than we need. Have you got it ? "

Jon realized with a shock that this voice was certainly not Miss Ballinger's. It was a younger, more attractive voice, and one which he had never heard before. There was a pause before Mr. Grandon replied :

" I have got something . . . something important, but I do not know what it means."

" Let me see," said the strange voice quickly. " All right ! All right ! No need to hold on to it like that. . . . I only want to look at it, and I shall have to take it to her, anyway, so I may as well see it now. . . . You know that you're not to be seen with her or even to know her at present, so you'd better hand it over to me at once. If you don't I'll tell her you kept it from me and you know you won't like what happens then. . . . Come on. Let me see . . . But this doesn't make any sense at all . . . ' nt 8 April 7.' . . . Wasn't there something else ? Are you sure this was all ? "

Mr. Grandon sounded a trifle sulky and Jon could picture

Dolphin and his mother and what he thought of the old house and whether he had explored it all yet.

" I'm interested in old places and old things," she said, " so be sure and let me know if you find any old papers or maps. And be sure that you don't take 'em to a junk-shop in Hastings or Rye. Bring 'em to me. I'll buy 'em from you."

Just then a bus came down past the church, and when Jon saw that it was marked " Rye " he called a hurried " Good-bye " and thankfully escaped. He swung himself on to the step as the bus slowed down for the sharp corner, and Miss Ballinger raised a brush in salutation and called :

" I shall come over and see you soon. . . . Yes, you will see me in Rye one day ; but you and your cousin must come and have tea with me in my bungalow. . . . Don't forget ! Good-bye."

Jon sat back and wiped his forehead. What a lucky escape from all those questions ! He began to wonder whether Miss Ballinger had seen him pass her on his way to the mill and decided to wait for him to come back before asking him all those questions. But what did she know about it all . . . unless Penny was right and she was the mysterious " she " referred to by the woman who had met Mr. Grandon at the mill ? He'd got plenty to tell Penny to-night, anyway, he thought as he got off the bus at the bridge and climbed the steps of Trader's Passage.

Penny was leaning against the wall at the top, pulling a tamarisk to pieces. There was a brooding look in her eye and she spoke before Jon could open his mouth.

" Don't tell me," she began. " Don't tell me now, because I can't bear it. I can see you've had a marvellous time. I can see by the silly grin on your face that you've had all the adventures. I knew you would. You choose Winchelsea mill yourself, didn't you ? You jolly well knew that I'd have a miserable time. Tell me now before we go in to supper. Who met him ? "

" I don't know who it was, Penny. I never saw her."

" You didn't see her ? You went all that way and found the place and saw Slinky. . . . I suppose you *did* see Slinky, didn't you ? . . . Oh, you did ? But you didn't see the ' her ' ? But, of course, you didn't *have* to see her because it was Miss Ballinger, wasn't it ? "

was careful to put his weight on the sides of the steps and not in the centre, where they would be weakest, and although he felt one of them give under his feet he managed to get his hands on to the edge of the floor and pull himself to safety. Even as he scrambled up he heard voices and the sound of running footsteps. He had only just been in time.

When he got off his knees he saw that he was in a round room with a great wooden shaft running through both floor and ceiling. There were so many cracks and splits in the wooden walls that the place was quite light, and Jon noticed at once a big trap-door with a ring in the floor. He examined this carefully, but it fitted closely, and it was obviously much too heavy to lift. He put his ear down in the dust, but could hear nothing, and then moved over to the great shaft. This, of course, could not fit the floor so closely, and there was a crack about half an inch all round, but he tried in vain to see through this. Then he lay down full length, and with his head against the massive oak shaft and his ear to the crack, found, to his excitement, that he could hear every word which was being spoken below.

" Lucky for me that the rain came just then," he thought, " as otherwise they would have stayed outside."

A woman's voice was speaking.

" Well, don't let's spend any more time in this foul place than we need. Have you got it ? "

Jon realized with a shock that this voice was certainly not Miss Ballinger's. It was a younger, more attractive voice, and one which he had never heard before. There was a pause before Mr. Grandon replied :

" I have got something . . . something important, but I do not know what it means."

" Let me see," said the strange voice quickly. " All right ! All right ! No need to hold on to it like that. . . . I only want to look at it, and I shall have to take it to her, anyway, so I may as well see it now. . . . You know that you're not to be seen with her or even to know her at present, so you'd better hand it over to me at once. If you don't I'll tell her you kept it from me and you know you won't like what happens then. . . . Come on. Let me see . . . But this doesn't make any sense at all . . . ' nt 8 April 7.' . . . Wasn't there something else ? Are you sure this was all ? "

Mr. Grandon sounded a trifle sulky and Jon could picture

him fingering his little moustache as he said : " There are other papers, and I know where they are ; but she must be patient. There mustn't be any signs or suspicions of burglary. . . . This is not going to be as easy as I thought, but I tell that to you and not to her, you understand. . . . But this paper that I have found ? It must mean something, I think, because it is really old."

" Where did you find it ? Tell me quickly because I must get back and tell her."

" Those children—and I do not like those children at all and particularly that brat of a girl—have been given the Trader's room at the top, and they are up to something, but I have not yet had time to make sure. . . . I think they have the other papers in a box which they are careful to keep locked. . . . I was in the room this morning when they were out. . . ."

And here Jon nearly whistled in amazement. He was still positive that the outside door had been locked when they went out to church. His leg was fast going to sleep and he shifted it gently as Slinky went on :

" . . . . and this scrap of parchment was on the floor. One of them must have dropped it, I suppose. . . . I would have you know that these children are not fools . . . they are not as I thought they would be, although it is true that I have had no experience of children of their age. . . . They are a nuisance, and may even be dangerous, and I am thinking that they may know much, but are not aware of the meaning of their knowledge. . . . We must find out quickly what this paper means . . . as quickly as we can."

" Yes," the other voice replied quietly, " and *you* must find out at once if these children know anything. And if you cannot find out for yourself we must take other steps. She will say that, I know. It is vital that we know what they know at once."

What Slinky would have replied to this quiet threat Jon never knew because at that moment he nearly cried out with the sudden sharp pain of cramp in his leg. Instinctively he bent his leg and began to rub the calf, but his shoe scuffled across the floor and he heard the woman's startled exclamation, " What's that ? "

Jon bit his lip to stop himself crying out as he heard Mr. Grandon say, " Only rats. Any old place like this is alive with 'em ! " and then laugh as his companion screamed and ran outside. Mr. Grandon followed more slowly, but Jon was in such pain that although he crawled over to the opening, he dared not trust himself to the steps until the pain was easier. When he could walk again, he found the steps were difficult, but he managed the descent somehow without hurting himself.

The storm had passed now and the sun was shining brightly again as Jon made his way carefully along the sunken road and back into Winchelsea. He passed a few people, but there was no sign of Slinky. He was wondering whether there was another way out of the town without passing the lookout when he realized that it didn't matter now whether Miss Ballinger was there or not, as she had not been the person with whom Slinky had made the appointment.

She was still there, however, and called out to him as he passed.

" Good evening, my young friend," she boomed at him over her easel. " So you have soon found Winchelsea. Come over here and tell me what you think of her. . . . And where is the little red-head ? ' Penny,' I think you called her. . . . Ah, yes ! Penelope, no doubt ! A headache, eh ? Dear, dear ! Such misfortune on such a lovely day. So you are exploring on your own ? Come closer, my boy, and tell me if you recognize the old gate. Twenty times I have painted this at different seasons of the year, and it never looks the same. . . . It is the light off the levels, but I shall never be satisfied. . . . What are you telling me ? That you have been exploring on your own ? And what have you been exploring, my young man ? Look at the dust on your knees ! "

In horror Jon realized that she had seen something which he had not noticed himself ! He was wearing shorts to-day, and his brown knees were grey with the dust of the old mill.

" I don't know where I've picked that up, Miss Ballinger, unless it was climbing an elm tree this morning after a wood pigeon's nest. . . . I like your picture very much indeed. I think it's wonderful."

She went on with her painting ; but while she worked she fired all sorts of inquisitive questions at him about the

D

Dolphin and his mother and what he thought of the old house and whether he had explored it all yet.

" I'm interested in old places and old things," she said, " so be sure and let me know if you find any old papers or maps. And be sure that you don't take 'em to a junk-shop in Hastings or Rye. Bring 'em to me. I'll buy 'em from you."

Just then a bus came down past the church, and when Jon saw that it was marked " Rye " he called a hurried " Good-bye " and thankfully escaped. He swung himself on to the step as the bus slowed down for the sharp corner, and Miss Ballinger raised a brush in salutation and called :

" I shall come over and see you soon. . . . Yes, you will see me in Rye one day ; but you and your cousin must come and have tea with me in my bungalow. . . . Don't forget ! Good-bye."

Jon sat back and wiped his forehead. What a lucky escape from all those questions ! He began to wonder whether Miss Ballinger had seen him pass her on his way to the mill and decided to wait for him to come back before asking him all those questions. But what did she know about it all . . . unless Penny was right and she was the mysterious " she " referred to by the woman who had met Mr. Grandon at the mill ? He'd got plenty to tell Penny to-night, anyway, he thought as he got off the bus at the bridge and climbed the steps of Trader's Passage.

Penny was leaning against the wall at the top, pulling a tamarisk to pieces. There was a brooding look in her eye and she spoke before Jon could open his mouth.

" Don't tell me," she began. " Don't tell me now, because I can't bear it. I can see you've had a marvellous time. I can see by the silly grin on your face that you've had all the adventures. I knew you would. You choose Winchelsea mill yourself, didn't you ? You jolly well knew that I'd have a miserable time. Tell me now before we go in to supper. Who met him ? "

" I don't know who it was, Penny. I never saw her."

" You didn't see her ? You went all that way and found the place and saw Slinky. . . . I suppose you *did* see Slinky, didn't you ? . . . Oh, you did ? But you didn't see the ' her ' ? But, of course, you didn't *have* to see her because it was Miss Ballinger, wasn't it ? "

He shook his head. " No, it wasn't. But I have seen her as well."

Penny put her head in her hands.

" Don't explain, Jon. Please don't tell me. I'll tell you what a *marvellous* time I've been having instead. No, listen. You must listen. I got caught in the rain and lost in that farmyard place and chased by a goat. Then I lurked round that horrible old mill for half an hour and got ordered out of the field by a *beast* of a farmer. And for the rest of the time I've been waiting and waiting for you, Jonathan dear ! "

But before Jon could tell her his story Mrs. Warrender came out to find them. And after supper they neither of them felt they could leave her. Once, under the cover of the radio, Penny whispered, " Meet you in our room at midnight," but Jon frowned and shook his head. " Too late. I'm too sleepy. But if you'll knock at my door about seven in the morning I'll come up."

She grimaced her dislike of him and then nodded agreement to his last suggestion. Soon after the News, to her Aunt's surprise, she went up to bed. She didn't care to admit it to Jon, but she was tired, too, and although she was keen to share his news she did realize that the early morning would be better fun.

But she nearly came back to find him when, at the bottom of her little staircase, she collided with Mr. Grandon—who was coming *down*.

CHAPTER V

MONDAY: BEACH VIEW

ON was no good at waking early, and although he had
so much to tell Penny about his adventure in the old
mill, he was fast asleep when the breakfast gong sounded
next morning. Oddly enough, Penny also overslept for once,
and was still looking sleepy when she came down just before
her cousin arrived in his usual tousled condition.

" I thought you were going to wake me . . ." they both
began together, and then laughed when Mrs. Warrender
asked them whether they would like breakfast earlier in future.

" Not for me, thanks," Jon said. " It's Penny who likes
the early morning walks. She walks in the dew to keep her
feet white! Did you know that, Mother? Don't you
remember that Mr. Grandon found her shoes? She dances
with the fairies in the morning, the sweet little thing!"

Penny choked with fury.

" It would do him a jolly lot of good if he did some dancing
in the morning," she spluttered. " He's *awful*, Auntie. He
just lies there in sloth. . . . And what's it to do with him
what I do in the morning before breakfast?" she demanded
as a fierce afterthought.

" What are you both going to do to-day, anyway?" Mrs.
Warrender asked. " Why don't you take some sandwiches
and go out and explore while the weather is fine? There
are wonderful sands at Camber, and there's the old castle,
too, although I haven't been there yet. I can't do much
with you to-day because the first guests arrive this afternoon."

" Oh dear!" Penny sighed. " What a pity! I don't
think I'll like the *Dolphin* so much with strangers about.
All right, Auntie—I know we're not supposed to see them
and get in their way. We'll be good, I promise. . . . But
what are they like?"

" That's something we shall never know until they arrive, Penny. Until they come they are only names. And you mustn't talk about our guests as if they were—well, specimens ! " she laughed.

" Well, I'm not going to worry about them," Jon said as he reached for the toast. " We three will stick together whatever happens, and we've got our room upstairs when you don't want us down here, Mother. . . . Come on, Penny. Buck up. It's a good scheme to go out for the day."

As soon as Mrs. Warrender had gone to see about their sandwiches Penny looked up and said :

" You can arrange what you like, Jon, but I absolutely refuse to do anything until you've told me what happened to you at the mill. Shall we go upstairs ? I wish to goodness that I'd wakened up like I usually do ! I'd have soon had you out of bed this morning ! "

Jon got up. " No," he said. " It's a grand morning. Let's go out and I'll tell you everything. . . . Come on, little girl ! "

They went over to their favourite wall and looked out over the swaying tamarisks to the marsh, which was very green in the morning sunshine.

" Jump up," Jon said. " Let's sit on it and face the street so that we can see what's coming. It's a bit knobbly, but you'll get used to it," and he hoisted her up beside him.

Then he told her his story. He told her how surprised he had been to see Miss Ballinger in Winchelsea and how he had only just got to the mill in time. Penny didn't interrupt very much, but she shuddered in sympathy when he described crawling under the mill and nearly fell backwards off the wall in excitement when he got to scrambling up the broken steps.

" What I'm so wild about," Jon added at the end of the story, " is that my leg hurt so much that I couldn't get down to see the girl who was with him. She sounded young, but, of course, you can't tell from just a voice."

Penny slid off the wall. " I can't stick it any longer, Jon. I wouldn't mind it being knobbly, but there's a spike where I'm sitting. I knew you'd have all the adventures, and that's why you sent me to the mill with the goat. I know it is. Anyway, I'm sure we're right about Miss Ballinger. She's in it. She knows all about it. I always thought so, and now I'm sure. She was the one they had to take the papers to."

" But why should she send the girl when she was sitting only a few hundred yards away herself ? " Jon asked. " Why go to all that trouble ? . . . Still, I must admit that she's a very odd person. She was most curious about us again when I spoke to her on my way back. By the way, she's going to ask us to tea. Can't think why. Shall we go ? "

" Of course we will. I wouldn't miss it for anything. But the greatest mystery of all is how Slinky got into our room and took the clue while we were at church. He must have another key, and I suppose we shall have to ask Auntie to let us change the lock. But it will be difficult to explain why we want it done, won't it ? P'raps you could do it yourself ? You're such a handy little chap, aren't you ? Jon, I bet that footprint in the dust was Slinky's ! He's been there lots of times."

" Maybe he has, but I don't think he's ever been able to open the box. I suppose I must have dropped the clue when we rushed out to church. I'm awfully sorry, Penny. It was jolly careless of me. I think I'll slip up now and get the map. It's safer with us than in that room, and we'll have another good look at it when we're out. . . . You go and see if the sandwiches are ready and don't forget a bottle of something because picnics always make me thirsty," and he wandered off indoors, leaving Penny still leaning against the wall.

She was wondering whether it was worth going into the kitchen yet when she noticed a boy wobbling down Trader's Street towards her on a bicycle. There was nothing very remarkable about the boy except that he looked dirty and was riding his bicycle without using his hands. Now this was something which Penny had never been able to do, and secretly she was rather ashamed at her lack of prowess. The boy had one hand in a pocket and the other held a half-eaten apple, which he stuffed into his mouth just in time to use his brake as he reached the *Dolphin*. He looked over to Penny and jerked his head towards the hotel.

" Where's door ? " he asked curtly.

" In the wall," Penny answered sweetly. " It always is."

The boy glowered at her and muttered something which she couldn't hear, and got off the bicycle. Then he took a letter from his pocket and after some intense mental effort turned in under the archway. He didn't look like an errand boy, and as Penny was by nature very curious she followed him into the yard, where he was now standing on the cobbles looking sulkily first at one door and then at the other.

"I wonder if I can help you?" Penny asked in her very best manner and held out her hand for the letter. The boy looked at her with deep suspicion and then said:

"You live hereabouts?" and when Penny nodded he rather reluctantly handed over the envelope. Penny gasped. It was clearly addressed in a small but tidy handwriting to "Jonathan Warrender, *Gay Dolphin*, Rye," and marked in addition, "Bearer to await reply."

"You just wait here and I'll bring you the answer in a minute," she said, and dashed in to find Jon. She met him coming down the stairs whistling cheerfully, with the map roll sticking out of the inside of his coat pocket.

"Hi, Jon! Come here. I've got another letter for you. Come over by the window and read it. A boy on a bicycle brought it."

"If a boy brought it I don't suppose it can be another from Great Uncle Charles," Jon grinned. "Or perhaps it cancels all the other letters we've got upstairs and now we've got to start over again. What do you mean? A boy brought it?"

"He's outside waiting for an answer," Penny hissed. "You are stupid sometimes, Jon. Buck up and read it."

So John crossed over to the window and slit open the envelope while his cousin stood on tip-toe and tried to read the letter over his shoulder.

"Winchelsea.

"Dear Jonathan,

"If you and your cousin can spare the time this afternoon I should be very happy if you would come and have tea with me. You may like to explore in this direction, and I shall be glad to see you and perhaps tell you some more stories of the Ports and the Marsh. I hope you will be able to tell the lad who brings this that you will be coming.

"Please give my kind regards to your mother.

"Sincerely yours,
"E. M. Ballinger."

"P.S.—My bungalow is the fourth to the west on Winchelsea Beach, past the little hill at the end of the Beach Road."

You pretend to shudder, but you love it really. . . . No, Penny, I think we ought to leave the gibbet and that district for a whole day. We should have to start back for Winchelsea almost as soon as we got there. Camber Castle is much nearer and four tracks meet there, but, somehow, I feel that needs a day to itself, too, though we could start there now, if you like. . . . No, I'll tell you what we'll do to-day. I want to see the old harbour, so let's go to Camber Sands by the river and walk back to that little hill at Winchelsea Beach along the coast. I expect there's a bridge or a ferry over the mouth of the river. . . . There's Fred ! Let's ask him."

" Yes," Fred told them. " There's a ferry right enough. He's never side you want him, but you've only got to holler for him and he'll come over. . . . Don't be forgetting the visitors 'ull be here time you're back, Master Jonathan, and you won't go banging about in the lounge, will you ? "

So they went and said " good-bye " to Mrs. Warrender, and then Jon folded up the map so that it fitted properly into his pocket, took up the knapsack and led the way down to the iron bridge that crossed the river on the other side of the town.

Penny panted after him.

" I do wish you wouldn't start off at such a pace with those stupid long legs of yours, Jon. You only do it for swank, and if you want to walk by yourself you can go by yourself this way and I'll go by the Castle, and we'll meet for tea at the Ballinger's place."

" It's funny how the children get older," Jon said. " Seems only the other day you were eleven. You'll have to grow up a bit, Penny, if you want to take your proper place in the world," but he waited for her good-naturedly and rumpled her head as she came alongside. " I just don't know what we're going to do about these ' earthen vessels,' Newpenny," he went on. " I haven't got an idea, and, you know, we might wander over two counties and never find a clue."

They were crossing the bridge now and, as this was the first time they had explored this part of the town, they stopped for a minute to look down at the brown water filling the river as the tide came in. On this side of Rye they were on the edge of the real Marsh and could see at once that it was different from the levels round Winchelsea. It was wider and bigger in every way and stretched, as flat as a table, as far as they could see to the east. The road upon which they were standing disappeared in the clear distance and no hillock even broke the monotony of the vivid green flats in front of them. Faintly through the still air, came the constant calling of thousands of sheep.

" Green and white," Penny said quietly. " Green and white. Those are the colours of the Marsh, aren't they? I love this place, Jon. I love it already. You could get lost out there just as easily as the Sahara . . . but we'd better get on if we're going to the harbour. Have you still got the map ? "

Jon nodded, and they came down the slope of the bridge which set them above the low level of the Marsh, and went off along the east bank of the river towards the sea. They reached the little town of Rye Harbour after an hour, and walked on to the wide, white stretch of Camber Sands a little further on and had their lunch on the top of the dunes.

" What a place for smugglers to land their goods," Jon said. " There's miles of these sands and the Excise men wouldn't be able to guard all of then. I suppose they would hide behind the dunes and hope to catch the smugglers as they led their loaded ponies over to the marsh. Let's look at the map again. . . . You see, there's one track marked leading inland from the dunes, and I expect that was secret and not an obvious gap. And if there's even a little hill somewhere inland, I bet that's where the gibbet stood—they always hanged 'em as high as possible so that everyone could see—and that was where five tracks met. . . . We'll have to find that one day."

" I've found it," Penny cried. " There *is* a little hill over there, but it's a long way off. Come and look."

Jon looked over her head along the line of her pointing hand, and it seemed as if there was a slight rise in the ground about half a mile inland.

" No time to go there now, anyway," he said. " Let's get down on the sands in the sun and eat, then the haversack will be easier to carry."

" Wish we'd brought bathing things," Penny said. " We never thought of it somehow. We'll come here again and swim, Jon."

" If she has that will prove it," Jon agreed. " But she'll be clever if she gets as far as ' earthen vessels ' !   I tell you what we shall have to do, Penny.   We must pretend to be quite innocent and try to lead her on if she keeps on asking us questions. . . ."

" She'll do that," Penny interrupted. " She's always asking questions and that's why we're asked to tea. You're right, Jon. If we stay simple long enough she'll give herself away. Would you like me to be a bit silly ? You know—not quite, *quite*. . . ."

" For goodness sake, don't play the fool, Penny, or you'll spoil it all. Let's make up our minds not to talk too much and maybe she will give herself away. This is a rum place, isn't it ? "

The bank here was very high and behind it the grassy levels seemed, in contrast, to be much lower. The track upon which they were walking was bordered on their right by a lagoon, which looked as if it filled as the tide came in. Before them rose the steep little hill which Penny had seen ten minutes earlier, and on the seaward side of the hill was a row of squat cottages. A rough road ran inland towards Winchelsea from the beach and beyond that again were some modern bungalows and some ramshackle huts made out of old railway carriages.

Penny wrinkled her nose in disgust.

" I don't think much of this," she said. " I remember now that Fred didn't seem very keen on it that first afternoon."

" What I can't understand," Jon said, " is how she can live here if she's an artist. It's all so ugly. And yet we know she's an artist because she sketched you for some extraordinary reason ! . . . Fourth along, she said in the note. Come on and let's get the party over," and they turned on to the beach and trudged west along the shingle.

" There she is," Jon said. " Waiting for us. Don't forget what we said and don't play any of your silly tricks whatever she says or does."

Penny composed her face into what she fondly imagined to be a smile of innocent welcome as they approached the little gate of " Beach View."   Jon raised his hand in greeting as Miss Ballinger, bareheaded and with the usual cigarette dangling from her lips, waddled out to meet them.

" Just beginning to wonder if you'd lost your way," she boomed. " Glad you could come. How are you, my dear ? I met your Jonathan yesterday and he was good enough to admire my work. . . . Come along in. . . ." and she led the way down the shingle path edged with large stones towards the faded green door of the bungalow. Although it was called " Beach View," the name had no justification. " Bank View " would have been more truthful, for these ugly little holiday homes were built behind the shelter of the shingle bank and it was not even possible to view the sea from the front windows. Penny turned as Miss Ballinger fumbled with the door handle and looked back. Suddenly she shivered and clutched the rough tweed of Jon's sleeve. The sun had gone in again and the wind had risen and was howling over the top of the bank. A few forlorn, yellow sea-poppies bowed their dainty heads in the shingle by the path, but it was not altogether the chill of the wind that made her shiver. It was something that she could not explain even to herself—a feeling of fear and foreboding and of something she did not understand.

Jon must have realized her dismay or sensed something himself, for as she stepped into the hall behind Miss Ballinger's broad back his hand gave hers a reassuring squeeze. This was quite enough for Penny ! Her chin went up and she fought back the instinct to turn round and run from this ugly little house and the hard, shifting shingle and go back to the open green levels which she already thought of as home. She flashed a grateful look over her shoulder to Jon and then laughed naturally as Miss Ballinger apologized for the size of the hall.

" Not much room here, I'm afraid, but that's my fault and not yours. . . . Trouble is I'm too big for the house. . . . Come along in here and let's have some tea," and she opened another door and led the way into a room with a cheerful fire in a miniature kitchen range and a table loaded with cakes and jam.

When they compared notes later they both agreed that their hostess was very entertaining and for half an hour at least she did not ask them many questions—or none which were difficult for them to answer. The tea was wonderful and, as they had had nothing but sandwiches since breakfast, they did full justice to it. Miss Ballinger herself enjoyed food also and Penny watched her in admiration, for experience had taught her that women of her size tended to avoid nourishing meals and concentrate on toast and the like. But Miss Ballinger was presumably past caring what happened to her figure !

In between slices of cake she talked to them again about the Cinque Ports and the Marsh, and when they had finished and she had lit another cigarette she invited them to see some of her work.

There was no doubt that she was a clever artist, and for a time they were both fascinated by the sketches and paintings that she selected from piles of canvases stacked untidily on the sofa in the front-room. Here were impressions of the Marsh in all its changing moods, of the quiet tree-shaded streets of old Winchelsea, and of the cobbled highways of Rye.

" Why, here's the *Dolphin* ! " Penny called excitedly. " You must have painted this from our wall."

" Yes, I did, but that's some years ago now," the older woman explained. " I did that when I was staying there once, but I'd like to do a better picture one day. Has your mother decided when she's going to open ? " she asked Jon.

" We're opening to-day," he said. " I hope you'll come while we're at home."

Miss Ballinger nodded. " I'll ring up your mother some time or come over and see her. I'm fascinated by old places and old things. I collect old maps and papers, and my house in London is full of them. You must both come and see them one day. . . . And that reminds me that you can do something for me before you go back to school."

" Of course we will, Miss Ballinger," Penny said sweetly. " We'll do anything we can, won't we, Jon ? "

Miss Ballinger had her back to them as she spoke, and was standing by the window, but she turned at Penny's remark and her glasses flashed so that they could not see the expression in her eyes.

" I'll tell you what you can do for me, then," she said. " Just now I'm making a collection of old letters, books, documents and maps—I'm particularly interested in maps —dealing with this district. I get all my stories of the Marsh and smugglers from papers I have already collected, and I'd like you to help me to find some more."

" I don't quite see how we could help you do that," Jon said. "Of course, we would if we could, but we're not likely to find any old papers or maps."

Miss Ballinger turned again to the window.

" I never pass a secondhand or antique shop without going in and nosing round. . . . Quite astonishing the things I've found in shops. . . . There are several shops like that in Rye, and I thought you might look round for me. . . . I'd pay well for anything you found like that. A little ready cash is always useful at school, I've been told, and if you like I'd be glad to pass over a few pounds now for you to go shopping for me."

" Oh, Miss Ballinger ! " Penny exclaimed as she nudged Jon so violently that he staggered. "We couldn't *possibly* do that ! Why, we wouldn't know what to buy ! And besides, we hardly ever pass any shops ! Of course, if we *did* see anything at any time we'd be only too glad to tell you about it, but I know Auntie wouldn't like us to take any money, would she, Jon ? "

Before Jon could answer their hostess said lightly, " Never mind, my child ! Don't worry yourself. But just remember I'm interested if you find any such documents *whenever and wherever* you may come across them. I'm a very keen collector, and collectors, you know, will give almost anything to get what they want."

Although the last words were spoken with a smile as she turned again to look at them both, Penny sensed a warning or a threat behind them, and when Miss Ballinger spoke again, quite softly, she moved instinctively a little nearer to Jon.

" And that reminds me," their hostess was saying. " Didn't you tell me on the train that your mother was keeping some old papers for you to see ? Are you *sure* you haven't anything which you could sell me, Jonathan ? Perhaps some of those old documents which are quite worthless to you would be just what I'm looking for. If I come over one day soon perhaps I could look through them ? "

" What papers do you mean, Miss Ballinger ? " Jon answered innocently. " I didn't say we'd looked at those old things yet, did I ? "

" Didn't you ? How very odd ? I wonder what made me think you had. How very extraordinary. . . . *Have* you looked at them yet ? "

"Well," said Jon hesitantly, "we have found one or two old papers, and there was a map, too, wasn't there, Penny? But, of course, we couldn't let you have any of *those*. After all, Miss Ballinger, those are ours, and we wouldn't want to sell them, if you see what I mean?"

"I don't see what you mean at all," Miss Ballinger snapped so sharply and with such a distinct change of expression that Penny jumped. "There's no reason whatever why you two children shouldn't let me have those old papers. They're worthless to you, I'm sure, but they must be just the sort of document I want. . . . And the map? . . . I'll tell you what I'll do, my young friends, I'll give you five pounds for that map!"

"But, Miss Ballinger," said Jon, "we couldn't take money like that! Of course we couldn't!"

"It was only a scrappy old thing, wasn't it, Jon?" Penny went on. "Just a lot of little sketches and some red crosses and dotted lines."

"Red crosses?" Miss Ballinger interrupted. "Are you sure of those, because those are the sort of maps I'm always looking for. Where is it now? Could I see it?"

"Knocking about at home somewhere," John said carelessly. "I can't quite remember what I did with it. Can you remember, Penny?"

"No, I can't; but you're jolly careless, Jon."

"Oh, well, I suppose I'll find it somewhere some time."

"Now, listen to me. That map may be worth a lot of money, and I think you'd better go home at once and see that it's safe, and then perhaps you'd let me see it some time. Just bring it along, or I'll come over if you'll send me a post card. I'll soon tell you what it's worth!" and she turned to Penny and went on: "When's your birthday, my dear? Would you like that painting of the *Dolphin*?"

"Well," Penny replied rather taken aback, "I've just had it. In July, actually. . . . Of course, I'd like that picture of yours, but I couldn't possibly take it. Not *possibly*, thank you all the same."

Miss Ballinger waddled to the sofa, found the picture, rolled it up and pressed it into Penny's unwilling hands.

"Nonsense, my dear! Glad for you to have it. Take it, please, and all I ask is that you remember me if you find any old papers. I'll buy *anything* you find. . . . Funny

about your birthday, but somehow I thought it was in April
. . . April the seventh, to be precise. . . . No ? . . . Can't
imagine how I came to think that was the date. Perhaps
it's yours, Jonathan ? "

But not by even the flicker of an eyelid did Jon give away
that April the seventh meant anything to them.

" No, it's not mine either. I expect you dreamed it,
Miss Ballinger. I dream dates sometimes. . . . Come on,
Penny, we must be going because we've got to walk to
Winchelsea along that road we saw by the hill, and we'll
get a bus from there."

" Thank you *so* much for having us," said Penny, shaking
Miss Ballinger by the hand. " We have enjoyed it so. . . .
You must come and see us some time."

" Thank you," their hostess said grimly. " I most
certainly will ! "

" Keep quiet. Go steady," Jon muttered as they left
" Beach View " and shuffled through the shingle again.
" Don't let her see us talking and don't try and look
mysterious. Just look slightly soft, like you usually do ! "

But when they were out of sight and had turned on to
the road they both started to talk at once.

" She gave herself away, Penny. I knew she would !
She was clever about the birthday date, though, wasn't she ?
I know jolly well nearly I gave the game away myself at
that."

" What date ? What did she mean, anyway ? " Penny
said wonderingly.

Jon clapped both hands to his head in despair. " April
the seventh, you idiot ! The date on the clue. Don't you
remember ? "

" Oh, of course ! " Penny laughed. " I'd forgotten about
that stupid scrap of paper."

" Forgotten about that stupid scrap of paper ! " Jon repeated, as if in a trance. " She's forgotten already. Don't
you realize that everything is proved now ? It shows that
Slinky passed the clue to someone else, who passed it on
to Miss B. There's no doubt of that now. She thought
we might give ourselves away when she mentioned April the
seventh. I nearly jumped, but she was watching *you*, luckily
for me. No wonder it didn't affect you ! "

" I just thought she was mad," Penny said complacently.

" I always hated dates, anyway, and I never remember them. . . . I say, Jon ! She does want that map, doesn't she ? What do you think she would have done if she had known it was in your pocket ? "

They were walking now on a rutted track leading inland from the beach. Just before it joined a more important road they moved aside to make way for a cyclist, who looked at them curiously as she pedalled down towards the bungalows. She was a very pretty girl, of about twenty. Her gleaming hair fell straight to her shoulders under a bright blue scarf which was tied carelessly over her head. Her lips were scarlet and her skin a delicate golden brown. She was wearing a white mackintosh and sandals on her bare feet, and Jon turned to look at her as she passed.

" You'd know her again, wouldn't you ? " Penny said coldly as they reached the road.

Jon looked at her in surprise, but had the sense to say no more.

They were still talking about Miss Ballinger a quarter of an hour later and had nearly reached the corner of the road under Winchelsea hill, where they hoped to stop the bus, when the sound of a bicycle bell behind them made them jump apart.

" Thank goodness I've caught you up," said a pleasant voice, and they turned to see the girl in the white mackintosh. Before they could answer she came up behind them and went on, " I've got a special message for you from my aunt, Miss Ballinger, and she asked me to be sure to catch you up. It's for you, actually," she said, turning to Jon and smiling radiantly.

" For me ? " he said doubtfully. " Why just me ? "

Penny blessed him for this and moved round to his side so that the girl no longer had her back to her.

" I'll tell you why. It sounds crazy, I know, but I was to tell you that after you'd gone she thought about that old map that you said you'd found, and the more she thought about it the more certain she was that she wanted it for her collection." She stepped a little closer to Jon and said quietly : " She wants that map so badly that she'll swop it for a motor-bike ! "

" A what ? " Jon gasped.

" A motor-bike ! And you can choose it yourself ! Bring

her the map, she said, and you can go and buy the bike when you like. . . ."

" The bus, Jon. Here's the bus," Penny interrupted. " Come on, Jon. We *must* catch it ! "

Jon came out of his dream.

" Thanks for telling me," he said, " but we must catch this, Good-bye ! " and he started to run after Penny.

" Cheerio ! " the girl called. " Let her know quickly, won't you ? Any bike you like, she said."

They caught the bus, but it was very crowded, and Jon had to stand by the door, while Penny sat on the edge of a seat farther up. She was almost shaking with rage at the stupid way Jon had listened to the girl. Even now he was looking vacant as he held on to the strap and swayed with the bus.

He waited for her at the bus-stop and they climbed the steps of Trader's Passage in silence. Penny didn't feel like starting a conversation and Jon still seemed in a dream.

At the top, though, outside the *Dolphin*, they both saw the same thing and stopped. A little black Scottie dog with one ear cocked was sitting solemnly under the archway regarding them with curiosity.

" I said we wanted a dog here," Penny whispered, " and now here he is. He's wonderful ! Here, little black boy ! Here ! . . . Oh, wake up, Jon, do ! Anyone might think that girl was a witch and had put a spell on you ! "

" I don't know about a spell, Penny, but, you see, I nearly met her before."

" What do you mean—*nearly* met her."

" I did nearly meet her. That was the girl who met Slinky at the mill. I'd recognize her voice any time."

CHAPTER VI

TUESDAY: ALLIES

"ONLY twelve more days and then school again," Penny said at breakfast next morning, "and we've got a lot to do still. I do hope you don't mind us being so busy, Auntie? We don't seem to be doing much together, but you do understand, don't you?"

"Yes, I do! But you did come to church with me on Sunday, although you weren't very pleased about it! I can't come out with you this week very well now that these people have come, but we will have a day together before you go back. I think the weather may break soon, so you had better get out as much as you can. Where are you going to-day?"

"Camber Castle. We both want to see it. I've been reading about it in some of those old books."

"What old books?" his mother asked.

"The books in the box—the Great-Uncle-Charles' box upstairs—of course."

"I've been very good," Mrs. Warrender smiled, "and I haven't once asked you what you have found. Anything interesting yet?"

"Nothing really, Auntie," Penny broke in quickly. "Of course, we shall tell you immediately we've got any *real* news. . . . If you're going to see Cookie about our lunch, darling, you do think you could drop a hint about those meat pies we had yesterday? They were super. I think we could eat three each if you don't mind us suggesting it. . . . And what are these new people like? I mean the people we are not allowed to see!"

"I think they're nice. There are some children, too, and a dog. I didn't really reckon on a dog, and I don't think the best hotels have them."

"We met the dog last night," Penny said. "He's a darling, and I covet him. I would like to mention that when, just before Christmas, you are both worried about what to give little Penny, you needn't worry any more. I want a little dog just like that one. . . . Are you listening, Jon ? "

"Oh, yes, I'm listening. We can't help listening when you keep talking. Don't take any notice of her, Mother. Next week she'll want a concertina. I remember the time when she asked for a milk-cart and a horse. . . . Don't worry, little girl. Wait till Christmas morning comes and see what you find in your stocking ! "

Mrs. Warrender smiled and put her hand over her niece's brown fingers for a second as she got up from the table.

"It wouldn't be fair to tell you when he gave up a Christmas stocking," she said, "but I *will* tell you one day, darling, if he doesn't behave himself. . . . Just let us know later on if you change your mind about the dog. . . Have a good day and don't be late for dinner this evening."

Two hours later Jon and Penny had left the Winchelsea road by a farm gate and were heading towards the grey bulk of Camber Castle rising ahead of them like a rocky island in a green sea.

"I've got a feeling," said Penny pensively, "that something is going to happen to us to-day. I feel it in my bones. I think we're going to discover something thrilling at Camber."

"Something has happened to us every day so far," Jon replied, "but I want to explore this place, too. The map showed four tracks meeting there, and I've been thinking, Penny, that an old ruin like this might have some secret passages——"

"Or a secret dungeon," Penny interrupted. "That's what I'm hoping for."

"I was reading up about the castle in bed last night," Jon went on. "Nothing much ever happened here—no fierce battles, I mean—but it was built right on the edge of the sea. I think the land jutted out from Winchelsea and that the castle was nearly an island. . . . And I tell you what, Penny. I nearly told Mother everything at breakfast this morning. You mustn't think I'm backing out, but I don't see much chance of us getting nearer to

any treasure with our clue, and I don't like this business
between Miss Ballinger and Slinky and that girl who tried
to bribe me."

" You looked quite goofy at her, anyway," Penny said
quickly.

" What do you mean ? I was just surprised at being
offered a motor-bike."

" Well, I've never seen anyone look like that, even at
the idea of a motor-bike," she retorted ; " but it doesn't
matter now. What's more important is that you *promised
and swore* not to say anything to Auntie. You know you
did, Jon. It's not like you to back out. Maybe it seems
difficult now, but I'm sure we shall find something soon,
and remember, too, that old Uncle Charles told you in the
letter that your mother wasn't to be worried. We must
wait a few days more, Jon. Let's do it on our own . . .
get out of the way, you fat thing ! " The last words were
spoken to a large ewe which was the last of about twenty
to scamper across their path.

They crossed yet another dike by the usual plank bridge
before Jon spoke again.

" It's not that I don't want us to do this together, Newpenny. It's just that the whole business looks more serious
than we first thought, and if we're not bright enough to find
the answer to ' earthen vessels ' before these other people,
then we shall be to blame for not telling the grown-ups—
especially if there really is a valuable treasure. Don't you
see that we ought not to risk losing anything for Mother's
sake if we could find it by telling her what we have discovered so far ? "

Penny had no immediate answer to this and Jon looked
at her in surprise. Her chin was up and her grey eyes gazed
across the levels to the sea. The wind whipped her hair
back from her face, which, for once, was very serious.

She climbed another fence and sat on the top rail before
she said quietly, " I know we ought not to risk anything
if it means losing the treasure, but you said yourself that
we were a step ahead of the Ballinger gang—I've just thought
of that name for them. I think we're quite clever enough
to deal with the old woman, and Slinky, too, if we go on
pretending to know nothing. There isn't really anything
they can *do* as far as I can see. . . . And besides, Jon, I've

made up my mind that we've got to do this without grown-ups. It might make it easier if there were more of us, because I think we ought to be watching Slinky and Miss B. all the time. It's by watching them that we might find out a lot."

Jon looked at her in admiration.

" You mean we might drop them an innocent hint and let them do some of the thinking for us ? "

Penny nodded brightly, although she hadn't really thought as far ahead as that !

" We're nearly there now," Jon went on. " But I'll tell you what we'll try and do presently—when we've had our sandwiches perhaps. We'll go through everything we've discovered so far—I'll write it down if I've got my note-book—and we'll talk it over sensibly and see if we get any nearer that way. That's what real detectives do, and I've meant to have a shot at it once or twice—hop down and let me get over."

They were close enough now to see that the castle walls, viewed from the outside, were still in fairly good condition and that the building itself was very much bigger than they had imagined. The round, squat central keep did not rise very high above the outer walls, but what struck them most forcibly was the castle's loneliness. It did not seem as if it could ever have been of any use standing, without even a moat, in the middle of a grassy plain with sheep grazing under its battlements.

When they came up to the gap in the walls which once had been a gateway they saw that nothing but the central tower remained inside. Sheep were nibbling on the very ground where Henry VIII's garrison may have sat down to eat, ivy climbed the walls from which armoured sentinels had watched the Channel, and from the crumbling mortar of the keep lusty wallflowers were swaying in the wind.

They stood for a moment in the big, grassy space. The sun beat down upon them, and they were sheltered, too, from the breeze which was rustling the leaves above them. The only sound was the monotonous baaing of the sheep and the ceaseless song of the larks overhead.

" I wouldn't like to be here at night," Penny said at last. " I wouldn't like it at all. It's all right now with the sun-shine, but I wouldn't like it at night."

" You said that three times. Nobody is going to ask you

to come here at night unless you come to watch one of the others, and it was your own idea to get them to work for you, wasn't it? . . . Now let's be sensible. The map showed four tracks meeting here and the path we've just used was one of them. This must have been a splendid place for a smuggler to hide treasure if he wanted to get rid of it quickly. It would be easy to defend, too, if it were attacked, and I believe there's a good chance that something is hidden here. I can't get over the idea, Penny, that ' earthen vessels ' means that whatever the smuggler's saved from capture was *buried* eventually. I think it is safe to assume that the clue suggests that. . . ."

They were leaning now against the wall of the keep and Penny looked at him solemnly. " Oh, Jon ! " she said softly, " you've no idea how I *admire* you when you speak like that ! "

" Like what ? " he said suspiciously.

" Like—' it is safe to assume that the clue suggests,' " and she laughed and fled from him round the keep.

For the next hour they explored the walls from the outside. They looked to see if any of the great stones within their reach were loose or whether any showed strange markings or signs. They searched, too, along the ground at the foot of the walls, and once Jon went down on his hands and knees and scraped the sand from a bare patch in the hope that he might find a trapdoor.

" You're not overworking yourself," he said savagely as he looked up from his lowly position. " It's no use just wandering vaguely round after me and standing by while I do all the hard work."

Penny looked distressed.

" I was just thinking," she replied, " that's it's nearly time we stopped for lunch. You look very hot and over-tired, Jon, and you're getting bad tempered, too. . . . And you're not fair either. . . . I've broken my nail picking and scraping at those beastly stones, and I've given you lots of good ideas. But there's just one thing I won't do, and that's go grubbing about in nettles. I'm no good at nettles, and I come up in the most fearful blotches and I've only got socks on. How sensible you were to wear nice thick stockings ! "

Jon got up and laughed. " You've always got an answer,

haven't you ? I'm tired, too, so let's find a place to eat.
I wonder what's the best way to find out if the walls are
hollow ? A castle like this might have had secret passages
in the walls, and perhaps the entrance would be bricked
up now."

" We could look round the walls from the inside presently
and see if any of the stones look new," Penny said as Jon
stepped out of the nettle-bed.

" And suppose they do ? "

" I s'pose we'll have to get a bulldozer and knock the
walls down, but I know it would be difficult to keep that
secret. . . . Don't worry, Jon. I still feel that something is
going to happen to us to-day. You'll feel better after some
of these meat pies."

They found an ideal picnic place inside the castle on the
top of a high grassy bank that rose, in once place, to within
two feet of a part of the outer wall that faced due south.
Here they were almost as high as the sentinels who once
would have paced the ramparts on the look-out for invaders.
They were sheltered here from the wind that sang among
the broken stonework, and Penny flopped down and stretched
herself on the sweet-smelling turf which was gay with tiny
nodding scabious and little red and yellow blooms of Lady's
Slipper.

She sniffed rapturously. " It's lovely ! " she said.

Jon was already unpacking the haversack. " What's
lovely ? Can you smell meat pie ? "

" No, I didn't mean that. I meant everything. I love
the smell of the sea and the marsh and the sheep. And
I love being here in the sunshine and listening to the birds,
and I love the *Dolphin* and the fun we're going to have and
to-day is one of the days that I feel I never want to go back
to school again."

" You'd better have something to eat," her cousin said
rudely. " You can't be feeling well. . . . As soon as we've
finished we'll do as I said and write down all the things we
know about the Ballinger and Slinky."

A quarter of an hour later, when they were ready to talk
again, Jon brought out his notebook and pencil and began
his task. Penny was not very helpful, for she was feeling
pleasantly drowsy ; but as Jon thought aloud she was not
called upon to say very much.

" I'm going to write down what we're sure of," Jon began. " We don't want to put down queries and what we think *may* have happened. . . . First of all, we know that Slinky and Miss Ballinger and, of course, that girl, are all convinced that there is a treasure to be found either in the *Dolphin* or somewhere near. We know, too, that they have the clue on the scrap of parchment which Great Uncle Charles left for me, but we don't know whether they have deciphered it. Another thing we're certain of, is that they want the map in particular and would go a long way to get hold of it."

" They even sent a messenger after it who made you look goofy ! " Penny murmured as she lay on her back with her eyes closed.

Jon continued as if he had not heard the last remark.

" Another thing we're sure of, is that Slinky has a duplicate key to our room, and until we get that lock changed he can go in there and nose around whenever we're out."

" He can't unlock the box, anyway," Penny said, " and there's nothing else in that room, is there ? "

" If he wanted to see inside the box badly enough I expect he could have another key made. . . . I've only just thought of that, but perhaps we ought to keep the box in my bedroom."

" What I think," Penny went on dreamily, " is that we ought to watch them all, all the time, and sooner or later they'll think of something that we haven't, and then we can nip in first and get the treasure."

" Very practical and helpful ! " Jon said. " Thank you very much. Now there's another thing. We found the letter and the clue in the Bible and that started us off, but I don't think they will even get the same start."

" You're guessing now," Penny said brightly. " You can't put that down because it's not certain. Anyway, they're quite likely to guess that ' nt ' means New Testament. Of course I know it might mean lots of things as well, but they *might* guess. . . . Jon, this is absolutely heavenly. Look what I'm doing ! Am I looking too absolutely heavenly ? "

Jon looked up from his notebook. While he had been talking she had reached round and picked a small bunch of lilac scabious and was now strewing her face with the flowers.

" You'll always look more beautiful with your face covered, darling ! " Jon retorted. " And you'd better rouse yourself because we shall have to get back to work soon."

" Just be quiet for a minute, Jon, and listen. There's a sort of hum like you get in a field in summer. It's wizard. Listen."

With a sigh Jon put his notebook on the grass beside him, lay back and closed his eyes. Perhaps Penny was right. No reason why they shouldn't take it easy for a few minutes. . . . Sun was lovely, too. . . .

" Can you hear, Jon ? There's the sea about a thousand miles away and the wind all the time, and the sheep and the bees and that noise of insects something like the noise in a shell."

" Midsummer hum they call it," Jon murmured.

" Of course it's silly and babyish," Penny whispered, " but somebody told me when I was little that only those who can see fairies hear this music."

Jon had no answer to this, but he was warm and comfortable, and when he closed his eyes the world slipped away.

Penny was asleep already.

They slept for an hour and in that time several things happened. High up under the walls they could not be seen from outside, and only from inside by someone who came right round the keep and then looked up to their eyrie.

Penny was the first to wake. The sun was still pleasantly hot on her face and glowed pinkly through her eyelids, which for a moment or two she kept blissfully closed. Then she heard a voice which seemed vaguely familiar and sat up in surprise. Her grey eyes opened wide as she brushed away the scabious still clinging to her hair. Kneeling on the turf facing her about two yards away was a boy of about sixteen, who was laughing at her as he put his finger to his lips and nodded towards Jon.

" Sorry to wake you up," he whispered, " I didn't realize you were here till I started to climb up. Do you mind ? I want to listen to what's going on down below there without being seen. . . . If you want a bit of fun, peep over the top here with me and watch. . . . That funny old thing doesn't know what she's in for ! "

Penny looked at the stranger with interest. He seemed to be a very nice boy—brown hair, dark eyes and very white teeth in a tanned face. Like Jon, who was now grunting a

"CALL THAT DOG OFF!" ROARED MISS BALLINGER. "TAKE HIM AWAY AND YOURSELVES TOO, YOU HORRIBLE LITTLE NUISANCES"

little and rousing himself, he was wearing corduroy shorts. A camera-case was slung over his sports shirt.

The voice which had seemed familiar was still rumbling in the distance, but before Penny could get to the parapet to look over Jon sat up and rubbed his eyes. He looked so astonished that Penny giggled and pushed him back on the grass.

" Not a word," she hissed with her face six inches from his. " Just be quiet and listen and look over with us. . . . Something's happening down there and I think Miss Ballinger's in it. . . . I heard her voice."

Jon polished his glasses violently.

" Who's this chap, anyway ? " he whispered. " How did he get here ? "

" Same way as we did, I expect. He'll tell us presently. . . . Come on," she said urgently, and beckoned to the new-comer, who crawled up between them.

" Sorry to disturb you," he said to Jon as he came up to them, " but maybe you'll enjoy the joke. Most people do —the first time ! "

Slowly and very cautiously the three of them crawled to the edge of the wall, raised their heads and peeped over. Almost directly below them Miss Ballinger was sitting at her easel with her back to the castle walls. She was waving a large paint brush in her right hand and booming in her loud voice at two children who were standing one on each side of her.

" I do not like inquisitive children and I ask you both to go away. And I would like you to go a very long way away and take your objectionable little dog with you," and with the last words she gestured with the paint brush in the direction of a black Scottie dog which Penny felt certain she had seen before.

It was at once evident that this action of Miss Ballinger's was a mistake, for the dog, which had previously taken a dislike to the large woman, first bowed his head to the ground between his front paws and growled and then leapt upon the paint brush, seized it and pranced triumphantly away. In about five seconds the handle of the paint brush was a tangle of splinters, while the oily end was tossed into the air as if it had been a rat.

" Take the brute away," Miss Ballinger roared as she got

like a big ice each.   Now here's half a crown. . . . Just run along and get yourselves a big tub each. . . . Here you are, my dears."

The twins regarded her coldly.

" No, thank you," said Mary.   " We don't care much for ices. . . . Not in the afternoon."

" Not enough to go running back to Rye for, anyway," her twin added.

" And besides," Mary went on.   " We're not allowed to take money from strangers."

" Of course," Dickie continued brightly.   " If *you* would like an ice our big brother David is about here somewhere and p'raps he'd run back to Rye for you."

" He's not as interested in art as we are, you see," Mary took up the tale, " an' sometimes he's a bit difficult about runnin' errands and that sort of thing, but he's a Scout and he has to do his good turn. . . ." her voice died away as Miss Ballinger jumped up from her stool and raised both hands above her head.

" *Brats !* " she stuttered.   " *Disgusting brats !   Will you go away ?* "

Mary put the dog down.

" Mackie, darling," she said, " don't take any notice of her.   She's rude."

" *Rude !* " screamed Miss Ballinger and knocked the easel over.

Dickie politely helped to set it up again, while Mary examined the daubed canvas critically.   Miss Ballinger snatched it from her, broke it in half across her knee and flung the pieces away and joyfully the little dog pursued them !

" Get out of my way, both of you," she went on between clenched teeth.   " Just get away before I lay my hands on you. . . . Yes, I'm going ! "

" Can we come too ? " Dickie asked innocently.   " I want to see how you paint."

Mary picked up the paint-box which was dropped at this question.

" No, Dickie," she said.   "I don't think we ought to do that, however much we want to.   I think that would be wrong because David told us to stay here till he came.   He was going to try and take a photo of a bird or something and I expect he'll be back soon. So I'm afraid we shan't be able to come with you after all. I'm so sorry, but it was nice of you to ask."

" Look," Jon whispered. " I think she's foaming at the mouth now. This is grand. I wouldn't have missed it for anything."

" Most people like the first performance," David murmured. " That's why I woke you up. It was rather a nerve really. I do hope you didn't mind ? "

" Not a bit," said Penny politely. " I wasn't really asleep."

" Liar," said Jon. " You went off first. Listen ! Whatever is that kid saying now ? "

Dickie was speaking.

" I'm sorry you've got to go. We really are. I wanted to see how you made a picture out of all those measurings."

Miss Ballinger, who now seemed to have objects hanging from all parts of her person like a Christmas-tree, turned and faced the little boy.

" Measurings ? What do you mean, boy ? " she asked sharply.

" Well," said Dickie innocently. " Mary and me were behind that little tiny hill over there."

" Acksherly," Mary added, " we were Indians on the warpath . . . neither seen nor heard. . . ."

" Well, anyway," Dickie went on, " we saw you come along that path and put your tripod thing up there and then get a tape measure and string or something and go crawling along the walls measurin' and writin' things down in a book."

Jon and Penny looked quickly and significantly at each other.

" Yes," Mary was saying. " That's right. What did you do it for ? "

The noise that Miss Ballinger now made cannot be described in words. Certainly she snorted and afterwards they agreed that she laughed a sinister laugh, but she did *not* answer the question. Instead she turned her back on them, picked up the folding stool, put it under her arm and waddled away in the direction of Winchelsea.

" There you are," said David. " That's the end of the Morton Twins act. As the R.A.F. say, ' You've had it ! ' "

" I don't think you ought to tell them anything, David—not without Peter and the others, anyway. What we did is secret. Besides, I don't know that we like that big boy, do we, Dickie ? "

" No," agreed her twin. " I don't think we do. Of course we talk. We can't stay dumb all the time, can we ? And another thing. What's it to do with anybody where I go to school ? "

This time David laughed.

" You're too cheeky anyhow, Dickie. Now just be quiet, both of you, and behave yourselves."

" Just wait a minute, David," Mary broke in. " Excuse us, please, but you've got to explain to your friends about us." Here she turned her back to her big brother and went on, " Dickie and me do everything together in the holidays and we'd do everything together in term time too, only they won't let us go to the same school. I don't suppose that ever before twins did things together like we do ! We have lots of fun and all sorts of adventures and we'd like to have some with you, too, if you don't spoil things by bossing us about and interferin' . . ." and she smiled so radiantly at Jon that he actually blushed in surprise, before muttering :

" Sounds like an ultimatum to me."

But the impulsive Penny liked them all. David she had been sure of from the moment she had wakened and although, as Jon said in his blunt way, the twins did have a lot to say and seemed very sure of themselves, she admired their loyalty to each other and the way in which they had routed Miss Ballinger. She looked up at them, standing a little defiantly side by side, and noticed that the lips of both were set in a stubborn line and for all their rather babyish talk, she felt that they were both older in their ways than they pretended to be.

Anyway, it would be stupid to spoil a new friendship with a squabble, particularly as these three were Mrs. Warrender's guests, so Penny reached up and pulled Dickie down on the grass beside her.

" Thanks for coming to share our adventures," she said. " Let's all stay here while the sun is still shining and have some chocolate. I've got a packet somewhere. . . . Unless you'd rather run back to Rye for an ice, David ? " she added.

" So you heard that, did you ? " Mary said, as she sat down by Jon and pulled the dog on to her lap. " Did you hear that, twin ? People are always listening secretly to us and it worries us very much. . . . Thank you, very much. . . . Can Mackie have some, too ? . . . He likes chocolate. It nourishes him ! "

" Why do you call him Mackie ? " Jon asked. " It seems an extraordinary sort of name for such a decent little dog— if you don't mind me saying so."

" Macbeth is his real name," David explained.

" Why ? "

" Lots of people ask that," Mary said. " It's 'cos he murdered sleep when he was tiny. . . . That means he barked a lot and kept Mummy and Daddy awake one night. . . . He didn't like that fat woman, did he, Dickie ? He hated her."

" When he hates people it means they're bad," Dickie said. " He's never wrong. . . . Or not often, anyway. I didn't like that woman either and she *was* snooping along and measuring the walls and she didn't like us seeing her. We only came yesterday and I think there's something mysterious going on already."

" Tell us about this castle ? " Mary said. " Is this the sort of castle where fair damsels sat and embroidered and waited for their knights to come riding home to them ? "

Jon looked at her in surprise.

" I shouldn't think so," he said. " Why ? "

" I like that sort of castle," Mary replied simply. " I read all I can about castles like that. Sometimes I just pretend I'm one of the ladies waiting for my knight to come home from the wars. He wears my glove in his helmet as a gage. . . . Oh well ! What shall we do now ? "

" Let's have some tea," Dickie said promptly. " That's what I want more than anything."

" So do I," Penny agreed.

" A good idea," said David, " and I've got a better one. I saw a jolly looking teashop up by the church this morning. Let's all walk back now and you two come and have tea with us there. Will you ? Please do."

" I will if I sit next to Jon," Mary said. " He doesn't like us much yet, but he soon will."

So they tidied up and buried the waste paper and set off

David's eyes were bright with excitement.

" Grand," he was saying. " Go on. Tell us more. This is like old times again. Oh, gosh ! If only Peter could be here."

" Send a telegram for her," Dickie said. " Stop everything till she comes. And the other members, too. We need them ! "

" Members ? What members ? " Penny asked as David paid the bill and got up to go.

" We've got a secret society of our friends," he said. " That's what Dickie means."

" Well, I wish we were members," Penny said impulsively. " I'd be proud to be a member of that."

David looked at her thoughtfully for a moment but said no more as Jon went on to tell them of the connection between Miss Ballinger and Mr. Grandon and of the girl in the white mackintosh.

They strolled up Trader's Street together and even the twins were quiet and listened carefully as Jon told them of the maps and of Miss Ballinger's attempts to bribe him.

" Can't you show us ? " David pleaded.

" Not out here," Jon said. " But, of course, you can see it some time when nobody else is about. . . . I've just had a grand idea though ! Penny and me have a secret room of our own up under the roof at the *Dolphin*. It's our very own and nobody else can get in because I've always got the key with me. Let's all meet there at midnight to-night and I'll show you the map and the other papers, and we'll make some plans. . . . But what about these kids ? They can't very well come, can they ? "

Jon soon realized that this suggestion was a mistake. When he had given way and Penny had promised to be responsible for calling them, Mary said :

" And I was just getting to like you ! You can't do things like that to Dickie and me. We come in on all the big things and you've got to remember that."

" Don't worry," Dickie added. " We won't let you down, partner. But Penny will have to wake us."

And so it was agreed that Jon should call David in Room 5 at 11.30 and Penny would do the same for the twins in No. 8 at the same time if she could keep awake.

" But it will be a strain, Jon ! Can't you do them all,

because although I wake easily, I'm not any good between eleven and twelve. . . . But I'll stay awake to-night if I have to prop my eyelids open. . . . I promise."

Then Mr. and Mrs. Morton drove up and Jon just had time to say :

" Better not let anyone know we're all in on this. Silly of us to talk here really, I think. Slinky might see us and that's not very clever. You go in now with your people, and we'll call you about eleven-thirty—or earlier, if all is quiet and everyone has gone to bed. Try not to talk at dinner about us meeting you, or else Slinky will hear about it. . . . See you later then. . . . Wear rubber shoes."

When they had gone Penny said :

" That was fun, Jon. I'm so glad you decided to recruit them. I was *willing* you as hard as I could—I practically prayed—and I'm sure we shall be able to do something with them. Don't you think so ? "

Jon nodded. " Maybe. But don't say too much yet. Let me do the explaining to-night. Come on. Time to change, else we'll get into more trouble."

    ❋   ❋   ❋   ❋   ❋

Penny stayed awake until some time after eleven. It was, as she had said, a very great strain to do so and when she was at her sleepiest she put her head out of the window in her effort to keep awake. At last it was time. She had not undressed so the moment the hands of her watch showed 11.30 she reached for her torch, opened her door quietly and stepped on to the creaking stairway. All else was quiet and as the light was burning in the corridor she switched off her torch. Her journey down the stairs and along the carpeted corridors was rather nervy, but she found No. 8 without difficulty. The door was unlocked, of course, so she turned the handle and slipped in.

Both twins were fast asleep with their clothes bundled on chairs beside their beds. They looked very babyish asleep, but Penny was ruthless, and when they realized why she had come, they were quick, quiet and sensible and were into shorts and jerseys almost without saying a word.

They crept out into the lighted corridor and stood stock

still when there came a sound of a match being struck somewhere below them. The twins shrank against the wall as
Penny whispered under her breath, " Still. Don't move."

Then a board creaked round the next corner and Penny
thought, " It's all up now ! " and wondered what explanation
she could give. Behind her, the twins' eyes were bright and
big with excitement, but neither of them moved. For a
moment she considered opening the door nearest to her and
slipping inside, but before she could decide two shadows
slipped round the corner to be followed by Jon and David !

A suppressed giggle came from Mary and Penny whispered :

" What are you going this way for, you chumps ? Buck
up ! There's someone downstairs ! "

" Must have lost my direction," Jon muttered. " Sorry !
I remember now. It's the first turn on the left for your
stairs, isn't it, Penny ? "

She nodded. " Hurry ! " she urged. " Do hurry."

Jon turned round and padded back along the corridor with
David, and Penny followed with a twin on each hand. When
they came to her staircase Jon stopped and whispered, " Lend
me your torch, Penny. Mine's nearly out and we must see
properly to open the door."

She passed hers along and saw David grin at her as the
beam flashed across his face. Behind her the twins twittered
with excitement as they climbed the narrow stairs. She
closed the door of her room as they passed it and called up
to David, " I suppose you've got matches for the lamp,
Jon."

" There are some on the ledge over the fireplace," he
whispered back. " Do you mind if Penny comes in front,
David, and holds the torch for me while I unlock the door.
She knows the way round here."

So Penny squeezed past and held the torch while Jon
fumbled for the big key in the pocket of his dressing gown.
In the background there was a peculiar tap-tapping and
Mary whispered :

" It's Dickie's teeth. He's not scared. Only excited.
Do buck up there, big Jon, 'cos we're getting worked up
behind here."

The beam of the torch focused on the lock as Jon fitted
the heavy key and turned it. Penny stepped back as Jon
pulled the door towards them and then swung the beam over

his shoulder into the room. It was very dark, for there was no moon to-night, and in order to guide Jon she shone the torch across to the fireplace to guide him to the matches. But as the little yellow spot-light reached the panelled wall at the far end of the room there was an odd click and then Penny screamed and the torch clattered to the floor. For a moment she was so frightened that her knees went weak and she leaned against the door-post. In the darkness she felt Jon stoop for the torch and then his arm slipped across her shoulders and gave her a clumsy squeeze.

"Did you see her, Jon?" she whispered. "Just her face . . . against the dark wall. . . . Did you see her too, Jon. . . . Tell me you did?"

The torch flashed on again and Jon held it steadily so that the beam shone on the wall by the fireplace.

"There's nothing there now," he said shakily. "But I saw that face, too, Penny. It was Miss Ballinger."

CHAPTER VII

TUESDAY NIGHT: TRADER'S PASSAGE

"IT was Miss Ballinger's face," Jon repeated in a whisper. "A face without a body. . . . but of course, that's nonsense. It couldn't be ! "

" It looked like that," Penny said with a shudder and then David, on the little landing behind her, broke in sharply :

"What are you two burbling about ? Do get out of the way and let us in. Isn't there a light somewhere ? "

And from behind him came further plaintive comment. " It's pitchy dark and it's jolly cold and we can't see a thing because of you big ones. . . . Are you frightened of the dark, Jon ? "

At that Jon stepped forward, still with the torch shining on the wall, and picked up the matches from the ledge by the fireplace.

" Sorry ! " he said. " Come in quickly. Take the torch now, will you, David, and bolt the door on the inside. . . . I'll soon have the lamp alight. . . . Penny ! There ought to be some dry wood down there. Try and get a fire going, I'm cold and we might as well be comfortable if we're going to talk."

While he was speaking he lit the lamp which shed a comforting, golden glow round the old room, and Penny busied herself at the hearth. She was thankful for the job Jon had given her as her teeth were still chattering from the shock of a few minutes ago and she did not want her new friends to see how shaken she was. When she turned round, it was to see the twins seated side by side on the table swinging their legs. David was standing by Jon the other side of the fireplace where they had seen the apparition.

"You're going to tell us your secret, aren't you?" Mary began and Dickie said, "This place is fun. Does it belong just to you two?"

Jon nodded but before he could answer, David interrupted again, and Penny couldn't help thinking that he did certainly know how to manage things!

"I don't think the kids saw it," he said. "But I did. Don't worry, Penny! I'm sure it was real." He turned to the twins. "Did either of you two see a woman's face with big glasses up against the wall here when Jon shone his torch through the door?"

Dickie and Mary glanced meaningly at each other.

"I've explained once," the former began patiently, "that we couldn't see a thing 'cos it was dark. . . ."

"And you great lumps were standing right in the way," Mary continued.

"And how could there be a woman's face there, anyway? Do talk sense, David. There aren't any pictures or a mirror. I s'pose you were just dreaming as usual."

"But Penny looks as if she saw something horrid, twin," Mary said quietly. "*Was* there a face, Penny? We'll believe you—even if it's magic."

Penny, who had now got the fire alight, got up from her knees and faced the boys. She felt better now.

"Yes," she said. "It was Miss Ballinger's face. The woman artist you baited at Camber to-day. I saw it. Jon saw it and David saw it and if you'd been big enough you'd have seen it too. . . . I suppose it was a trick to frighten us. . . . P'raps it was a mask."

"No, it wasn't," Jon said. "It was real. It blinked. It was peering sideways into the room, wasn't it, David?"

"Nowhere she could have hidden, here in the room, is there?" David asked.

"See for yourself," Penny replied. "There's nothing here except our precious tin box and table and chairs."

"If you all saw a face on the wall I think it's jolly unfair that we didn't," Dickie complained.

"We're always missing things 'cos others are selfish," Mary added. "But I'll tell you something, and I bet I'm right."

"*We're* right, twin," Dickie corrected her. "We both thought of this. I know we're right . . . Go on!"

" We'll, we think there's a secret passage behind the fireplace and that rude old Miss What's-her-name heard us coming and was just skipping off when Jon opened the door. I 'spect—*we* 'spect—that she was trying to see who we were when the torch went on like a searchlight and surprised her. . . ."

" . . . And then she slipped into the passage and closed the secret panel and that's how she vanished, just like an old witch," Dickie finished triumphantly.

Jon beamed at them and swung Mary off the table.

" Of course you're right ! Don't you think so, Penny ? That explains everything, doesn't it ? "

" Yes, Jon. I think they're right. It would explain how Slinky got in here on Sunday and stole the clue. . . ."

" Yes, and it explains the footmark in the dirt, too ! You're a bright girl, Mary ! Sorry ! Dicky, too, of course. You're both bright and we weren't clever, Penny, to miss something so obvious. . . . Now, come on all of you and see if we can find the secret of the panel. . . . Stand there a sec. Penny and I'll go and look from the door and see if that's the right place. . . . Yes, that's it. I'm positive."

" If you're right," David said, " there must be something to push or pull on this side, else she couldn't have got back."

" Unless she left the door open," Penny said as she began to run her fingers up and down the smooth panelling.

The twins went down on their knees and began to search the wainscot.

" 'Straordinary thing," Dickie said, " but adventures just happen to us. Wherever we go they just start, don't they, twin ? "

" Yes, but I wish I knew what all this was about. I just happened to think of this secret passage business 'cos it looks that sort of house. But what I want to know is, why ? "

" Why what ? "

" Why we're doing all this, you silly ass, Dickie. I mean, I can't see why. . . . You'd better tell us everything, Jon. Just tell us why that painter woman should *want* to come up to your room. . . . Unless she's living here, of course," she added as a bright afterthought.

Jon, David and Penny were working feverishly now to find some catch or part of the smooth woodwork which would prove to be the key to the panel, and as they searched

Jon told them about the clue and " earthen vessels " and of how they were sure that Miss Ballinger had not yet deciphered this.

" Let's see if there's anything on the carving of this ledge," David said as he moved over to the window. " But I think we'd better be quick, because if there's a passage, then our large friend got safely away five minutes ago, and we shall never catch her. . . . I say, Jon and Penny. It's jolly decent of you to have let us in on this adventure, and you can trust us not to breathe a word. You do know that, don't you ? I told you some of our adventures and we'd like to help you all we can without making the grown-ups suspicious. . . . And don't worry about these kids. I promise you that they're all right for all their talk. . . . They'll be careful, too."

" They're jolly useful at this very minute," Mary hissed triumphantly. " I've got the place ! Watch me. . . . Watch us, I mean."

They saw her poke her finger into a small round hole where two floorboards reached the panelling of the wall. She put out her tongue, as she always did when concentrating—and Penny put hers out, too, in sympathy—and pressed hard. There came a muffled click and slowly, very slowly, the panel adjoining the fireplace swung outwards into the room, disclosing a dark cavity within. And as it opened there came, too, a breath of dank, cold air—a smell of fungus and wet wood and decay.

" Give us the torch," Mary called excitedly as she peered in. " We must have a light. . . . There are steps going down. Who's coming ? "

Dickie climbed in after her, and then David reached in and pulled them both out again.

" Just wait a minute and don't forget yourselves. You're neither of you Captain here and you could spoil everything with your chatter. Suppose there's someone a little way down there listening to you ? "

" If there is, I bet he's jolly frightened of us by now," Dickie muttered protestingly as he was hauled out. " Don't be so rough, David ! We're only trying to help you, just like you said we all could."

Jon then closed the panel softly to within a quarter of an inch of the latch and beckoned them to the centre of the room.

"Now," he began quietly. "Let's decide quickly what's the best thing to do. We know the way in, so if we like we can go back to bed now and explore this passage properly in the morning. Or we can explore it now, but if we do I think we'd better get at least two more torches, and we'd all better put rubber shoes on if we've got them, because it looks and smells damp in there. Thanks to Mary—sorry! and thanks to Dickie, too, of course—we've solved the secret of how Slinky and Miss Ballinger got in here; but it seems to me it's a bit late to let these kids hang about now. Don't you think it's much more sensible to come up after breakfast and explore?"

"May be more sensible in one way, but stupid in another," David said promptly. "Miss What's-her-name may have left a clue now which ought to be followed up at once, and if we wait till morning we may miss it. Let's go while the trail is red hot! Much better. Don't you agree, Penny? . . . As for the twins, Jon, it's decent of you to be worried about 'em, but look at their faces and you'll see you've said the wrong thing."

"I'll just say *one* thing," Mary spluttered. "If you do just one single thing to keep us out of this now, we'll yell and scream until the whole house wakes up and discovers us."

"You've got to learn," Dickie added, thrusting out his jaw, which made him look rather silly, "that we're always in things. We do everything you others do. If we're kept out, like you said just now, then there's an awful row and we run away, or something just as serious. Please don't be silly."

"And another thing," Mary added. "Unless we go in with you big ones at once and explore this passage now, we'll . . . well, I won't say what we'll do till we do it, but you'll be sorry!"

Jon looked annoyed. He could not get used to these twins; but before he could grumble Penny said quickly:

"David is right. Let's get ready at once and explore while the scent is hot. Golly! My heart is banging with excitement! How are your teeth, Dickie? Have they stopped chattering?"

"Course they have. I've got 'em clenched with rage!"

"All right then," Jon agreed. "But we do want another torch. This battery is nearly finished. Who's got one?"

" We have," Mary said. " Sorry we forgot it. I'll go down for it."

" I'll come with you," Dickie said. " But let's be quick."

Jon, who wanted to change his dressing-gown for a sweater, went with them. While they were away Penny crouched with her ear against the open panel, and David paced up and down behind her.

" I can't hear anything," she whispered, " but it does smell mouldy. I wish the others would buck up. I say, David, I was jolly glad you suggested that we explored this to-night. I couldn't have slept a wink not knowing. . . . And there's another thing. I'd love to hear some more about that secret society of yours some time. . . I've always wanted to belong to one. P'raps we could start one here ? "

David laughed. " I'll tell you one day, but there's nothing against us having you in if the other members agree. . . . Here they come."

" We wanted to wear masks," Mary hissed as she slipped into the room again, " but Jon said anyone would know us whether our faces were covered or not. I can't think what he meant. . . . An' Dickie's teeth started again. You are a nuisance, twin ! "

Jon was bolting the door from the inside when David said :

" I wonder if we ought to do that, Jon ? You don't mind me suggesting it, do you, but if we go down the passage and for any reason can't get back the same way, we wouldn't be able to get into the room to-morrow by the ordinary way, would we ? "

Jon slipped the bolt back quickly. " Thanks," he said, " that's sensible. . . . Now then, I'll turn the lamp low and then we're ready. Who shall go first ? "

" You," said David promptly. " It's your passage, any-way. Penny next to you with a spare torch, then the two nuisances and then me in the rear to keep them in order and with the other torch."

This seemed to be the best plan, so Jon opened the panel and stepped in. His torch showed a narrow stone stairway leading down to the right at the back of the fireplace. Penny, immediately behind him, took his left hand and he noticed how cold her fingers were. Then David whispered :

" We're all in now. What about the panel ? I'd better leave it open, hadn't I ? . . . Bother it ! It's closed itself.

these papers long ago. . . . You can also let me know whether these children can be bribed. I believe everybody can be bribed one way or another, and it is up to you to find a way to make these children part with the papers. I must rely on you for that."

Grandon sounded sulky when he replied.

" That's easy for you to **say**. I tell you that I don't like dealing with those children. It's not what I've been used to. Kids ! Fancy putting me on to watching kids ! "

Here Penny felt the twins shaking with stifled laughter.

"And another thing," Slinky went on. " It's not safe for you to come here at night like this. You know perfectly well that you might be recognized on the way home, even if nobody sees you here. . . . All right ! All right ! Don't get worked up. How did you get on at the tea party, by the way ? "

Miss Ballinger did not seem to like this question, and hesitated before saying :

" Most satisfactorily. I found out something, of course, but I am not sure that I am the best person to deal with them. I do not like children, but here, in the hotel, you have many opportunities, and if you cannot find the map and papers upstairs or in that box—you will have to get a duplicate key of that box and search it of course—then you must somehow get the necessary information from the children. Meanwhile, I shall continue my own investigations in the surrounding country. . . . Now I must go, and *not* by the front door. Trader's Passage for me, and be advised to remember what I have said. . . . I am very serious."

Jon turned round and shone the torch up the stairs again. " Back," he whispered urgently. " As quickly as you can, David. Get out of sight round the corner. Buck up, Penny. Push those kids up in front of you."

Penny had no choice, for he put his hand on her back and forced her up the stairs. David had been quick to realize the position and had already hauled Mary up the winding steps and Dickie was quick to follow. The rumble of Miss Ballinger's voice came nearer as Jon squeezed round the turn in the stairway and switched off his torch. Penny's hair was tickling his cheek as she said under her breath, " What shall we do if she comes this way ? "

" Quiet," he whispered. " See the light. The panel's opening." They crushed themselves back against the stone wall as the thin line of yellow light widened and was then obscured as Miss Ballinger squeezed through the narrow panel into the passage below them.

Dickie was gritting his teeth to stop them chattering, but Mary might have been carved from stone. She confessed later that she was saying her prayers !

Then they heard Miss Ballinger say curtly, " Well, good night. Two days, I said. Communicate in the usual way," and then there was a click and they were in velvety darkness again until Miss Ballinger switched on her torch. They all held their breath in an agony of suspense until they heard her heavy footsteps going away from them down the steps.

" Oh, gosh ! " Dickie whispered. " That was awful. I felt quite sick. . . . I still do acksherly."

Jon sat down on the steps and pulled Penny down beside him, and they heard David say, " Just pull yourself together, Dickie. You can't be sick here and you know it. If you can't come on an adventure like this without being a nuisance you ought to have stayed in bed. What do we do now, Jon ? "

Before Jon could answer Mary had something to say.

" Now, don't you start on that bullying again, David. I don't see how Dickie can help feeling sick and it's jolly honest of him to say so, I think. . . . Just you leave him alone. . . . Just because we're the smallest here you start on us. . . . Sorry, Jon. What shall we do now ? "

" We shan't hear any more to-night, anyway," he said after a pause, " and we've certainly got something to go on now. I vote we go back to our room, where it's warm, and plan what to do to-morrow. These kids ought to be in bed, anyway ! "

" I'm not going back to bed for anybody," Dickie protested. " I'm going to follow that woman down those steps and see where they lead. And another thing. We don't like the way big Jon keeps saying we ought to be in bed, do we, Mary ? "

" We loathe it," Mary replied. " It's just that he doesn't know any better."

Penny got up from the stone stair.

" It's jolly cold sitting down," she said. " And I think

that the panel had closed behind David, who had not been able to reopen it.

"That was unintelligent of me," he admitted, "and it was stupid to forget it before we came up again. . . . Shine the torch somebody and let me see if I can find the latch which will do the trick."

But he was unsuccessful. Both torches began to dim; the twins got fidgety and Dickie's teeth began chattering again, and even Penny was worried as they searched and fumbled for the secret catch.

"Trouble is," Jon said, "that the catch seems to work from the *inside* and that hole which Mary found is lower on that side than it is on this, and that's why we can't get at it here. . . . The only way to find it would be to heave up these floorboards and I s'pose nobody has got a strong knife ? "

Nobody had, and Jon sat back on his heels in despair. Then one torch flickered and went out and Mary said :

"I'm not very keen on this. Shall we go right down the passage again and then come up the steps outside and knock at the front door ? We're tired now, aren't we, twin ? "

"I don't know about you chaps," Dickie yawned, "but I'm going down to wake up Slinky. He'll just have to let us through his room. If he tries to be funny, I'll just fix him. . . . Come on. Mary and me are tired, and it's all because David hasn't been clever with this secret door. . . . But he *would* do it himself ! "

"Don't be crazy, Dickie," David said. "And don't show off. You know perfectly well that we can't go and wake him up. He'd give the whole game away and that would be the end of everything for us. . . . Golly ! This torch is going now. I'll switch it off while we talk."

"We've got to do something, anyway," Penny replied. " 'Cos we can't sit here all night in the dark."

"There are three things we can do," Jon said. "We can stay here in the cold, we can walk back as Mary suggested and try and get into the *Dolphin* without waking anybody, or do what Dickie says—and I think the last suggestion is the best."

Dickie yawned again so loudly that everyone else did the same.

"He can't do anything to us, anyway. We're too many

THE PANEL SUDDENLY SWUNG OPEN. MR. GRANDON STARTED
BACK IN ASTONISHMENT

CHAPTER VIII

WEDNESDAY: ROMAN'S ISLE

DOWN the dark tunnel Penny fled. Her feet stumbled on the rough floor and her hands were scratched on the walls. Far, far ahead was a pinpoint of light, and she knew that if she could only get out into the sunshine amongst the tamarisks she would be safe—safe from Slinky, who was coming after her so silently and with such horrid purpose. She had always hated and feared him, but neither of them now wasted their breath in words.

If only Jon would come! Dear, funny old Jon wouldn't fail her if he realized her danger. . . . Slinky was very close now . . . the loose stones hindered her and pressed through the thin soles of her sandals . . . her legs were too tired now to carry her forward, and the little spot of light seemed as far off as before. She could go no further, and then, just as she made one final, special effort, a hand grasped her shoulder and with an agonized cry of " Jon! Jon!" she woke.

For the first few second she was too bewildered and frightened to know where she was. Her heart was thudding against her ribs and she realized that she was half out of bed with her head hanging over the edge. The hand that she had felt so unmistakably in her dream was still holding her shoulder, but a voice she knew and loved was saying:

" Penny! Darling, what is it? What's the matter? Why did you shout like that for Jon ? "

Penny rolled over, sat up in bed and hugged her aunt.

" I'm so sorry," she said. " Did I really shout for Jon ? You won't ever tell him, will you, Auntie ? Promise you won't. . . . Darling, it was terrible! I had a nightmare. . . . I was being chased down the passage by Sl. . .! Well, I was being chased, anyway. You know how *awful* it is, don't you ? "

Mrs. Warrender sat on the bed and pushed back Penny's red curls and looked gravely into her grey eyes.

" You've no business to be having nightmares like that, Penny. Are you sure you feel well ? You look tired. Do you know the time ? It's nearly nine, and I've had to wake Jon, too, for he was dead to the world. . . . What have you two been doing ? " she added suspiciously.

" Nothing, darling," Penny said quickly, clasping her knees. " At least that's not quite true. Nothing that we can tell you about now, so please don't ask me yet. . . . You won't ask us, will you, Auntie ? . . . And I'm so sorry we're so late. I was jolly tired yesterday, but I can't think why Jon should be ! "

" Can't you ? " Mrs. Warrender asked quietly. " How odd. I think I must talk to Jon again. Be as quick as you can now, because I'm keeping your breakfast hot for you."

Penny put her face right under cold water twice to try and wake herself properly, but she yawned several times while she was dressing and did not feel very fresh when she went down to breakfast. She did hope that Jon would be there first because she was not looking forward to a further conversation alone with her aunt, who seemed to be getting rather suspicious. It was silly of him not to wake up at the proper time. If they went on making mistakes like this they would spoil everything !

Then she remembered Slinky's threat to tell Mrs. Warrender and Mrs. Morton about last night's adventure. Perhaps he had already done this, and that was why her aunt had seemed so quiet and suspicious just now ? And yet it did not seem likely that he would risk doing such a stupid thing merely out of spite, particularly as he must have been certain that Jon would betray him if forced to do so. Then she remembered David, and those amazing twins, wondered if they had overslept, too. She also remembered how, for all their sometimes silly talk, both Dickie and Mary had behaved splendidly last night and been no trouble at all ! They were good fun and good friends.

She paused outside her aunt's sitting-room and listened hopefully. Jon was down, for she could hear his voice raised rather querulously, and as Penny recognized this sign she was certain that unless he was supported he was in the mood to give everything away ! As she was determined to make a bright and jolly entrance she stepped back into the hall, took a deep breath and then almost danced into the room.

Her aunt gave her a welcoming smile, but Jon barely looked up. He was attacking an egg morosely and just muttered, "Hullo, Penny!"

"What's happened to you this morning?" she asked brightly. "Did you oversleep, too?"

At this he glared at her so fiercely that his mother looked up in surprise.

"I'm not quite sure what is the matter with you two this morning," she said, "but you're both very over-tired. Have you been up in that room of yours at night when you ought to have been asleep? I hope you haven't been silly? I've been wondering lately whether I ought to have let you have those old papers? You're not getting into trouble with them, are you? If you have you must tell me."

"Of course not, Auntie!" Penny began brightly, but before she could say more Jon put down his egg-spoon and said:

"Well, Mother, I think perhaps we ought to tell you. . . ." And then two things happened. First, Penny kicked out under the table in the hope of reaching her cousin, and then there was a knock at the door and Mr. Grandon came in. He looked more sallow than usual this morning and his black eyes flickered quickly from Jon to Penny as he said quietly to Mrs. Warrender:

"Excuse me. The telephone. They insist upon speaking to you and say it is urgent. . . . I am so sorry. I did not know that you were still at breakfast. . . ." He held the door open for her then, when she had gone out, he turned to Jon and Penny and put his finger to his lips.

As soon as he had closed the door Penny opened her mouth to speak, but Jon whispered:

"Quiet for a minute. He may be listening outside."

Penny tiptoed to the door and put her mouth to the key-hole, took a deep breath and blew through it!

"If he's there now that'll give him earache!" she announced with great satisfaction, then turned like a fury on her cousin.

"Now then," she went on, "you were going to give in, weren't you? You were just going to tell her, and I bet Slinky *was* listening outside then and invented the telephone so that you would be interrupted. It's too bad of you, Jon!

You know you promised you wouldn't tell her. . . . If Slinky is so keen to keep you quiet it shows he's afraid and that he won't tell about last night. . . . And that gives us a better chance to use *them*, doesn't it ? "

" Look here, Penny," Jon said, " this is all very well, and I agree with every word you say, but I still think this business has got too serious for us and that Mother ought to know that this beastly man Slinky is an accomplice of Miss Ballinger's. She ought to know, too, that this proves there *is* a treasure and that they tried to bribe me with a motorbike. . . ."

" Jon ! You know you promised that we would do this without the grown-ups, and now we've got the Mortons to help there's no need to be afraid of anybody. We'll find the treasure without grown-ups. I know we will."

But Jon just shook his head obstinately.

" You're afraid ! " Penny taunted. " That's what it is ! You're in a funk about the whole business. . . . I tell you what I'm going to do ! I'm going to find David and tell him that even if you back out now I'll stand by him and help him to find the treasure in spite of anything the others can do with *your* help. . . . It's no use you looking mad and getting red in the face and spluttering. . . . I know jolly well that David would see this through on his own. He's not the sort to go to grown-ups, and I never thought you were until the last day or two ! "

Jon was furiously angry. He was not used to this sort of taunt from Penny, and he didn't like it at all, and was still trying to find a dignified and suitable retort when Mrs. Warrender returned.

" Odd about the telephone," she said. " When I got there the caller had rung off. What's the matter with you, Jon ? You look red. Never mind ! Don't tell me. . . . By the way, I've got a special message for you."

" Me, too ? " asked Penny.

" No, it's not for you ; it's for Jon. You weren't mentioned, Penny. I've just seen Mr. Morton in the lounge, Jon, and he tells me that you have already met his family."

" Yes," Penny broke in. " Yes, Auntie, we did meet them, but we didn't know who they were at the time. They're jolly, and I think we shall be friends."

" Well," Mrs. Warrender went on, " you know I didn't

F

really want this to happen, but they seem to like you, too, so I suppose it's all right. . . . Anyway, Jon, Mr. Morton asked me to ask you whether you would like to go with them to the golf links this morning—his boy David is going, too—and stay to lunch with them at the club-house? Mr. and Mrs. Morton are both keen on golf, and I think they want you two boys to caddy for them. It's nice of them to ask you, so I should go if you're not too tired!"

"Too tired, Mother? What do you mean?"

"You look tired, and you are tired. Neither of you could wake up this morning, and you've been up to something, I know. . . . Anyway, I said that I thought you'd be glad to join them, and you're to meet them in the lounge in half an hour."

"And what about me?" Penny asked plaintively. "I think it's jolly unfair, Jon going off and having a good time without me. What am I going to do?"

"I'll think of something," her aunt said quite grimly for once, and Penny had the grace to grin sheepishly at Jon across the table.

"I'm not interested in walking round with a sack of golf clubs on my back, anyway," she said. "Have a good time, Jon, and I'll see you this afternoon, I expect . . . unless I decide to do something on my own."

Soon after this Mrs. Warrender left them, and when the door had closed they both started to talk at once.

"I'm sorry I got into such a bait about telling Auntie," Penny began, and Jon said:

"Do you think Slinky really was listening outside the door? . . . Oh, that's all right, Penny. . . . It's just that this business is getting me down a bit, I s'pose. . . . We'll give it a bit longer. You keep your eyes open here and watch Slinky particularly, and David and me will have a talk about last night and see if we can get any more brainwaves. And keep an eye on those twins, too, and don't let them go up to the room until we're all there. . . . Do I look very tired? You look awful."

"You look bleary, too," Penny replied. "No wonder Auntie was so suspicious. I should think some fresh air will do you good."

Later, when Jon went out into the lounge, the twins introduced him to their father.

" Decent of you to come and help us," Mr. Morton said as he shook hands. " I hear you've met these rascals already ? "

" Good morning, Jonathan," Mary said sweetly. " I hope you slept well."

" *We* heard noises in the night," Dickie said. " We were a bit disturbed and we overslept a bit."

" It must be this house," Mary added. " It's very old, isn't it ? "

" Let's ask that nice Mr. Grandon while they're out. He'll tell us all about it," suggested Dickie, and his father looked at them both suspiciously.

" No twins' tricks now," he cautioned. " I like Mrs. Warrender and the *Dolphin*, so don't start any of your games or we shall be asked to leave . . . and now here's Mummy at last, so we can start. This is Jonathan, and I've told him we're grateful to him for coming. David is helping to get the car out."

Jon liked Mr. Morton at once. He liked them all, and when they went out into the sunshine together he realized that he was going to have a jolly day, but he had no idea how exciting it was going to be.

David was just driving the car under the archway into the street with Vasson beside him, so they followed him out.

Penny was sitting on the wall swinging her legs and Mrs. Morton went over to her.

" You must be Penny," she smiled. " I've heard a lot about you already. You and Jonathan must come out with us for the day soon. We'll make up a party. And if you've nothing better to do to-day, my dear, just keep an eye on those awful twins of mine, will you ? All right ! All right ! I'm coming ! Thank you, Vasson. What a lovely day ! "

" Best get your game in quick," Vasson replied as he closed the car door and stood back. " Wind's rising and weather's breaking up. Moon's full to-night and tide be highest of the year."

" He doesn't sound very cheerful," Mr. Morton said as they bumped softly over the cobbles of Trader's Street and turned round the church. " But it looks a lovely morning for a holiday to me."

They crept out between the great round towers of the Land Gate and then over the river. The green of the Marsh was vivid in the clear sunlight, and ahead of them, as they turned off the main road into a lane, the thin strip of shingle across the bay gleamed bright and yellow, while the lighthouse at Dungeness sparkled like a tiny white star.

" Hope you didn't mind coming," David whispered at the back. " The parents wanted me, anyway, and I thought we could have a yarn while we went round with them. Trouble is you're not allowed to talk when they're actually hitting the ball. Seems silly, but they're very particular about this. Did you oversleep, too ? "

Jon nodded. " A walk round will do us both good. I'm only half awake now. Do you think Slinky has said anything to your mother ? We don't think he's spoken to mine. He signalled to Penny and me at breakfast as if he was going to stay quiet. . . . But we've got to do something soon, David. You see, it's jolly worrying for me because it's my mother concerned in all this. I nearly told her everything at breakfast, only Penny kicked me in time. . . . If your people don't want us this afternoon, p'raps just the two of us could go back and try and work things out again. We must get the meaning of ' earthen vessels ' before they find out. . . . I say, David, are you allowed to drive this super car ? "

" Not really. I can drive, of course, but they're a bit difficult about it. Don't seem to think I'm old enough. It's easier than learning to ride a horse, though. Peter taught me to do that."

" What's that about Peter ? " Mrs. Morton said over her shoulder. " You'd like Peter, Jonathan. We asked her to come down here with us, but she wouldn't leave her father. You must both come up to Shropshire some time and meet her and the others."

The car was bumping now along a rough track leading to the club-house, and as they got out David whispered :

" I wrote to Peter and told her about you and Penny last evening. We shall hear from her soon."

Jon was not quite sure what was meant by this, but he did realize how jolly and friendly these people were and how fortunate it was that the Morton's were the first guests at the *Dolphin*. As they followed the grown-ups across to the first tee he thought of Penny on guard at home and missing the fun here, but comforted himself with the thought that she was probably enjoying herself already and that Slinky would not have much chance of eluding her.

David showed him how to carry a bag of golf clubs comfortably across his shoulders, and it was not long before Jon had forgotten all about treasure and earthen vessels. As they tramped across the springy turf and over the dunes the wind freshened and before long the sun disappeared behind the clouds which were piling up from the south-west. The colour of the sea changed to dark green, and far out across the sands the tumbling waves were flecked with white foam, and by the time they were back at the club-house the first silver spears of rain came driving sharply at them from the sea.

" Vasson was right, then," Mr. Morton said as they went in. " Doesn't look as if we shall get much more golf to-day. How quickly the weather changes down here."

The meal was good and the boys were hungry, but they both felt sleepy by the time the coffee arrived. Jon was almost nodding when he realized that Mr. Morton was talking about the Marsh.

" . . . We must explore it properly," he was saying. " We'll organize some expeditions. Did you know, Jon, that there's an old priory at Bilsington which is haunted by a prior who tells his red-hot beads in the shadows ? Strangely enough, there is another ghost in the same building—the ghost of a poor old woman who was murdered by her husband when she dropped a tray of china downstairs ! I read that almost every night you can hear the sound of china being broken and that once, not so very long ago, thirteen clergymen were called in to try and lay this ghost."

" Did they manage it ? " David asked.

" No," his father replied. " I remember that part well because only twelve turned up, so their efforts were in vain. And remind me to tell Mary that it is not so many years ago since the Marsh folk believed in witches and witchcraft, and that there are still some cottages past which an old farm-hand refuses to drive his horses."

" We've read a lot of the smuggling stories, too," Jon said. " Didn't the Romans land on the Marsh ? Do you know any stories about them, sir ? "

He had no particular reason for asking this question and had no conception that Mr. Morton's answer would give him his brilliant idea.

" Yes, Jon, there's no doubt about that. Roman remains

have been found in the Marsh, I believe, and many of them in this district. A mound in flat country like this is conspicuous, and somebody told me that many of these odd-looking hillocks have already been opened by experts."

" What do they find ? " David asked. " Bones ? "

" Yes, bones and old Roman coins and fragments of pottery."

Fragments of pottery ! Pottery made of clay ! Earthen vessels !

Jon nearly fell off his chair with excitement as he turned to see whether the same idea had occurred to David. But his friend was stifling a yawn and rolling the remains of his bread into pills and Mrs. Morton was looking through the smoke of her cigarette at the raindrops beating against the window.

" But, sir," Jon said as quietly as possible, as he polished his glasses, " can you tell me some more about the Romans and lend me a book ? What sort of pottery would be in these old graves ? Would they put their gold in them, do you think ? "

Mr. Morton laughed. " You sound very keen ! I'm not an expert on this, old chap, but I think they did bury gold in pottery jars with their dead. I suppose the money was intended to help them on their journey. If you are going treasure hunting on the Marsh for Roman remains though, you had better read it up before you go. Anyway, I'm sure that jars of gold coins with Roman markings on them have been dug out of some of these old mounds, but I expect you have to get permission before you start your own excavations."

" I suppose that lots of these little hills and ridges round here might be Roman forts or burial places ? " Jon persisted and winked hard at David who seemed at last to realize that these questions meant something.

A sudden gust of wind shook the windows as Mrs. Morton stubbed out her cigarette.

" I'm sorry about the weather. What are you boys going to do ? We're going to stay on here for a while and play cards. Would you like to wait for us or go home on your own before it gets too bad ? There's a bus, I believe."

Jon nudged David and said, " I think I ought to get back home, thanks all the same. Penny is on her own you see, and I might be able to help Mother."

" I'll go back with you, Jon," David added, taking up his

cue quickly. " I suppose you wouldn't let me have the car, would you, Dad ? I'm sure someone would give you a lift home later."

" You're right as usual, David," his father replied. " We wouldn't let you have the car."

Outside, when they left the shelter of the Club House, the force of the wind nearly lifted them off their feet. The rain had stopped now, but behind the roar and worry of the gale they could hear the angry muttering of the sea.

" Let's climb to the top of the dunes," David panted as they leaned against the wind. " It'll be grand up there, and you can tell me what's happened. Have you had a brainwave ? "

. They struggled forward in silence until, behind the shelter of the dunes, they could speak without shouting.

" Of course it's a brainwave," Jon said. " I know what earthen vessels are now. I bet the treasure is buried some-where in one of those old Roman vases your father was telling us about. It was probably easy enough for a smuggler who knew the Marsh to unearth one of those old burying places and find a pot with Roman coins. . . . We'll have to puzzle it out, David, but I think we are really a bit further on. . . . Do you really want to drag me up to the top of this bank ? I think we ought to get home. I want to look at the map again. . . . Oh, all right. Come on then."

They pulled themselves up the bank of slippery sand by clutching tufts of grass, while the wind roared over their heads. Once on the top, though, they were exposed to its full fury and flung themselves down full length in the grass. Jon raised his head to look out to sea and felt the sting of flying sand on his face.

" Gosh ! " he gasped. " I've never been in a wind like this. Put up your hand and feel the sand. It's coming in like rain—and look at the sea, David."

The tide was on the turn and big, angry crested waves were racing in over the flat sands. The horizon was a bright, clear strip of light above the brown sea, but dark clouds filled the rest of the sky. The world was full of wind. They were alone in a world of roaring and booming, a world in which the wind seemed a live and tangible thing as it whipped the sea into a fury, whirled microscopic grains of sand from the beach and whistled through the grass that was levelled round their heads. A few gulls wheeled and hovered against the force of the wind while their plaintive mewing was tossed inland and lost in the tumult of the gale.

" That chap Vasson knows how to read the weather," David gasped. " This is grand, isn't it ? Now what do you suggest, Jon ? Do you think we'd better get back to the *Dolphin* ? "

" Yes, I do. I think we ought to look at the map again and check up on the hills which it shows. Come to think of it, David, Camber Castle is on a mound and we caught Miss Ballinger messing about round there. Then, the two windmills are built on mounds and both of those were marked on the map. And there's a gibbet on a little hill round here somewhere. Penny wants to explore that and— I've got it, I believe ! There's one little hill marked specially and that's on Winchelsea beach just by those bungalows where the Ballinger lives ! "

" Maybe you've got something there," David agreed. " Let's get back and rout out the others and see if there's anything we can do to-day. . . . I hope it won't rain again, though."

" If it does," Jon replied, " we can all go up to our room and have a fire and make some plans for exploring all these mounds properly. Come on ! Let's try for the bus," and they scrambled down from the dunes and were almost blown off their feet as they made for the road on the other side of the Club House.

" Pity they wouldn't let me have the car," David said as they scrambled into the old bus which was already nearly full. " They're jolly unreasonable. I shall have to drive them in it one day, so why not now ? "

In between the jolts of the bus and the roaring of the wind they agreed that parents were often difficult and somehow this reminded Jon of Penny and he realized that, after all, he had missed her to-day. She would have enjoyed the top of the dunes.

The bus put them down by the river and as they climbed the steps of Trader's Passage another scurry of rain rushed over the levels and lashed the sturdy walls of Rye, that had stood fast and firm against so many gales.

Vasson was standing under the archway looking out to sea and nodded when he saw the boys.

" You were right about the weather, Mr. Vasson," Jon remarked as he wiped the raindrops from his glasses. " I've never been in a gale like this before."

The porter shook his head. " Nor never may again," he muttered. " I've seen but two more like this and each time there's been trouble. There'll be trouble to-night, I'm thinking."

He sounded so serious that the boys looked up at him in surprise. He was still looking out to sea, with blue eyes narrowed to slits and the wind blowing his scanty hair over his brown forehead.

" What do you mean by trouble ? " Jon asked.

" It's the tide, Master Jonathan. Her allus comes high this time o' year, but with this wind at her back it 'ull be mortal rough in Channel. Fishing boats have been coming home all day and I hear tell that no sooner were some of the lads safe ashore afore they was warned for lifeboat."

" What do you mean ? Warned for lifeboat ? " David asked.

" Crews of lifeboats are mostly fisher chaps," Vasson explained. " There's a lifeboat down at the Harbour yonder and another at Hastings. . . . Chap just come off the bus tells me they're standing by already there. . . . But that's not main trouble, for we've not many chaps at sea now. Step over here and I'll show you," and he led them out of the shelter of the arch to the wall at the end of the street.

" Now look," he said, pointing in the direction of Winchelsea beach. " That's where the levels seem to be lowest —back there behind those pink boxes they calls bungalows— and it's just along there from Cliff End to Camber where the bank is weakest."

" Do you mean the high bank that keeps the sea back ? " Jon said.

" I mean the bank wot's meant to keep the sea back," Vasson said gravely. " 'Tis nobody's business to see to it seemingly, and if once it goes—and go she might in weather like this with the tide at the full—there's nothing to save thousands of acres of best grazing in the country and nothing to stop the sea coming up here again."

" Gosh ! " said Jon. " But has the big bank ever broken there ? "

" Once. But tide was on turn and some chaps were ready

to fill up the gap and not much harm done—but there'll be plenty watching there afore long. I be going myself later if missus 'ull give me leave. Some of us are allus on call for this trouble."

" I say, Mr. Vasson, could we come with you ? " David asked. " Could we ? We'd be jolly useful."

Vasson shook his head. " I would'na risk takin' you."

Jon grabbed David's arm and ran back to the *Dolphin*.

" Let's find the others first," he said, " and then we'll persuade Mother to let us go. . . . Oh ! You'll have to ask your people, of course. I forgot that. Perhaps your father would come, too, and take us in the car and then that would make it all right. I wonder where Penny is ? "

" P'raps she's sitting outside your room on guard," David suggested. " I don't expect Mr. Grandon will get far without her to-day. P'raps she's tied herself to him ! You'd better go in your side and see if you can find your mother, and I'll go over into the Lounge and see if the twins are there. I suppose Penny will be with them."

Jon paused with his hand on the door.

" But we were going to study the map, weren't we ? We'd better do that upstairs in our room where we shall be safe. I'll meet you in the lounge in five minutes, and if the others are there, see if you can find out where Slinky is and I'll do the same here."

Jon found his mother in her sitting room and she switched the radio off as he came in.

" Hullo," she said. " Have you had a good time, and did they get their game in before the gale ? Where's David ? "

Jon explained and then asked where Penny was.

" Penny ? Didn't I tell you ? She's gone into Hastings in the car with the twins and Mr. Grandon."

" *Mr. Grandon ?* " Jon nearly shouted.

" Yes. And why not ? I thought it was rather decent of him. I'm not sure whether I was right to let those twins go, too, but they wanted to go and I don't think Mrs. Morton will mind. It seemed a shame for them to miss the fun."

" Fun ? " Jon gasped as he sat down on the nearest chair. " What fun ? Why have they gone ? "

" Don't be stupid, Jon. I keep telling you. Mr. Grandon had to go in on business to-day, and as Penny was mooching about all over the house after you'd gone and looking particularly gloomy, he asked me whether he could take her and the twins with him. I thought she was a bit stupid about it at first, but the twins were very keen and as Penny said she'd promised Mrs. Morton to keep an eye on them, she went off cheerfully enough in the end. And that reminds me that she was very anxious for me to tell you where they'd gone for some reason or other. . . . Now are you satisfied ? Why are you looking so worried, Jon ? They can't come to any harm, and anyway they'll be home at any minute, I should think. They were having lunch in the town and said they would be back for tea. . . . Now, where are you going ? "

" Only to find David," Jon said as he made for the door. " I'll be back soon, Mother. . . . Don't worry. I'm not worried. Only surprised ! "

David looked up eagerly from his chair by the wood fire in the lounge, but before he could speak Jon had told him the news.

" Now, why on earth has she gone trailing in there with him for the day ? " he finished breathlessly. " Can you see any sense in it ? "

" Didn't you tell her to keep an eye on him ? " David said. " I'll bet anything she's got suspicious and gone with him for a jolly good reason. Penny's got her head screwed on the right way. She'll come back with something you'll see. . . . I say, Jon, I bet she's got an awful temper with that red hair of hers, hasn't she ? "

" She certainly has," Jon agreed fervently thinking of the scene at breakfast this morning—and of other occasions, also ! " You should just hear her when she really gets worked up."

" She was jolly bright last night imitating the Ballinger, anyway," David continued, warming to his subject. " I think she's a grand kid. I bet she's putting Slinky through it."

Jon looked at him with some suspicion, but said no more on this subject. He was thinking that Penny's temper was nothing to do with David, anyway, and was just wondering whether to go up for the map when the telephone bell began to ring. Vasson was presumably still outside watching the weather so Jon walked over and lifted the receiver.

" Press Button A please, caller," came a thin voice from the Exchange. Then, " You're throu-u-u-gh."

" *Gay Dolphin*, Rye," Jon announced, feeling rather bored.

" Oh ! May I speak to Mr. Jonathan Warrender, please," came pleasantly over the wire in a voice Jon seemed to recognize.

" Jonathan Warrender speaking," he said feeling himself go rather red in the face.

" Isn't that lucky," the girl said. " How are you, Jonathan ? We did hope we should catch you. You know who it is speaking, don't you ? "

" You're Miss Ballinger's niece, aren't you ? " he muttered rather ungraciously.

" That's right ! But listen, Jon. I'm really speaking for your cousin, Penny—and for us all, too, of course—but specially for Penny. Can you and your friend come over here right away and have tea with us ? The twins are here, too, but your cousin says you must come because she's got important news . . ." and here the girl laughed musically . . . " news about some treasure or something equally exciting."

" Who is it ? What's she talking about ? " whispered David who had come over to his friend's side.

Jon shook his head and put his finger to his lips. The girl was speaking again :

" I know it's a rotten day, Jon, but it's not raining now, and if you'll come I've got the car, and I'll come and meet you and pick you up on the road."

" Where's Penny ? " Jon asked suspiciously. " Why doesn't she give me her crazy messages herself. She's all right, isn't she ? "

" Of *course* she's all right. She's at the Bungalow helping my aunt to get the tea, and she asked me to come up to the call box to 'phone. I've got the car, you see ! ' Tell him to come over at once with David Morton ' she said, ' and tell him that they *must* come, and be sure to bring the maps and papers. Tell him it's important ' was the last thing she said. . . . Oh, no it wasn't ! There was something else that seemed mad to me, but I s'pose you'll understand. . . . Something about a date. . . . April something or other. . . . but I say, you *will* come, won't you, Jon. . . . I'd like to see you again. . . ."

" Very well," Jon said slowly. " Thank you, very much. We'll come as soon as we can. We'll be on the road in about ten minutes. 'Bye," and he walked away from the telephone, looking very worried.

CHAPTER IX

WEDNESDAY: PENNY AND THE
TWINS IN TROUBLE

PENNY sat swinging her legs on the wall at the end of Trader's Street and watched the car containing the Mortons and Jon disappear round the corner. A steady wind from the sea behind her ruffled her curls, and she stifled a yawn and waved to Vasson, who grinned at her as he went back under the archway.

Somehow Penny did not think that the morning was going to be very exciting. She was tired and the more she considered her instructions from Jon the less she liked them. She did not relish the prospect of watching Slinky; neither was she very keen on her rôle as nursemaid to the twins when she wasn't being a detective. Not that the twins needed much nurse-maiding, but Mrs. Morton had asked her specially to keep an eye on them and Mrs. Morton was very nice. All the same, it would have been fun to have gone with the boys.

The wall began to feel uncomfortably hard. She jumped down and wondered what she would say if Mrs. Warrender questioned her again on last night's adventure, about which she seemed so suspicious. And suppose her aunt asked her to go shopping—how could she watch Slinky then ? Perhaps the best plan would be for her to avoid her aunt while looking for Slinky; and as she would have to search the house for him, perhaps the twins would be able to help, after all. It was also going to be very difficult to follow him around and with a sudden shock Penny realized that unless she sat upstairs in their room, she would never know if he used the secret passage. She could hardly disappear for the whole morning, and Jon had particularly asked her not to let the twins go upstairs by themselves, so she could not very well leave them on guard in the room. It was all very difficult.

She was still frowning as she strolled under the archway and met the twins and Macbeth coming out into the sunshine.

" Hullo, Penny ! What shall we do ? " Dickie began.

" Those two beastly boys have *slunk* off without us," Mary added. " Shall we disappear and have an adventure of our own ? Dickie and me do that sometimes. You can come, too, Penny. We like you."

" Where can we go in secret ? " Dickie went on, and then added out of the side of his mouth—" Can we go up to the secret room, Penny ? "

Before Penny could answer, her aunt's door opened and Mr. Grandon came out. The twins smiled at him winningly, but he gave the three of them an odd glance as he crossed over to the hotel entrance. He stopped on the step and turned quickly while Penny was wondering what to say.

" And what are you going to do this lovely morning, Miss Penny ? " he smiled, showing his teeth under the little black moustache. For a moment only she was taken aback ; then she said : " How nice of you to be so interested, Mr. Grandon. As a matter of fact, I was just saying, when you came out, that I would like to come round the hotel with you. I mean, would you show me how everything works and what you do in your office all day ? "

" Could we come, too ? " Mary chimed in.

" I'd like to see how you plan meals," Dickie added. " Eating always interests me, and I get jolly hungry in about half an hour's time. Do you mind if we come with Miss Penny ? "

He said " *Miss* Penny " without a suggestion of a wink, but Mr. Grandon did not seem to notice. With one hand on the door handle and the other fingering his moustache, he looked down at the three children thoughtfully.

" I do not think that would be a very good idea," he said softly, with half-closed eyes. " You would interrupt me when I am most busy. . . . You are going out exploring ? . . . It will be a beautiful morning, I think. . . . You will all be better out of doors, perhaps ? "

Penny shook her head as she met his eyes bravely. " You can't frighten us, Mr. Grandon, and we don't know yet what we're going to do."

" And we wouldn't tell you if we did know," Dickie added rather rudely.

Mr. Grandon laughed at this. " I will try and think of something for you all to do to-day. . . . It will never do for you to get into mischief. . . . Mrs. Warrender would not like that, I know," and before either of them could answer the door closed softly and they were alone.

There was a long silence and then, as if at a secret signal, the twins extended their tongues towards the door. Penny was still flushed and frowning when Mary said :

" What a beastly beast, Penny ! I think he wants us out of the way."

" D'you think he's going to search our room—your room, I mean ? " Dickie said.

" I don't know," Penny answered slowly. " He was foul, wasn't he ? I felt a bit scared of him when he threatened us like that. I think he does want us out of the way so that's a jolly good reason for us to stay at home. . . . Come over here, you two, and I'll tell you something."

She peeped into Vasson's cubby hole, but the porter was at his duties elsewhere, so she patted the step, already warmed by the sun, and the twins sat down one on each side of her, and listened as she went on.

" Before Jon went he asked me to watch Slinky and somehow we've got to do it. He may try to get us out of the way, but we've got to be sure he doesn't go prowling about upstairs."

" Can't we all sit up there and play a game or something," Mary suggested brightly.

" Ass ! " said her brother. " I s'pect that's just what he'd like. Soon as we're out of the way he'd hop off somewhere else and do some digging or something that he doesn't want us to see."

" All right, twin. I only just thought of it for a minute. Don't be so cocky."

" The best thing to do," Penny broke in hurriedly, " is for you two to hang about the hotel and keep an eye on him while I guard the room. I think I'll stretch some black cotton across the secret panel and the door, too, and then we'll know if anyone goes in while we're away. You know what I mean, don't you, Dickie ? "

" Do I know what you mean ? " Dickie repeated scornfully. " Do we know ? We know everything like that. We've done it lots of times."

" What you say is not what we'd like to do at all," Mary said. " I think it's a feeble idea. It's all the fault of those boys going off like that with Mummy and Daddy. They ought to have stayed with us and then we could have done something proper about the treasure. . . . All the same, I 'spect you're right, Penny. Come on, Dickie! Let's go and hunt him out and watch him."

Penny never learned exactly how the hunt had been conducted because when she inquired later the twins interrupted each other and told such incredible stories that she felt almost sorry for Slinky! Before they parted, though, she rummaged about amongst the rubbish on the bench at the back of Vasson's room and found some pins and a reel of black cotton. She was particularly pleased about this, as there was now no need for her to go to her own room or to search her aunt's work-basket. Then they all went back into the hotel and Penny waited on the stairs while Dickie crept up the passage which led to Mr. Grandon's office. He looked so guilty when he tip-toed back again that Mary giggled.

" Be quiet, can't you ? " he hissed. " He's in there. The door's closed, but I can hear him mumbling on the telephone he's got in there. I thought I heard the bell ringing when we were outside."

" Hang about, then," Penny whispered as she ran up the stairs. " Watch what he does and follow him if you can. I'll come and join you as soon as poss. . . . If he goes into the other house you can be pretty sure he's gone to his room to use the passage so one of you had better run up and tell me if I'm not down. Do you know the way, Mary ? All right. Come up with me now as far as the staircase and then you'll remember. If he does go to his room I'll sit up there quietly and wait for him ! "

" You're very brave," Mary murmured as she followed Penny upstairs. " I should be afraid to be up here alone waiting for that panel to open all quiet and slinky. . . . Oh, yes . . . thanks, Penny. I'll remember now. . . . The staircase is the first on the left after Room Nine. . . . Trouble is, of course, that Room Nine is not easy to find, but I'll remember. . . . 'Bye, Penny. Come down soon, and don't worry. We'll watch him, and we'll find the treasure, too ! Come on, Mackie ! " and she bounded down the stairs with the little dog at her heels.

Penny went up the narrow stairs past her own room and unlocked the big door. It swung slowly back with a slight squeak and she stepped into the room. Everything looked the same and last night's ashes were still in the fireplace. It seemed a long time ago since she had lit this fire after seeing Miss Ballinger's face glaring at them from the opposite wall, yet it was only a few hours ago. She wondered whether the catch that worked the secret panel still worked, so, after bolting the big door behind her, she crossed the floor and put her finger into the little hole that Mary had found in the wainscot. She felt the catch and pressed it and the panel opened to let in a gust of cold, dank air. She shuddered and stepped into the narrow passage after making sure the panel would not swing back and imprison her.

There was enough light for her to press a pin about nine inches above the ground into each wall and then stretch a length of black cotton taut between the two so that anyone stepping, however cautiously, up the passage could not avoid breaking the thread or pulling out the pins. Then she stepped back into the room, sucked the top of her thumb which she had used for pressing in the pins, and looked rather pleased with herself. After closing the panel she fixed another thread trap across the inside wall and then repeated the same trick across the little landing at the top of the stairs. There didn't seem much else that she could do up here, so she locked the door again, hid the key in her room and went down, deciding to leave the ashes in the grate for the time being.

In the long corridor she ran into Mrs. Warrender.

" What are you wandering about up here for, Penny ? " said she brightly. " I was hoping to find you because I want you to go down to the High Street for me. It won't take you more than a quarter of an hour. You don't mind, do you, darling ? "

Penny shuffled and said awkwardly, " It wouldn't do this afternoon, would it ? I mean, of course, I'll be glad to go, but just now it isn't actually a very *good* time for me to go if you know what I mean, Auntie."

" I don't know a bit what you mean. It's nothing really important, is it ? Why can't you go ? "

" Oh, I'll go, of course. It's just that there was something I ought to do upstairs. . . . Have you seen those jolly twins, Auntie ? "

" Yes," said her aunt sharply, " I have seen them, and they're behaving very badly. I'm surprised that Mr. Grandon didn't send them off, but when I saw them just now they were talking together at him at the door of his office. Why do you want them ? "

" Mrs. Morton asked me to keep an eye on them, that's all, and I was just going to look for them. . . . I'll just tell them I'll be back soon, and then I'll come to your room for the message."

But on second thoughts, when she got downstairs, she decided to leave the twins undisturbed, as they were apparently doing their work well and might be put out if she interrupted them. As she crossed the lounge she could hear their shrill voices, and she grinned to herself as she crossed the yard and waited for Mrs. Warrender in her room. The note was soon written, and Penny went out determined to get back as soon as possible. As she ran down Trader's Passage she noticed how the wind was rising, for here, on the edge of the town facing the levels, there was nothing to break its force as it came blustering in from the sea.

She had to wait a few minutes for an answer to the note and was back at the *Dolphin* again within half an hour.

" Thank you, Penny," Mrs. Warrender said. " I've got a surprise for you. Personally, I think that it's extremely good of Mr. Grandon, but he has offered to take you and those Morton twins into Hastings in the car. He has to go into the town, and as you seemed to be rather at a loose end he thought you might like to go, and as he has included the twins very specially in the invitation, I've taken the risk of accepting for them. I don't think Mr. and Mrs. Morton would mind, do you ? "

Penny gasped. " He *asked* us to go with him, Auntie ? Are you sure he suggested it ? "

" Of course I'm sure. He came over specially to ask me, and I must say those twins seem to have taken to him, for they're following him about all over the place. I only just managed to close this door on them, but they were waiting in the yard when he came out. He seems to like them and has offered to take you all out to lunch."

Penny just did not know what to say or do. If she went she would certainly be able to keep an eye on him, but there were so many things to consider. Was this just a trick to get them out of the way while Miss Ballinger searched somewhere else ? Would Slinky try and maroon them or play " Babes in the Wood " and then dash back and continue the search ? Penny knew that only last night he had been instructed to get the secret from them ; perhaps he was now going to try and bribe them while the boys were out of the way. Penny was sure that the three of them could cope with anything like bribery, but she was very puzzled.

" You don't seem very keen to go, Penny ? Why are you looking so worried ? I thought you'd like the chance of the trip. You haven't got to be with him all the time, you know. After lunch you three can arrange to go off on your own and meet him later. He says he wants to be back at tea-time."

" Do the twins know, Auntie ? What do they think of the idea ? "

" They're thrilled about it ! I heard the boy say he'd been looking forward to spending the day with Grandon and that it would be wizard to go with him. I can't think what he meant about spending the day with him, but they both seem to like him, as I say. I think they're getting the car out now, so you'd better go and get ready."

" All right, Auntie. Thank you. I can't say I like the little man very much, but it will be fun to explore Hastings ! Will you settle with him after about the lunch, 'cos I don't like him paying for us."

Mrs. Warrender laughed. " Of course I will, silly ! "

" And will you tell Jon *directly* he comes back where we've gone ? " Penny pleaded. " Please do that, because it's most important. Promise ? "

" I promise, but I don't suppose he'll notice that you're not here, Penny ! "

" Will you tell him, anyway, please ? You will, won't you ? " and with that Penny ran upstairs to change.

When she came down the car was in the yard with the twins in the front seat. Mary had Macbeth on her lap. Mr. Grandon was not to be seen.

" Oh, gosh ! We've been doggin' him," Dickie hissed as Penny opened the door. " He was angry at first, but people aren't angry with us for long, 'cos we just don't take any notice."

" Once he had a telephone call and pushed us out of the

Penny listened to him entranced, for he became more and more excited as he talked and the old car bounced and bumped and rattled as he pressed the accelerator pedal. Weird cries of encouragement came from the back seat as the twins urged him to even greater efforts.

"Atta boy, Mr. Grandon! Step on it, brother!" was Dickie's contribution.

"Never mind the bus, Mr. Grandon," Mary yelled. "Just swish by it!"

And swish by it he did, with his hand on the button of the horn. Penny turned round in time to see the bus driver shaking his fist at them, and then they ran over a chicken. But what was a chicken to Mr. Grandon in his present mood? When she tried to tell him what he had done he burst into song and bent forward over the wheel as if he was in a racing car, so she leaned back and hoped for the best.

"Has he gone mad?" Mary yelled in her ear as the car swerved on two wheels to avoid a respectable old dame on a bicycle.

"Tra-la-la! Tra-la-la!" carolled Slinky, and the car rocked again as he turned his head sideways and laughed. "No, my little one! Not mad! But when we have a holiday we should enjoy it. . . . Now we must crawl again, for we are near the town. . . ."

After this exhibition Penny treated him with more respect. She was still wondering what the real purpose of the invitation could be and trying to make some sense out of his extraordinary mood, when he pointed ahead and said seriously:

"There is the sea again at the bottom of this road. See how the horizon sinks as we go down the hill. It is strange, Miss Penny, but ever since I was the age of those two behind us I have felt strangely moved by a road that leads to the sea as this one does. . . . I remember a road like this down which I trotted with my mother the first time I had ever seen the sea. . . . I remember the smell and I remember how the sea got nearer and how suddenly we came to the end of the road and there was the edge of the sea for me to play in . . . Ah well! it is no use remembering these things now. . . . You would like to stop for a minute, perhaps?" and here he turned the corner on to the Front and stopped by an ice-cream barrow, while the twins gazed at him with humble respect.

" Perhaps you would like to walk along the Parade to the Pier," Slinky went on. " I will meet you in half an hour, and please don't be late, as I have much to do later," and almost before Penny had nodded agreement he had let in the clutch and glided away.

" Well ! " said the twins together, " what do you think of that ? "

Penny shook her head. " I don't know what to think. Everything is upside down. If we didn't know what we do know about him we'd think he was quite decent ! . . . I say, something has happened to the weather, chaps. It's going to rain like fun in a moment, and the wind is worse than ever. . . . Let's cross over and look at the sea."

The tide was low, but the waves were racing in over the sands and breaking in fury over the rocks. Storm clouds filled the western sky and the force of the wind seemed to grow every minute as they leaned over the rails and watched the seagulls twist and turn over the deserted beach. Then came the first sharp stinging raindrops.

" Lucky we brought our raincoats," Mary said. " We wouldn't have only your nice aunt said we must. This is rather beastly, isn't it ? We shan't be able to do much here after lunch if it's like this. Poor darling Mackie can hardly walk in this wind ! "

" Don't let's worry about *after* lunch," Dickie said. " Let's have lunch first and then do the worrying."

" Well, we can't stay here and get wet through," Penny agreed. " We'd better get on a bus or something."

Then they noticed that under the Parade on which they were standing was another covered walk open to the sea and that they could reach the Pier this way in shelter. Dickie was fascinated by the concrete walls of this underground parade, which were studded with the coloured fragments of broken glass bottles and china.

Mr. Grandon was waiting for them as he had promised in a shelter by the Pier. He had no raincoat and looked rather miserable and cold in his smart grey suit.

" I have parked the car," he said. " Let us go and eat, and I promise you that because I know well the manager of this hotel that we shall be specially served." He turned to Dickie and added slyly, " Not as well served as you are at the *Dolphin*, young sir, but well enough, I hope. Come ! "

Castle. This is Richard and Mary Morton, and they are friends of ours, now staying at the *Dolphin*."

Dickie got to his feet.

" I remember o' course," he said. " You were going to teach us how to paint."

" But hadn't got time and had to hurry away," Mary added. " But, good morning, all the same."

" And we're very pleased to see you again ! " Dickie concluded the duet triumphantly.

Miss Ballinger, still with a set smile on her face, seemed to gulp slightly before she spoke.

" This is fun, isn't it ! "—and here Penny felt Dickie step gently on her foot under the table—" I wonder if you would all have pity on a lonely old woman who was going to have her lunch alone and come and join me ? Would you ? I should be so glad of your company."

Mr. Grandon protested rather feebly, but Penny felt uneasy. Somehow she was certain that this was not a chance meeting and although the invitation was cordial enough, she wished most fervently that the boys were with them. She was responsible for the twins and although she knew really that nothing could happen to them in broad daylight in a crowded restaurant, she knew that Miss Ballinger was determined to find the Dolphin's treasure, and was convinced that they could lead her to it. They knew enough about this woman now to know that she was not to be treated lightly. Penny recalled that odd shudder of fear and distrust which she had felt when she first crossed the threshold of *Beach View*.

Dickie was speaking now and looking up at Miss Ballinger cheekily. " It's jolly nice of you to ask us to lunch, but we've been asked once already by Mr. Grandon. . . . I s'pose they wouldn't let us have two lunches here, would they ? "

This remark eased an awkward situation and everyone laughed except Mary who said :

" You're a disgusting, greedy little pig, twin, and I'm ashamed of you."

Then, before Penny could make any further protest, the waiter appeared again and they soon found themselves seated round a larger table with their new hostess who had her back to the window. She gave them a very good meal— a meal so unusual and so satisfying that even Dickie was reduced to silence. Penny was too worried to say much, but she did notice that Slinky kept very quiet and this, of course, was in keeping with the part they now knew he had to play with Miss Ballinger.

It was while the grown-ups were having their coffee, however, that Penny noticed the weather. From where she was sitting she could see the Parade and part of the beach, but for the last hour she had been too busy listening to Miss Ballinger and keeping a guard on her own tongue to realize that what had seemed to be a storm was now a raging gale. The horizon line had vanished ; sky and sea were merged into a grey blur and the windows were drenched with spray whipped from the waves nearly two hundred yards away. Occasionally gusts of rain rattled against the panes and the window frames trembled with the force of the wind.

" We shan't be able to bathe now," she said to Mary regretfully.

" We shan't be able to do anything much except go home," Mary replied. " But we have had a lovely lunch and thank you very much indeed, Miss Ballinger."

" I'll tell you what I want to do," Dickie said as he sat back. " I want to find a place where you drive little cars yourself and they all bash into each other. There must be a place like that somewhere round here."

" You couldn't do it," Penny protested. " You'd be sick. Nobody could eat as much as you have and go on a Dodgem. I'm not going to let you. It's dangerous."

" He can do anything like that," Mary said sadly. " It's astonishing, but he can ! "

" I've got a better idea," Miss Ballinger broke in. " The weather's too bad to do anything out of doors and I've done all my shopping. If Mr. Grandon would give me a lift home I should be very grateful and then perhaps you would all come and have tea with me and finish off the day nicely. Perhaps Dickie would come out with me now and help me choose some cakes."

Mr. Grandon murmured a polite acceptance—just a little too quickly it seemed—and the twins looked rather at a loss. But by now Penny's mood had changed. Perhaps it was the good lunch, but although she was sure that this meeting had been arranged, she no longer felt afraid. If they thought that they could bully Penny Warrender they were mistaken, and perhaps this would be a chance for her to solve the mystery on her own. It would be very sweet to go back to Jon with the mystery solved!

If she was clever she might find out more than Miss Ballinger realized, and in any case, no real harm could come to them. Miss Ballinger would not dare to hurt them and the meeting was not likely to be more than a battle of wits. She was sure, too, that the twins would back up her new mood loyally; so she turned to their hostess and thanked her as charmingly and naturally as she knew.

"Of course, we will give you a lift home, Miss Ballinger. I know my aunt would be very cross with us if we did not help you after your kindness. But I don't think really that we ought to stay to tea, because four extra is a lot now. . . ."

"Nonsense, my dear! Nonsense! I'd like these two rascals to see my little place and I might even give Master Richard here the painting lesson he's been asking for," and here she leered at Dickie who remained unmoved. "No! I'd like you all to come and as it is nearly three o'clock, perhaps we had better start now, if Mr. Grandon is not inconvenienced. . . . We will be in the hall in ten minutes, Mr. Grandon, if you will have the car ready."

And Mr. Grandon took these orders as a matter of course and after making his usual little low bow, walked quickly out of the restaurant, leaving Miss Ballinger to pay the bill.

Days afterwards, when they were discussing the adventure again together, Penny remembered that Slinky never made any attempt even to pretend that he had any special business to do in the town, but merely followed the instructions he was given.

Miss Ballinger was an unpleasant surprise to Macbeth, who gave tongue the moment he saw her in the hall. Mary tried to quieten him, but they were all glad when Mr. Grandon came up in the car.

Penny had to squeeze into the back seat between the twins, as Miss Ballinger chose to sit in the front.

"Is it all right, Penny?" Mary whispered. "Ought we to go?"

"Just follow my lead," Penny said under her breath, "and we'll beat them yet. I think they've found out something else and I want to know what it is."

"O.K. Pard!" Dickie muttered.

They drove along the almost deserted front and when they

stopped outside a pastrycook's and Dickie stepped out on
the pavement, he was blown sideways by the wind into the
shop porch. But not even this gale could shift Miss
Ballinger's bulk and she laughed as she helped him up from
his knees.

Just before they turned away from the sea up through the
old fishing town, they noticed a throng of people on the
shingle round a big shed and Mary, who could never resist
a crowd, begged Mr. Grandon to stop for a minute.

" Be quick then," Miss Ballinger agreed, " and if it's
somebody drowned come back at once."

Penny jumped out also, and as they scrambled over the
shingle with heads down against the wind, Dickie took one
arm and Mary the other.

" I only said that so that we could plot together if we had
to," the latter said. " Although I do want to know what
these people are looking at."

A specially fierce gust flung some stinging sand in their
faces and Dickie had to yell to make himself heard above the
roar of the wind and the crash of the waves on the shingle.

" Why does she want us to go to tea ? " he shouted. " I
thought she hated us. I b'lieve she still does really."

Mary pulled down Penny's head to her mouth.

" I'm sure she does, too. I don't like the way she looks at
us even when she's smiling."

This was a very shrewd remark and Penny had seen this
look more than once at lunch time.

" When we get to a 'phone box we'll ring up the *Dolphin*
and I'll tell Jon where we are and where we're going, but
don't you worry twins—Dickie will get a good tea, anyway,
and I'll take care of you. I'm not afraid of her ! "

By now they had reached the edge of the crowd and saw
that the big double doors in front of the shed were open and
that some men in oilskins were busy round an enormous
lifeboat. In a flash the twins had worked their way through
to the front rank of spectators and during a lull in the wind
Penny, still at the back, heard their shrill treble as they
demanded information. A big fisherman in a blue jersey
smiled at Penny.

" They be just getting her ready in case she be wanted,"
he explained. " There's no trouble yet, but it'll be a dirty
night with tide at the full."

" Is that why you've pulled all the fishing boats right up the beach ? " Penny yelled and the old man nodded. " Highest tide o' year to-night," he agreed. " There'll be trouble to-night surelye."

Then Penny felt a hand on her shoulder and turned to see an agitated Slinky behind her. He looked most unhappy in his light grey holiday suit which was already marked by the rain and spray, and his voice was shrill and peevish.

" Come quickly please, Miss Penny. This is no place to wait. It is cold and wet and Miss Ballinger is anxious to be off."

Penny looked him up and down.

" And what if she is ? We don't have to do what she wants, do we ? It's Mrs. Warrender's car, not hers. . . . We'll come in a minute, but the twins want to see the lifeboat."

At this Mr. Grandon looked almost scared.

" I know, I know, Miss Penny. But I am afraid of the weather and I think we should go and you will come, please ? "

Penny relented and dragged the protesting twins back to the car where Miss Ballinger greeted them with one of her nasty smiles.

Dickie explained as Mr. Grandon drove off that nobody was drowned yet, but that they were getting the lifeboat ready just in case.

Not much was said on the road. Once or twice the children noticed that Miss Ballinger made some remark in an undertone to Slinky but the noise of the wind and the engine was too great for them to hear what she said.

Just before they reached Winchelsea, Penny leaned forward and said :

" Please will you stop at the 'phone box. I just want to ring up Mrs. Warrender and tell her that we'll be with you for tea. She'll be worried if we're not back when we said."

Miss Ballinger did not answer, so Penny asked again.

" No need to telephone now, my dear. We'll only waste time. Let's get on as quickly as we can and then you'll be home more quickly in the end."

" We've jolly well got to telephone," Dickie said loudly. "You can't stop us. . . . Penny wants to ring up. . . . Please stop, Mr. Grandon. . . ."

But Slinky did not, or would not, hear, and by now they

were through the town and rushing down the hill under the Strand Gate to the level marshlands. The twins both turned to look at Penny and saw that she looked rather white under her freckles. Mary felt for the bigger girl's hand and gave it a squeeze while Dickie whispered, " What shall we do ? Shall we murder them both ? "

Penny, who felt scared for the first time, shook her head silently and wondered how stupid she had been to try and tackle this adventure without the others.

They were rushing now along the narrow winding road which led to the beach—the road along which she and Jon had trudged after their first tea-party at *Beach View*—and had just turned a sharp corner when Slinky muttered something under his breath and jammed on the brakes suddenly. A white-faced man in a sodden raincoat was standing in the middle of the road with his arms outstretched, and as soon as the car stopped he jumped on the running board on the driver's side. Slinky pulled down the window just enough to hear what he had to say. A furious gust of wind whistled into the car and Miss Ballinger said quietly to Grandon, " Drive on," and then turned to the children and engaged them in loud conversation so that it was impossible for them to speak or shout to the stranger through the door.

Penny saw Dickie reach for the door handle and, just for a second, she wondered whether they could all make a dash for it. But even as she considered the possibility her courage came back and she determined to see this through to the end. She put her hand over Dickie's and he understood, at once, and sat back. Meanwhile, although Miss Ballinger was still talking, Penny heard what the man was saying.

" Thanks for stopping. Do you mind very much turning round and taking me back to the nearest telephone. . . . We must have help and it's urgent. . . . They say the great bank will break to-night when the tide is high, but we can't do more without proper assistance. Sorry to bother you, but . . ."

" Nonsense ! " said Miss Ballinger loudly. " Absolute nonsense. Drive on at once," and without questioning these orders, Slinky let in the clutch and the car moved forward. The man gave a shout of fury and toppled back into the wet grass at the side of the road and when Penny looked through the window behind her he was shaking his fist at them.

" What did he mean and why couldn't we give him a lift ? " Mary asked. " I want to go back to Rye now, anyway, and I don't think I want any tea even if Dickie does. . . . And I don't like this weather."

" What did he mean about the great bank breaking ? " Dickie persisted.

" Just hysteria, my dears," Miss Ballinger replied. " Don't take any notice. No such thing could happen. We haven't time now to give strangers a lift and he had no right to stop us like that. I want my tea and so do you."

But Penny was not sure that it was nonsense. She knew what the man meant and she remembered Vasson's views about the weather changing and what the old fisherman at Hastings had said less than an hour ago. She remembered the bank, too, for she had walked along it with Jon and they had talked then about what would happen if the sea broke through. Of course, things like that didn't *really* happen, but perhaps it would be wiser to explain to the twins.

The car had left the road now and was bumping over the rough track that led to the beach. Penny remembered that this was where she and Jon had first met the girl in the white mackintosh. Ahead of them was the little hill with the black shed on top—the hill that was marked so clearly on the smuggler's map—and in its shelter Mr. Grandon stopped the car. He took a coloured handkerchief from his breast pocket and wiped his forehead. He was a bad colour and had lost the jaunty mood of the morning and Penny, trying to keep a cool head, realized how they had all accepted without question his domination by Miss Ballinger. Meanwhile the latter seemed to have recovered her hospitable mood as she turned round and smiled at the children.

" Now we'll enjoy our tea," she said. " Don't forget the cakes, Richard, and hold them safely. I think Mr. Grandon is right ; we can't drive any further in this weather. . . . Better lock the car, Mr. Grandon, and take care of the key for a lot of undesirable people appear to be about this after-noon. . . . Now then. Come along. Perhaps Penny will lead the way. . . . And the twins had better hold on to me as it takes more than a gale to blow me over."

The twins glanced at Penny, who nodded slightly. There was no choice now and no chance to run away and not much sense in it if they did. They were here and had better make the best of it. She leaned across Mary on her left and opened the door and got out. The wind flung itself at her like a mad thing. It took the words from her mouth and wrapped her raincoat round her legs. It howled and sang and blustered in triumph but at the back of its mad symphony was the constant roar of the waves pounding on the shingle beyond the great bank. She saw some figures moving along its crest and it seemed as if one of them was waving ; but Miss Ballinger, now with an astonished twin on each arm took the lead and, like a liner with two tugs, launched herself into the gale. Penny, after one glance at the disconsolate and sulky-looking Slinky, decided that she had nothing to say to him, and followed the twins. Macbeth, much worried by the wind, followed Mary sadly with his tail down.

It was desperately hard going along the shingle to the bungalow, but they got there at last and the door was opened before they reached it by the fair-headed girl whom Penny already disliked heartily.

As they crowded into the tiny hall the girl raised her delicate eyebrows to Miss Ballinger, who muttered shortly, " This is all. Any news of the others ? " and when the girl shook her head she led the way into the front room.

As soon as Penny crossed the threshold of this ugly little house for the second time she knew that she had made a mistake. When Mr. Grandon behind her closed the door and she heard the latch click home her heart began to thump uncomfortably and she felt sick with fear. Then she felt Mary's hand slip into her own and this brought her courage for they couldn't *really* do anything to them, although they might try to frighten them. She thought of Jon, too, and tried to think what he would so. With a sigh she realized that he would have had the sense not to come. Then Miss Ballinger—a changed Miss Ballinger—spoke, and her manner was sharp.

" Now then, I've no time to waste. No, Richard. This is not going to be the sort of tea party you anticipated. You two kids can take your bag of buns and eat them in the other room. It's Miss Penny I want. . . . Grandon ! take 'em into the back room and lock 'em in with their disgusting buns and that unpleasant dog."

Before she had finished speaking the twins pushed past

G

Slinky and stood sturdily at Penny's side. Macbeth, sensing the situation, showed his teeth and snarled.

" You just try and move us," Mary said as she stooped to pat him. " Just try—that's all we ask ! I don't know what you think you're doing and what this is all about, but we jolly well know that you're wicked. . . ."

" And we know some other things, too," Dickie said, and then stopped in alarm as Miss Ballinger, who was leaning against the mantelpiece lighting a cigarette, looked down at the little boy with a flash of her spectacles.

" Oh, we do, do we ? Perhaps we do ! Perhaps you had better stay after all."

" You can say what you like, but we are not going to leave Penny. You can't do anything to her. She's our friend and if any of you come near we'll . . . we'll . . . we'll fight you tooth and claw," Dickie shouted. Then he thrust his hand into the paper bag which he had forgotten to put down and produced a sticky chocolate eclair. " Now then," he went on. " Just you try it on—any of you—and see what you get ! "

It really was very foolish of Mr. Grandon to step forward just then in an effort to grab the bag, for Dickie promptly swung back his arm and launched the eclair with great success, right into the little man's astonished face. Apart from some oaths in a strange language and a suppressed giggle from Mary there was silence in the room. Even Dickie was awed by his own skill. Then :

" Get out of the way and don't be such a fool, Grandon," Miss Ballinger snapped. " You ought to have more sense. . . . Now let's waste no more time. You two children sit down there if you must and listen to what I've got to say to your special friend, and understand that the sooner I get what I want the sooner Mr. Grandon will take you home. . . . Now, Miss Penelope Warrender, take that stubborn look off your face and listen to me. You're old enough to know that I mean business."

A few minutes ago Penny had been frightened. Then, as Miss Ballinger began to show in her speech all the vulgarity that one would expect, she felt angry. She felt the blood rise to her cheeks and her hands begin to tremble with anger. Mrs. Warrender had told her years ago that she must try and conquer those fits of rage that so often seemed to go

DICKIE LAUNCHED THE ECLAIR WITH GREAT SUCCESS

with red hair, and she had not felt like this for ages. Then she began to go cold, but much calmer, and with the twins holding her hands she leaned back against the shoddy sideboard and listened while Miss Ballinger told an old story with a new variation.

She said bluntly that she intended to have the map which she was sure existed and any other papers which had anything to do with the treasure.

" I pay you the compliment, child," she said, " of not pretending. You and your friends know there is treasure to be found, and you know what I know. I intend to find this and am working for my friend here on his behalf."

" What friend ? "

" Mr. Grandon, of course. I have already told you that I am an expert on antiques, and Mr. Grandon has asked me to help him. What you children have not been told is that Mrs. Warrender's old uncle who owned the *Dolphin* intended Mr. Grandon to have this treasure because he had served him so well. When the time comes and the treasure is discovered we can produce a letter from Mr. Charles Warrender to prove it."

" That's a lie ! " Penny said indignantly. " You know it's not true."

" And how do you know it's not true ? " Miss Ballinger asked, flicking the ash from her cigarette.

Penny, too angry to notice the fair-haired girl flash a quick look at her aunt, unfortunately fell straight into the trap.

" How do I know ? " she stormed. " I know because I've seen the letter old Uncle Charles wrote to Jon in which he tells him that the treasure is for . . . Oh ! what have I said ? " and she put her hands over her eyes to hide the sudden, quick tears that came as she realized what she had done.

There was a long silence. Miss Ballinger regarded them with malevolent triumph. Slinky, by the door, shifted uneasily and then the girl who had been lounging in an easy chair flung her cigarette into the fireplace and laughed shortly.

" Now we know ! " she said. " I thought they had found something."

" Now we know," Miss Ballinger repeated with a quiet

innocence that made even Dickie shiver, while Macbeth, now tucked under Mary's arm, growled warningly.

" Grandon, throw that disgusting dog out. I won't have it here. Put the dog down, child, and don't argue."

But Mary, with her big eyes dark in her white face, only hugged her friend closer.

" You great bullying beasts ! " she stuttered. " Don't one of you dare to come near, else I'll make him kill you. We're not afraid of you, but wherever I go Mackie stays with me. . . ."

" An' wherever Mary goes I go . . ." Dickie added with chin up. " An' now you've made Penny cry."

" They *haven't*, Dickie," Penny protested violently and put an arm round his shoulders. " Not really, anyway. It's only because I'm so furious. . . . Anyway, what I said about the letter isn't true. I made it up. . . . Now will you let us go ? . . . We can't tell you anything about this treasure you keep talking about 'cos we don't know anything. . . . Just let us go now, please, and we won't say anything at home about it."

" Oh, gosh, won't we ? " said Dickie. " I can tell you you'll all be jolly sorry when we get out of this. You wouldn't dare do this if our father knew about it."

" No," Penny agreed. " And you wouldn't have dared played such a dirty, cowardly trick with Jon."

" Or David," said Mary stoutly.

" I see," said Miss Ballinger quietly. " But we are wasting time, and if we do not hurry the weather will be too bad for you to get home at all. I have a new suggestion to make," and she sat down suddenly at the table, behind which the children were still standing defiantly. " I do not enjoy this," she continued in a changed mood. " I like you children and admire your spirit. I have tried to be friends with you "—here Penny's arm tightened round Mary's shoulder—" but you will not let me be friends. Here, then, is my last suggestion. You children can help us more than you know, so let us get the business over and done with, so that you can finish your holidays with plenty of jolly fun "—here Penny felt Dickie shudder—" and to do this I am prepared to make you a reasonable present each. Perhaps the twins would like nice new bicycles ? "

" We got 'em," said Dickie tersely.

"Or another little dog," suggested Miss Ballinger, with cunning which was sadly misplaced.

"Why should we want *another*?" Mary asked.

"And you, Penny? There is sure to be something you would like. Just tell me what and you shall have it in exchange for one simple little favour."

"And that is?" Penny asked with her head high.

"Just write a note *now* to your cousin Jonathan and ask him to come over right away with the letter you mentioned and all the other papers you found in the box in your room at the *Dolphin*. . . . If you write the note at once Mr. Grandon will take it to Jonathan and bring him back in the car, and then you can all go back together and enjoy yourselves and forget all this unpleasantness."

For just one second Penny weakened. Not that the bribes had any attraction for her; she was tempted by the idea that if they gave up the papers they would be rid of this vile Miss Ballinger. As for the horrible Slinky, she knew that when Mrs. Warrender heard the story she would soon get rid of *him*. Penny was feeling very weary. She had not had much sleep last night and she was tired of this adventure. She wanted her aunt and without Jon she felt very much alone.

And then, at the thought of Jon, her mood changed again and she remembered how she had been the one to keep the adventure alive and the one who had refused to tell the grown-ups. She couldn't give in now! How could she ever have considered it? With her head down she glanced at her three enemies.

Miss Ballinger, seated only three feet away, was watching her closely through her thick glasses. Slinky, now that he had wiped his face, was biting his finger-nails by the door, and the girl, who was watching Penny very carefully over a new cigarette, had a suspicion of a sneer about her mouth—the sort of sneer that suggested that after all Penny was no more than a grubby schoolgirl of little account—and that raised all the temper of the red-headed Warrenders.

Penny put a hand to her aching forehead and, with the gesture that Jon and Mrs. Warrender knew so well, flung back her head defiantly.

"I won't write anything," she said. "Even if we had the papers you keep talking about I wouldn't write for them.

Why should I ? You can't do anything to us, and you've no right to keep us here." She turned to Slinky. " As for you, Mr. Grandon, the best thing you can do is to take us home right away. . . . You called it a truce this morning, didn't you ? "

" Atta boy ! " Dickie murmured.

" Good old Penny ! " whispered Mary.

Miss Ballinger bowed her head in her hands. She suddenly looked dispirited and defeated and her niece watched her with growing astonishment.

" We'll go now," Penny said again more firmly.

" Very well," Miss Ballinger agreed. " Perhaps that would be best. I cannot keep you here, but I did hope you would do the sensible thing. . . . Mr. Grandon will take you home . . ." and she got up heavily from the table and turned towards the door.

Penny's eyes were bright with excitement. She had won ! They had beaten the three of them and in twenty minutes they would be home and this horrible bungalow would seem like a bad dream. She looked down at the twins as Mary put Macbeth down on the floor.

" It's all right, darlings. We're going home now."

But she did not see Miss Ballinger's quick gesture to her niece, nor did she realize how quickly Slinky and the girl slipped out into the hall. When she glanced up again Miss Ballinger was glaring at them round the half-open door.

" Now, listen, and listen for the last time," she snarled. " You will stay here until I have the papers in my possession. If you will not help me to get them I must use other methods, and there are still plenty of ways in which young Jonathan Warrender can be persuaded to bring them here to me ! "

" After her, Mackie boy ! After her ! " Mary shouted, and the little black warrior hurtled across the room as the door slammed and the lock clicked home.

" Quick ! " Dickie yelled. " The window ! We can get out there. Smash it ! " But even as he spoke Grandon and Miss Ballinger passed outside and slammed across two heavy wooden shutters.

The fading daylight was shut out and as for a moment the howling wind was lulled, there came the sound of an iron bar slipping into place, followed by Miss Ballinger's laugh.

CHAPTER X

WEDNESDAY: JON AND DAVID TO THE RESCUE

"WHAT'S it all about, Jon?" David demanded as they walked away from the telephone. "Who was it and where are we going, and why are you looking so fussed?"

"We've got an invitation to tea," Jon explained, "and I don't like it. It was that girl—that girl who said she was Miss Ballinger's niece—who tried to bribe me with a motor-bike. She says Penny and the twins are over at the bungalow now and they want us to join them. . . . She said that Penny wants me to bring the map and the papers and that it was very important. . . . What do you think?"

"I should think she's a liar," David said shortly. "I can't imagine Penny sending a message like that."

"Neither can I, but the girl said Penny had important news for us."

"Of course she'd say that. I don't believe a word of it, but I'm puzzled to know how those kids were persuaded to go to the bungalow."

"She said they met Miss Ballinger in Hastings."

"And Slinky took 'em in, didn't he? And your mother said it was Slinky's idea? Looks a bit odd, doesn't it, Jon? I think we'd better go. What does the girl suggest?"

"She telephoned from Winchelsea and says she'll pick us up in the car on the road. . . . She gave me a hint about April the eighth, you know. . . . Something has turned up, I believe, David. . . . Good old Penny! . . . She may have told the girl to mention April just to show she was on the track of something."

"That's possible," David agreed. "But didn't you tell

me that Ballinger & Co. had got this clue now even if they can't understand it ? That girl—I wish we knew her name —might have mentioned April the eighth to catch us."

" It may be a trap, but I'm going," Jon replied. " I don't like the idea of Penny and the twins in that foul bungalow. I hated it when we went. . . . Let's go, anyway ; but I'm not going to take any papers. . . . Seems to me we're like two boxers both trying to trick the other into making a mistake, but I do think we ought to go over and see what their game is."

" All right. It's after tea-time and Slinky isn't back, so I should think the story is true and that they really are at *Beach View.* My people will be back soon, too, I should think, and I'd like the twins to be home before they arrive. The weather is getting worse. Let's get our macs."

" I don't think I want to see my mother," Jon said. " She'll wonder what all the fuss is about, and it will only waste time if we begin to explain. Just wait a sec. while I scribble a note to drop in her letter-box over the way."

In the note he explained where they were going and that they would come back in the car with the others, and then they went out together into the gale. The wind sang and roared through the narrow streets and passages of the town and sky and sea alike were a dirty, muddy grey, except where a thin line of white showed where the waves were pounding on the beaches a mile or more away.

They stumbled down Trader's Passage to the river and stood for a moment to recover their breath, looking at the muddy water swirling under the bridge. Two men were talking in the lee of one of the tarred, drying-sheds, and one glanced up and saw the boys. It was Vasson, and he strolled over to speak to them.

" Where be you two going on a day like this ? It'll be worse afore long, you know, and it's not much fun walking about in this."

" Is there any more news, Mr. Vasson ? " David asked. " I mean about the lifeboats standing by."

" Not as I knows on, but chaps down at harbour all be ready. You be going down that way ? "

" No, we've got to go down to Winchelsea Beach to a bungalow belonging to somebody we know. Penny and the twins are there to tea."

Vasson pursed his lips for a whistle of surprise that was blown away in the gale.

" But you lads'll never get out there to-night. That beach is no place to be. If it goes on blowing like this— and blow it will till tide is full to-night—them folks in those liddle houses and shacks'll have to clear out, I'm thinking. Tide's turned, but she'll not be full till after dark, and they're real worried for the great bank, I hear tell."

" It's worse down there, is it, Vasson ? Do they really think something like that will happen ? "

" Aye, they do ! And you say those youngsters and Miss Penny are there ? Who took 'em there, I'd like to know. They went out this morning with that Mr. Grandon."

Before Jon could answer David nudged him. A shabby little green car was coming towards them down the road, and they could see it was driven by the girl in the white mackintosh. As soon as she recognized the boys she stopped. They called a " Cheerio " to Vasson, who looked both puzzled and angry, and ran down the road as she turned the car.

" Don't forget she's an enemy, too," Jon gasped as the girl leaned out and smiled at them.

" Glad you could both manage it. Decent of you to come. Hop in. . . . Coming in the front with me, Jon ? "

He pretended not to hear this invitation and got in at the back with David. The girl turned round and smiled at them.

" You must be David Morton ? Penny told me about you. You're not much like the twins, are you ? "

David grunted, but Jon was amused to see him redden. This girl made him feel like that, too ! Then she turned to him :

" You've got the papers and things, Jon ? Penny was very keen you should bring them."

Jon didn't hesitate, but nodded briefly. She smiled at him radiantly, but before she could speak he said : " What's all the fuss about, anyway, and why didn't Penny ring me up herself, and why hasn't Mr. Grandon brought the twins home as he promised ? "

" One thing at a time," she laughed as she let in the clutch. " My aunt met Mr. Grandon and the others at lunch in Hastings, and she asked them to give her a lift home and stay to tea. Apparently you people have got some old maps and papers which interest my aunt, and from what I hear Penny now wants her to see them. She didn't come and speak to you herself because she was helping to get the tea. I had the car out this afternoon and had just got back, so they asked me to telephone and then meet you. We haven't got a 'phone at the bungalow. As for Mr. Grandon or whatever he's called, he realized that Mrs. Warrender would wonder where he was, so when I promised to bring you all back later he left the twins and started just before me. Hasn't he passed you ? "

" Haven't seen him." Jon said suspiciously.

" We came down the steps," David explained.

" That accounts for it, then. Just as you walked down he would be coming up through the town. Now are you both satisfied ? I can't think why you don't like me, Jon. You're a suspicious sort of boy, aren't you ? I know you are. . . . You don't trust me."

Jon gulped. She was too clever for him and could even read his thoughts ! He mumbled something as the car turned into the narrow road under Winchelsea hill, which led to the beach, and nudged David. He could not forget that, however charming she tried to be now, she was the same girl whom he had heard plotting with Slinky in the old mill only a few days ago. And now she was pretending that she didn't know Mr. Grandon's name.

The wind was so strong now that it slowed down the little car and once actually lifted it off two wheels for a second when a sudden gust caught it broadside on. But their driver kept a cool head and laughed, with the usual cigarette between her painted lips.

" Getting a bit rough," was all she said.

They met several people on the road. One couple were pushing a small pram which contained a child and two suit-cases. A man was trying to cycle, but was blown off and couldn't get on again. He flung his cycle in the hedge and shouted something at them as they passed. The wind was bringing rain again now and the reeds and tall bull-rushes growing in the dike at the side of the road were laid almost flat on the water, which seethed as it was struck by the squall. Although the car was closed they could barely hear each other speak for the ceaseless, relentless roaring of the wind.

" Hold tight," the girl said, and swung the car off the road on to the rutted track along which Penny and the twins had been driven only about an hour before. The little car lurched and swayed as it headed straight for the great bank of shingle behind which the highest tide of the year was now thundering up the beach.

Some men, drenched and hatless, ran up the track and signalled the car to stop. The girl hesitated before braking, and one of them signed to her to lower the windows.

" What's the fuss ? " she said coolly. " I'm in a hurry."

The man's face was glistening with wet and he was fighting for breath.

" Turn her round," he gasped. " Turn her round quickly and take us to the nearest 'phone. It's urgent."

Another man pushed forward. " Buck up ! " he shouted. " The bank will go for certain when the tide's right up ! Some of it is shifting now, they say."

The girl hesitated, took the cigarette from her mouth and dropped it outside the window.

" I'm going to *Beach View*," she said at last. " We shan't belong, and then I'll drive back myself to the telephone."

Another man with a suit-case on his shoulder and a woman and young child at his side came up and pushed his way between the others now crowding round the little car.

" You kids get out of there," he shouted excitedly. " If you're not getting out there are those who will help you. We've got to use every car we can find to get out of here. We've got to hurry. . . . There's another car back there under the hill, but it's locked and we can't get at it. This will do for some of us."

" Lock your doors," the girl said quietly over her shoulder, and Jon saw her slip up the handle on her side so that the door was fast. The two boys did the same almost without thinking, but there was now such a commotion and noise going on outside that it was difficult to discover exactly what was happening. It was getting dark, too, and the rain blurred the windows.

When they compared notes later both boys agreed that the threatening crowd round the car was first broken up by the big lorry which came lurching along behind them. The track here ran on a ridge a few feet higher than the flat marsh on the left and yet lower than some shingly hillocks which rose quite sharply on the right. Although two small cars might have managed to pass each other, there was no room for the huge lorry which so suddenly loomed up behind them. Looking out of the rear window, Jon could see that it was piled high with what looked like bundles of faggots. The driver, now leaning from his cabin, switched on his headlights and kept his hand on the button of the horn. Several other men carrying spades and picks tumbled off the lorry and ran forward, and one of them put his hand on the door and shouted :

" We can't pass you. Get on or get out of the way. What's wrong ? "

" Nothing's wrong," the girl said, " except that these panic-stricken rats stopped me. Get back, all of you ! I'm going on."

Just at that moment, by some freak, the wind died down and, except for the roar of the sea, there was an odd, almost uncanny, silence. Voices, raised a few seconds before to be heard above the gale, now sounded harsh and hysterical. The girl sounded her horn to warn the excitable man who was still standing in the middle of the track. He was pointing urgently away to the left, where the great bank loomed over the sullen lagoon which Jon remembered seeing on the afternoon he had come with Penny to *Beach View* for the first time. The last gleams of daylight lingered over this pool and the ridge of the bank above as yet another man came running and stumbling madly towards them. Jon wound down his window suddenly and in the strange lull they heard every word as he yelled :

" She's going up yonder ! Up beyond the last of those huts where the men are. She'll be through soon and the water's coming up underneath the bank. . . . What are you waiting for ? . . ." and the remainder of the sentence was carried away by the wind which rose again to a shriek of triumph as Jon saw a great plume of spray thrown into the air high over the bank and then flung towards them in the gale until it spattered the windscreen.

" Out of the way, all of you," the girl shouted as she eased her left foot and the little car jumped forward amidst the shouts of those who were now hurrying towards them from the beach.

" The lorry is following us. They've got away all right,"

David shouted. " Gosh ! I wouldn't have missed this for anything."

" There'll be trouble when she stops the car," Jon muttered. " I'll be glad to see Penny and the kids, though, and get them home again. . . . Vasson was right again, wasn't he, David ? . . . Look at the crowd under the hill there. . . . they're smashing the windows of a car . . . Look David, I'm sure that's our car. . . ." He leaned forward and shook the girl's shoulder. "Here, you," he yelled. " I thought you said Grandon had driven home and passed us in Rye. That's our car there."

She wriggled her shoulder free.

" Strong boy ! " she said. "And my name's Valerie and you had better call me Val, like everybody else and not just ' you.' . . . Now, listen to what I say, because it's important. I'm going to drive down a little way on the shingle at the side of the hill 'cos there's not quite so many people there ! Before I stop, nip out, one each side and I'll lock the doors from inside. Don't let anyone get so much as a finger inside the car and I'll manage to lock my own door somehow and bring the key with me. . . . Are you ready ? Right ! Jump for it."

Neither of the boys attempted to argue for they realized at once that her suggestion was wise. As the car lurched on to the loose shingle in the comparative shelter of the hill, they opened the doors and jumped out. Jon stumbled and fell to his knees and as he got up a wild-eyed woman rushed towards them.

" Lend me your car," she pleaded. " We daren't wait any longer. Turn it round and take us back to Winchelsea." Before Jon could answer Valerie was beside him and locking the door handle. Then she turned to the stranger.

" We're just fetching some children," she shouted. " Don't tell anyone else and we'll try and give you a lift if there's room. . . . But don't tell anyone." Then she slipped between the boys and took their arms. " That will keep her quiet I hope," she went on. " Now buck up, for we've no time to waste. . . . Come along this way behind the bungalows."

Although they both felt wildly excited they were also rather scared. Jon was unhappy about Penny, and David, although he knew from experience that the twins were **very**

A STRANGE, SHAPELESS BULK DETACHED ITSELF FROM THE GLOOM
OF THE PORCH

" Now," she said. " Let's have no more nonsense. I offered you twenty pounds for all the papers and maps you have found in that old box in the top room at the *Dolphin*. . . . There's no time to argue now, so if you want more money I'll give you more, because I'm in a hurry, but I must have the papers at once. . . . I've got to be off."

" I wouldn't worry, Jon," Valerie drawled looking at her red finger-nails. " Just give her the papers and let's all get out of this."

They all had to shout to make themselves heard. The walls and floor were shaking with the pounding of the waves and the force of the wind and there was a strange smell of stale sea water in the house. But Jon was no longer afraid.

" I've got no papers or maps of any sort with me," he shouted as the house shook again, " and if I had they belong to us and to my mother and are nothing to do with you."

" You little liar ! " Valerie screamed and stepped towards Jon with her hand raised as if to strike him. " You have got them. You told me you'd got them when I met you."

" I didn't say anything actually," Jon replied. " And I wish now I'd told you right out that I hadn't brought any papers. . . . Anyway it doesn't matter what you say or do because even if there were any papers they are *nothing to do with you !* " and in his excitement he got quite red in the face and went close to Valerie and yelled at her. Miss Ballinger snarled something at the girl which sounded like " fool " and then David broke in.

" And what have you done with my brother and sister ? Where are they ? We've come to take them home."

" Yes, and where's Penny ? " Jon added. " Penny ! Penny ! " he yelled suddenly but the noise outside was too great for him to be heard outside the room. Miss Ballinger turned to Slinky.

" Go outside," she said, " and see how things are. Let me know at once if everybody else on the beach has left."

Grandon, with bent, shamed head, slipped past the boys and obeyed his orders.

" Now sit down you two and I'll be quick with what I've got to say. Give me those papers or promise me on your honour that you will give them all to me with any other information you may have found out in the morning and you shall go home at once with Penny and the twins."

" Are they in the house then ? " Jon demanded.

" Never mind where they are, but you can be sure they are safe with me and in my care and they can be exchanged for the papers I need—the papers and map which will lead me to the treasure."

" But you can't do that ? How dare you ? You can't keep them here like that ! Why ! Why, it's kidnapping, and you can go to prison for it. Let them out at once and we'll all go home. We'll walk if you like but we're going home and you can't stop us."

" But I *am* stopping you. . . . You cannot go now and I have the others safe and they cannot go either. And in an hour they say the sea will be through the bank. . . . You see, Jonathan, I need those papers and I intend to have them. Neither do I intend to be interfered with by a gang of rude, unruly and ill-mannered children. . . . Give me your promise, Jonathan—your word of honour for you both— and you can go home with the others at once."

Before Jon could answer the door crashed open and Slinky shouted excitedly :

" Come at once ! We must go now, for all have left the beach. A man with a megaphone is calling that the sea cannot be kept back much longer. . . . I am going. . . . I shall take the car. . . . If you are coming, come now. . . ." and his voice died away in a miserable wail. Jon and David looked him up and down with disdain. He was a contemptible figure with his smart grey suit creased and damp and dirty, and his shiny black hair hanging loosely over his narrow forehead. His eyes were wild and frightened and his fingers plucked nervously at his mouth and little black moustache.

" You coward," Jon said bitterly. " You miserable coward ! If you don't tell me where the others are and get them away at once you'll be responsible and I'll tell everyone —and you'd better not go back to the *Dolphin* else it will be the worse for you. We all know what part you've played in this."

" I'll be almost sorry for you when my father hears how you tricked the twins and Penny and took them into Hastings," David added.

Mr. Grandon glared at them, ran his fingers through his tousled hair and bolted out of the room. Miss Ballinger seemed to catch something of his panic for she grabbed her niece by the arm and drew her towards the door.

" Get out ! " she snapped. " We've got to go."

" But you can't leave them all here like this," Valerie began and then turned to the boys. " Don't be such a fool, Jon. Give your promise and we'll all get out of here."

" Get out yourself," Miss Ballinger roared, " and keep quiet, too."

She pushed her out into the hall and before the boys could move the door was slammed and locked.

Jon and David stared at each other and then the latter's face broke into a broad grin.

" Gosh ! " he said. " We're in for it now. . . . Come on, Jon. Try the door first and then the window. We've got to search the house for the others."

They rushed to the door but it was locked fast and while they were tugging at the handle they heard the front door slam.

" What dirty tykes they are ! " Jon gasped. " Get a chair, David, and we'll smash the panels in. . . . I wish I knew whether those kids were safe."

" Just a sec., Jon. . . . Let's try the windows first. . . . We can open them easily enough from here, but the shutters are fastened from the outside. P'raps the door will be less trouble, but let's hurry. . . . Can you smell water ? I can sniff something damp and the storm is worse than ever. The house will collapse if we're not quick."

Jon reached for the poker and had dealt the first smashing blow to the panel door when there was a noise behind them.

They wheeled round in time to see the wooden window shutters suddenly flung back and then something heavy hurtled through the glass and a large stone landed on the table. The wind tore and whistled through the broken pane. Something smaller followed the stone and fell with a clink into the fireplace and as David stooped to pick up a key Jon, open-mouthed with astonishment, realized that Valerie was outside and calling to them. Her voice came faintly through the turmoil, but although she had gone almost as soon as she had spoken, he thought he heard her say :

" They're in the front room. But hurry, hurry ! The bank is breaking and the sea is coming in."

CHAPTER XI

WEDNESDAY: NOAH'S ARK

W HEN the shutters closed out the light and they heard the iron bar which locked them fast clang into place, Penny and the twins were almost too surprised to realize that they were actually imprisoned in the front room of *Beach View*. Macbeth was still barking furiously at the closed door and the noise of the wind and pounding waves seemed to be increasing. The room was not quite dark; a thin line of light where the shutters did not fit showed them the position of the window, but as the light outside was failing fast Penny knew that before very long they would be in complete darkness.

Rather more sharply than she intended she said :

" Keep the dog quiet, Mary. He can't do any good by making that noise."

" That's all you know, Penny ! He's a jolly fine watch dog and he's saved us from an awful fate before this. He wants to kill that beastly woman and I don't blame him. I want to kill her, too."

" I want to murder Slinky," Dickie said coming over from the door. " I think really that he's the worst of them all. CAN YOU HEAR ME ? " he bawled as nobody seemed to take any notice of him.

" Be quiet, Mackie ! Come here ! " Mary said, and although she spoke softly the little dog obeyed at once and came over, wagging his tail but still growling quietly. Mary picked him up and he licked her face.

" You're a brave boy, darling, but just keep quiet now, 'cos we're going to have a council of war. . . . I don't care for it dark like this, do you, twin ? "

Dickie was fidgetting between the window and the door.

" No, I don't like it. I don't like the way the sea keeps

banging away outside there. This adventure reminds me a bit of that Mrs. Thurston at Appledore.[1] Do you remember how she locked us in the bedroom ? "

" Yes, I do, Dickie. And David rescued us through the window. P'raps he will again. . . . I wish we could see. Where are you, Penny ? "

" I'm here. Don't worry. We'll soon get out of this. . . . Jon will come, you'll see ! He'll find out and come. I specially asked Auntie to let him know where we'd gone. . . . I say, twins ! You're not mad with me 'cos I didn't write that note are you ? If I'd written it I s'pose she'd have let us go."

" Course we're not," Dickie said stoutly. " We think you're jolly brave."

" I was *praying* you'd say ' No,' " Mary said. " And that just shows doesn't it ! But they can't do anything to us here, can they ? It's only the dark I don't like, and as we're all together we shall soon get used to that. We're not afraid of them, are we, twin ? "

" No, we're not. I'm going to break the door down now," Dickie replied. " Let's make so much noise that they'll have to let us out."

" Not much sense in that really," Penny said. " Let's try and get out by cunning. They won't take any notice of noise. Are you twins cunning ? "

Penny couldn't see him clearly, but she sensed that Dickie was grimacing wildly. She had already realized that he enjoyed acting a part and seemed to think that nobody would understand him unless he contorted his features to suit his mood.

" Are we cunning ? " he muttered and then, " But all the same I'm going to kick the door."

Unfortunately he forgot that he was wearing sandals and his yell of baffled fury was partly a cry of pain. Mary groped her way over to him.

" Hard luck, Dickie ! " she said. " Never mind. P'raps we could smash the window presently and if we have to make a noise we'll make Mackie bark again."

" Come here, you two," Penny said. " I've got a brain-wave. Let's camp under this table and make no noise at all. If we don't fuss I bet they'll soon wonder what's happened

[1] See " Mystery at Witchend."

to us and then they'll come and open the door. When they do we'll still keep quiet and if they look in they won't see us at first."

" What do we do then ? " asked the realist Dickie. " Overpower them, I suppose, by lurin' them under the table."

" I'm not sure what we do then," Penny said doubtfully, " but I think that if we keep quiet then they will have to do something. Let's try it once, anyway. . . . Come on ! "

They crawled under the table and Penny noticed that the strip of light at the window was fading fast. Macbeth seemed rather astonished that his friends should join him on the floor and Mary was uneasy about it all.

" I think maybe we ought to sing a bit," she said. " Just to keep our spirits up. This is the sort of time and place for us to sing."

" I know," Dickie said. " Like the early Christians before they were chewed up by lions in the arena. I read a book about that once. It was wizard."

" What shall we sing then ! " Mary continued. " P'raps ' Onward Christian Soldiers ' would be good, but I only know one verse. . . . or ' There'll Always be a Nengland,' or . . ."

" . . . or ' Roll out the Barrel,' which is a good tune," said Dickie, warming to the idea. " You'd better not do Christian Soldiers, though, 'cos we tried that once and Mackie doesn't like it. He howls."

" We won't sing anything," Penny whispered urgently. " Just be quiet. I believe someone tried the door."

Instantly the twins froze and Mary put her hand on Macbeth's collar. The window was rattling behind the shutters and the floor shook with the power of the waves thundering up the beach such a short distance away. They strained their ears to catch any other sound and suddenly the lock clicked back and a crack of yellow light showed as the door opened an inch. Penny slipped an arm round the shoulders of each twin and breathed, " Quiet ! Hear what she's got to say."

For a long moment there was no other sound from the door. Penny sensed Miss Ballinger standing there and waiting for them to beg her to let them go.

" Let her wait," she thought. " Let her do the wondering and the worrying. I know Jon will come presently."

Then they heard the hated voice.

" Are you listening, children ? "

No answer.

" Can you hear me ? . . . It's no use sulking and it's no use pretending you're not here. . . . Answer me ! "

Silence. Mary held her hand firm now over Macbeth's muzzle while the little dog trembled with fury.

" Very well ! Go on sulking then. Grandon ! Fetch me my torch from the bedroom. . . . These little fools are pretending they're not there. . . . Now listen. . . . Jonathan and the other boy will be here soon with the map and other papers, but it will save us all a lot of time if you, Penny, tell me all you know. Tell me if you know what ' nt 8 April 7 ' means ? "

Penny drew her breath in sharply and felt Mary's shoulders trembling against her arm. So they had not got as far as " earthen vessels " ! She almost laughed aloud in triumph ! How bucked the others would be when they heard this. She could not help wondering, though, how Miss Ballinger was going to persuade David and Jon to come over without the message she had refused to write. She was certain that the boys would find some way of rescuing them, but it was not likely that they would tell their enemies that they were coming. She supposed this must be another trick. Her head was already aching badly, but she knew she had got to do two things—to keep the twins from harm and to keep their secret for Mrs. Warrender. To-morrow, or to-night, when they were all safe again at the *Dolphin* she would, perhaps allow Jon to tell the grown-ups, and that would mean the end of Miss Ballinger, that odious girl and the miserable Slinky.

Miss Ballinger was speaking again. " The torch. Thank you. . . . Now will you children see reason and tell me what you know," and she flashed the beam round the room and then cried out sharply : " Come out of hiding. Where are you all ? " and then, just as the beam moved towards them across the floor, Mary whispered :

" Go on, Mackie boy ! After her ! Seek her, boy ! "

Macbeth needed no second invitation, but shot from his mistress's restraining hand like a little black bullet towards his enemy. At the same time Dickie crawled out and with

an exultant cry of what sounded like " Up the Lone-Piners,"
charged towards the door.

Then a lot happened at the same time. Miss Ballinger
shouted and kicked out to protect herself from Macbeth.
The kick, by an unlucky chance, caught Mackie just as he
was launching himself to the attack and bowled him over.
He yelped with surprise and pain and then again, with annoyance as Dickie, hot on his heels, fell over him. Miss Ballinger
in her fury dropped the torch, which rolled, still alight,
towards Penny, who was just emerging from under the
table. As boy and dog on the floor began to sort themselves
out, Miss Ballinger muttered something very unladylike and
slipped back into the hall, slamming and locking the door
again before Dickie could get to his feet.

Penny grabbed the torch and shone it on Dickie, who,
scarlet in the face with rage and humiliation, was beating
his fists on the thin panels of the door.

" If it hadn't been for your stupid little dog, Mary," he
yelled, " I'd have got her."

"And what would you have done with her when you'd
got her ? " Mary asked coldly. "And what do you mean
by calling Mackie *my* dog ? Isn't he *our* dog, and don't
we always do everything together, even if I do understand
him better'n anybody else ? Anyway, it's all your fault for
charging about like that. Mackie would have killed her
next minute. He will kill her next time, anyway, 'cos I
think she kicked him. . . . I don't think we've been very
clever, Penny, do you ? We weren't very cunning that time.
What do we do now ? "

Penny laughed. " Come in the camp again. . . . Actually
we've been quite clever. We've got the torch, and by what
she said they don't know as much about the clues as we do,
although they stole that bit of paper. . . . Come on, Dickie.
We mustn't waste this battery."

Dickie had his ear to the panel of the door and suddenly
turned and shouted : " She's come back ! I can hear her
outside. I think it's her. Look out, chaps ! She's going
to open the door again."

As the line of orange light showed again Dickie squeezed
behind the door so that he could not be seen by anyone
opening it from the other side.

" You see, it's no use behaving like that," came Miss

Ballinger's voice again. " Now, unless you, Penny, give me your word of honour that you know absolutely nothing about ' nt 7 April 8 ' or about any other clues you may hold, I shall tell the boys when they arrive—and they are on their way now—that you have all gone with Mr. Grandon, and then we shall leave you alone here in the bungalow when we go . . . and I presume you are old enough and intelligent enough to know what that means ? Come over here, child, and talk to me and be sensible."

She spoke in a cold, calm voice that frightened Penny far more than her shouting and blustering. For the first time in their adventure she had the feeling that Miss Ballinger really had them in her power and that she was crazy enough to carry out her threat. Penny had never before believed that a grown-up would really do this sort of thing, and she suddenly felt horribly defenceless and alone, for although the twins, with all their courage, were with her she knew that she was responsible for them, and the idea of being locked in this dark room in a deserted nouse with the storm raging outside and the possibility of the sea breaking through was not very inviting. At the time she did not realize that Miss Ballinger might be bluffing, for if Jon and David did come, whether they brought the papers or not, she would be no better off by lying to the boys and leaving the three of them alone in the house ! It was all very well for Dickie and Mary to reassure each other continually that they were not afraid of Miss Ballinger. That was an easy thing to say, but Penny was now afraid and not at all sure what to do for the best. After a moment's hesitation she whispered to Mary :

" Take the torch, Mary, and stay here. If she opens the door any wider, or if you can't see me against the bright light, switch it on. . . . Where's Dickie ? . . . There he is, behind the door. . . . And keep Mackie quiet again. . . . I'm going over to talk to her."

Mary grabbed at her arm. " Don't go, Penny. She's an old beast. She'll trick you. She'd never dare do what she says."

" I know she wouldn't," Penny lied bravely, " so don't worry. It's only that I want to hear what she's got to say. Here's the torch," and she walked over to the door, pushed Dickie gently out of the way and said quietly :

" Here I am, Miss Ballinger. I've told you already that I've got no maps or papers about any hidden treasure, so will you please stop bullying us and let us go. You know I'm responsible for these two and I must get them back home. . . . I know you were only joking about keeping us here, but it's a silly joke, all the same."

She could see Miss Ballinger's thick spectacles gleaming at her through the crack in the door, and she thought she could see Slinky behind her.

" I was not joking, my child. I have been trying ever since I came down here to make you children see reason, and I will not be trifled with any longer. . . . Now tell me what you know . . ." and with these last words she suddenly swung the door open and grabbed at Penny in the hope of dragging her into the hall. But Penny was just too quick ; as the arm shot out to catch her she ducked and pushed hard on the door, stepping back into the room at the same time. Then Dickie shouted and rushed forward. Mary switched on the torch and Macbeth once again dashed into the fray. Penny cried out with pain as something scratched her face, and then the door was slammed and locked once again and the prisoners returned to their camp under the table.

" I said it was a trick ! " Mary said indignantly. Then, " Oh, Penny darling—your're bleeding. What did she do to you ? "

Penny dabbed with a dirty handkerchief.

" Must have been her nails, I s'pose. She tried to get me out into the hall."

" She'd have tortured you," said Dickie solemnly ; " that's what she'd have done. Gosh ! What an awful adventure we're having ! "

So they settled down again with Penny between the twins and Macbeth with his head on Mary's legs. Penny felt that they should save the torch battery, so they sat in darkness. There didn't seem anything else to do, for although she knew very definitely that they were prisoners, she was equally certain that Jon would come and rescue them. For many years her faith in Jon had remained unshaken, and it was impossible for him to fail them now. For a time none of them spoke. Penny's thoughts were easy to guess, and for once the twins had nothing to chatter about. It would have been difficult for any of them to hear each other, for the noise of the storm was deafening. The house was shaking, soot was falling down the chimney and the floor trembled as the mighty waves pounded against the bank outside.

After a time Mary began to sing. She had a clear little voice which, for some reason which Penny could not explain, made her feel very choky. Dickie joined in as soon as he recognized " Christian Soldiers," but this only lasted one verse, and then they turned to more secular music. Mary knew plenty of songs, but was bad at remembering the words, which Dickie managed to make up, so it was a good concert. Penny joined in whenever she could, but Macbeth did not really care for it. They had to sing very loudly above the noise of the storm, and it was when Mary had switched to the nursery relic which began " I had a little nut tree, and nothing would it bear, save a silver nutmeg and a golden pear," when her voice suddenly quavered and died away.

" What is it, Mary ? " Penny shouted. " What's wrong ? "

She felt Mary's cold little hand on her shoulder and bent her head to catch her shocked cry.

" Penny ! The floor's all wet over my side. I've got my hand in water. . . . Penny ! Come and feel it."

They were sitting on cushions, but as soon as Penny leaned across and flashed on the torch Dickie yelled :

" It's this side, too ! Gosh ! We're being flooded out ! "

In the dimming light they could see a dark stain spreading over the thin, patterned carpet—spreading even as they watched—and over by the fireplace, where the boards were bare, water was sucking and bubbling up from under the floor. Penny felt her face go white and her scalp tickled with fear as she realized that the sea must either have broken through the great bank and be swirling round the house or else forcing its way up through the shingle. Dickie knew what it meant, too !

" The sea's coming in ! " he yelled. " We'll have to smash the windows and try the shutters again," and it was just as he was scrambling out that Penny, through all the turmoil, thought she heard a heavy crash which might have been the front door.

She tried to keep her voice steady as she shouted :

" Help ! Help us, whoever you are ! We're locked in the front room ! "

Mackie began to bark madly again and to make little angry dashes at the water bubbling in the corner by the fireplace. Mary scrambled off her damp cushion and climbed on the table as Dickie lifted a vase of flowers and threw it with all his strength at the window. Above the tinkle of falling glass Penny heard him laugh in triumph. He liked smashing things !

" Don't cut yourself, Dickie," Penny yelled. " Wait till I get the light on. . . . Right ! Now break the rest and we'll see if there's any way of forcing up that iron bar from inside."

" I'll jolly well . . ." CRASH went two more panes. " I'll jolly well smash the jolly lot . . ." CRASH ! . . . " and the iron bar and everything. I'm feeling jolly strong. . . . How are you, twin," over his shoulder, " are you all right ? "

" Can't hear you prop'ly," Mary yelled. " You're making such a beastly noise."

Now the wind whistled through the narrow gap between the shutters and Penny was shining the torch round the untidy room, when there came a heavy knocking on the door and a muffled shout. They all stood still—Dickie with a wooden cake-stand poised above his head ready for a new assault on the shutter, Mary on the table trying to dry Mackie's paws on her shorts, and Penny, by the fireplace, with the beam of the torch focused on the door.

" It's Jon ! " she shouted. " I knew he'd come."

And the lock clicked and the door opened and there was Jon's cheerful, bespectacled face, crowned with an unruly mop of hair, blinking and grinning rather sheepishly. Over his shoulder David was peering, and it was he who spoke first.

" Are you there, kids ? " and then, " All right, Penny ? "

Then Jon said, " I can't see you, but I s'pose it's you flashing that thing right on my face. . . . It would be ! Point it down ! . . . Quick now. Out this way. The great bank is breaking."

Dickie dashed for the door in his excitement, but Mary waited for Penny, who felt more like crying than laughing now that they were safe, and didn't know what to say as she splashed through the puddles to the hall.

Jon pushed Mary in front of him and grinned at Penny.

" All right, Newpenny ? Sure ? "

She gulped back the quick tears and nodded. When she could trust her voice again she said :

" Yes, we're all O.K. Where are those beasts who locked us in ? "

" Bolted, of course," David said over his shoulder as he fumbled with the latch on the front door. " Look out now, you kids, and hang on to me because I don't know what will happen when I open the door. . . . All right behind ? Right ! Here she goes ! "

There was a shattering crash as the wind flung the door back against the wall and the tinkle of falling glass as the coloured panes smashed to pieces. A picture fell and everything around them seemed to be shaking and collapsing as the gale filled the house with wind.

" Hang on to me, Mary, and put that dog down. He can walk, can't he, or don't his legs work ? "

" You are a beast to him, David," Mary replied. " You know how little and weak he is, and you've no *idea* what he's been through while you've been rescuing us."

" *Put him down !* " David roared.

" Very well, David dear," came the reply, so meekly that Dickie looked at his sister with anxious sympathy.

" Buck up, David ! " Jon urged from behind. " Down the side of the next-door house where we came up, and we'd better make for that little hill."

They struggled out into the wind, which tore at their hair and plucked at their clothes and whistled round their legs. The daylight had gone now and only a few streaks of angry red behind the black clouds showed where the sun had sunk in the west. And over in the east the full moon was rising over a wild and fantastic scene. As the children turned their backs to the sea it seemed as if they were alone in a wilderness of empty shacks and bungalows.

" The others can't be far ahead," David called over his shoulder, " and if we catch them before they can start the car, we'll force them to take us back with them. They dare not refuse when they see we've all escaped. . . . Gosh ! it's wet here. Careful how you go."

In between the bungalows the shingle now was loose and wet, but when they looked back the great bank was still holding, although the ground was shaking with the force of the waves. They turned to the right at the back of the bungalows and made for the foot of the hill where the cars had been left. Here the path had disappeared under a sheet of water which crept nearer their feet as they watched.

" Don't wait ! " Jon shouted. " Go straight through it. Don't worry about getting your feet wet. No time to waste ! "

They were half-way through and Dickie was up to his knees when he stopped.

" Where's Mary ? " he demanded.

They looked back and were just able in the gloom to distinguish her on the edge of the pool. She was stooping over something at her feet.

David was furious. " Silly little ass ! " he muttered, and then cupped his hands to his mouth and shouted :

" Paddle through it, Mary. Buck up ! Nobody will say anything if you get your feet wet. . . . Nothing to be afraid of. . . . Look at Dickie. . . . It's only to his knees now. . . ."

Mary shook her head and then lifted up Mackie. They could see that she was shouting, but her voice was not strong enough to be heard, so, still muttering, David turned and floundered back towards her.

" Hurry on, Jon," he called as he passed, " and take Dickie with you. . . . See if you can catch them before they start the car."

But Dickie insisted on going back with David for Mary, and there was so much confusion and argument that precious time was wasted.

Mary explained that Mackie did not like salt water, and would not even swim through it, and she refused to cross the pool herself unless Penny carried the dog. David then took Mary on his back, and Jon took Dickie, while poor Penny had to flounder through the water as best she could, with Macbeth snuggled under her arm. He was very appreciative of this service and licked her face before she put him down on the other side.

As soon as they were all safely over Jon and David raced ahead to the foot of the hill, but they were too late—far down the rough track that led to the road they saw the red tail-light of a car. They could not be certain that it was Miss Ballinger's, but there was no doubt that this was the last car to leave the beach and that they would have to trudge back to Winchelsea and safety.

" I doubt if these kids will make it," David said. " If Mary hadn't played the fool over the dog we would have caught them up."

Jon nodded. " I know. Do you realize that the Ballinger would have left the twins and Penny there in that place ? . . . Look, David ! The car has disappeared now, but there's something coming towards us down the track now. . . . It's another big lorry loaded with faggots."

The others came up now, and when Penny saw the boys' faces she knew that the car had gone. So they stood for a few minutes, a lonely little group at the foot of the hill. The rain had stopped and the rising moon gleamed sometimes through the gaps in the racing clouds, but all the air was filled with the mighty thunder of the waves behind them. They watched the lorry lurching towards them, and David wondered if perhaps they could wait until it was unloaded and then get a lift back to Winchelsea. Then the moon came out from behind a cloud again, and a man standing on the lorry suddenly waved his arms and shouted. They could not hear what he said, but Penny waved back cheerfully. He seemed 'ɔ get more excited and began to dance about on top of the faggots. The lorry suddenly left the track, swung sharply to the left and swayed off over the grass behind the big lagoon.

" He's gone mad ! " Dickie said sadly. " Poor old man. He's dancing mad. Look at him hopping now."

" He's pointing at us," Mary said. " He's rude. He's shouting. . . . What do we do next, David ? "

But David was staring over the twins' heads at the great bank towards which the lorry was bumping slowly. On top of the bank, against the skyline, they could see tiny figures labouring in the light of the headlamps of other lorries which were parked on the grass below. Jon was just about to remind Penny that they had passed the spot at which the men were working the other day and had remarked upon what would happen if the sea broke through when David gripped his wrist so hard that he peevishly snatched his hand away.

" Look ! " David shouted. " Watch the bank. I saw it move. Something's happening to it . . . it's changing shape. . . ."

Penny shouted against the noise almost without realizing what she was saying, clutched Mary close to her and screamed.

" It's breaking. . . . *The sea's coming through !* "

The next few moments were like a nightmare—a nightmare in which something terrifying rushes towards the dreamer who cannot move to save himself, and then, at the very last instant, wakes. But none of them could wake now, although it must have been a minute before Jon shouted :

" Quickly ! Up the hill ! "

They stood helpless and watched the tiny figures of men scatter along the top of the bank ; they saw the other men, from the lorry which had just passed them, jump out, run and climb the bank to join those already flying from that one spot where they had been working with planks and clay and bundles of faggots to repair the breach. They saw this part of the bank move—rather as an elephant might stir in his sleep—and surge a little forward. In the lights of the headlights they saw the top of the bank sink a trifle and then, in a mighty cloud of spray, a hundred feet or more of shingle collapsed under the weight of the waves, and the sea, for the first time for hundreds of years, came surging through the gap, spread hungrily over the nearby levels and crept slowly inland to take back its own.

At Jon's shout they all came out of their dream and followed him in a mad scramble up the sides of the little hill. Jon stopped, after a few steps, and held out his hand to Penny, who had stumbled and was limping with the pain in her knee. Poor David had a twin on each hand, and although he looked rather stern and cross, his young brother and sister were laughing and trying to turn round every few steps.

Jon paused for breath and pulled Penny up beside him. She slipped an arm through his and said :

" Let's wait here a sec. The water can't reach us here, anyway, and I want to see what those men are going to do."

David flung himself down at their feet.

" What do you think of that, chaps ? Do you realize that we're the only ones in the whole world besides those men on the top who saw that go and we could see better than they could ? . . . Could you believe it ? I hardly could."

" That's because you're not used to adventures, David

H

dear," Mary said. " Dickie and me don't think this is very exciting. . . . I mean this is the sort of thing we've had before, isn't it, twin ? "

" You know what we are, don't you ? We're marooned and maybe we'll be here for many days and nights and I'm sorry to mention it, but I'm hungry."

" You *can't* be, Dickie," Penny said. " It's impossible. . . . Oh, but you did throw one of your buns at Slinky. I'd forgotten that."

" That was stupid," Dickie agreed. " Just plain silly, 'cos I need that food now."

" Where's Mackie ! " Mary suddenly wailed and then, as she felt the little dog's cold nose against her bare leg, " Of course I didn't *really* forget you, my darling."

" What are those men going to do ? " Jon broke in. " Some of them are going down the bank to try and start the lorry. I s'pose it's not too deep there and if they could get it on the track down here the water may be shallow enough for them to get through."

They watched them struggle through the rushing water, climb up and then the lorry came back towards them. The driver was obviously making for the track and after two attempts with the water swirling round the axles, he managed to reach the higher level and turn the lorry inland. The man saw them and leaned out of his cabin.

" Can't wait now, but don't worry, kids ! " he shouted. " I've got to go back for help, but I'll send the lifeboat for you if need be ! " and they saw his teeth gleam in a friendly grin in the moonlight. . . . " Don't fret. . . . You're like old Noah in his Ark ! " and he pointed up behind them and the children saw that the little black hut which crowned the hill did look rather like a toy ark with its pointed roof.

" Good-bye," Mary called. " Come back soon ! " and " Good luck," Dickie shouted as the lorry splashed off.

They watched it until it turned into the road at the end of the track and then saw that the other lorries were almost completely under water. Some of the men who had been working on the bank were now going back to the gap, but there did not seem much they could do to stop the water until the tide turned.

Jon ran his fingers through his hair.

" We're in for it now, chaps, and in for the night, too.

It's like Dickie says, for we're marooned on an island. What shall we do ? "

" Climb to the top," David said. " That's what hills are for ! "

Now that the tide was near turning the wind was dropping in sympathy and when they reached the little plateau upon which the black hut stood, the moon sailed above the ragged clouds and they could see far inland to Winchelsea and all along the bank to Cliff End. Towards Rye it looked as if there was another break, but the flood water, although not deep, was still spreading over the grassy levels and still coming in through the gap.

They stood against the rough tarred boards of the hut and Mary suddenly lurched heavily against Penny, who looked down at the little girl in surprise.

" Tired ? " she asked quietly.

" . . . Um—just a bit," Mary nodded. " I'm funny in the legs, but don't tell the others. I'm gettin' cold, too. . . . How are your teeth, twin ? Chatterin' yet ? "

Jon and David moved away a few steps and started a consultation and Dickie turned round and smiled at his sister.

" Acksherly they are ! They've just started. What are we going to do ? I hope they don't rescue us too soon."

Penny smothered a terrific yawn. She was annoyed with the boys for whispering together and in the normal way would have had something to say about it, but now she stayed with the twins and fussed Macbeth until they came back. Jon grinned apologetically at Penny and gave her arm a friendly squeeze as he said :

" Sorry about that ! We're probably here for the night so we'd better try and make ourselves comfortable. . . . Let's see if we can get into the hut."

They crowded round the door which was fastened with a padlock, but David's big scout knife soon loosened the staple.

" It's a pity to break in, but I don't think anybody will mind really," said Jon as he swung the door back. " Stand back, you kids, and see if there's enough light to show us anything ! "

It was too dark to see much, but the smell which greeted them was not very pleasant—stale and fishy.

" Has *anybody* got a match or a light," David asked peevishly.

" P.S.—Again. There is also a little dog, but come quickly before we eat him."

Mary was so disgusted with the final postscript that she almost wept with rage.

" I'd rather let him eat me first," she protested. " Or *you*, you beast, Dickie ! You're not to send it like that."

But her twin dodged out of her reach, thrust the folded paper into the bottle, screwed up the stopper and ran down the hill. He put such effort into his throw that he nearly toppled into the water, but his face beamed with triumph when he came back.

" Dunno how it is, but that bottle has made me feel hungry. Soon I'll be thirsty."

" Stop talking about it and stop fidgeting about," David said. " Come and sit down here and keep warm."

And so, muttering to himself, the restless Dickie came back to the fire which was now blazing cheerily. They sat as near to it as they could with their backs to the rough sides of the hut out of the wind, which was at last subsiding. Mary, with Macbeth across her legs, was already asleep in the crook of Penny's arm. The fierce, flickering flames threw strong lights and shadows through her curls and when Dickie squeezed down between her and David she barely stirred.

" Why does she waste time going to sleep ? " he grumbled, but four minutes later David grinned to see that even the indomitable Richard had followed her example.

Penny, the other side of Mary, was next to Jon who was lolling back with his hands in his pockets, whistling softly as he watched the flames. The wind, though not nearly as strong, was still whistling round the hut, but the thundering of the waves was not so noticeable. It was a strange scene with the moon above and the water all round the little hill. Men were still to be seen on the bank by the great gap but, from where they were all sitting round their camp fire, they could not see the blazing ruins of *Beach View*.

After a long silence Jon said :

" Rum end to the day, Penny ! "

" Um ! " she agreed sleepily. " I hope you had a nice time this morning with David and Mr. and Mrs. Morton."

He looked at her suspiciously.

" It was all right," he said doubtfully, and although he may not have realized it, this was the right answer.

" I did what you asked me," Penny went on, " but they were clever about getting us into Hastings. I haven't told you all about that, have I ? Never mind. I'm too tired now. . . . I feel as if I'd played ten games of hockey without stopping. . . . I say, Jon ! What do you think Auntie will say about this. . . . Once or twice I've been wondering whether we ought to have told her all we knew."

Her voice was very drowsy and she hardly heard Jon's grunted reply. David leaned forward and flung two more chunks of wood on to the fire. A shower of sparks flew upwards and were scattered in the wind as Penny's red head nodded and then slipped down on to Jon's shoulder. He looked at her oddly, for a moment pursed his lips for a whistle which never came, and if he moved his arm so that she was a little more comfortable, nobody knew.

An hour later the tide had turned and the wind had dropped. Two big lorries and a fire engine with a searchlight and some trailer pumps came splashing down the still submerged track.

" You awake, Jon ? " David called.

" Yes—and nearly paralyzed. Little Penny's been asleep on me. . . . We'd better nip down and stop that chap. . . . Chuck some more on the fire and make a blaze so that they'll see. . . . Sorry, Newpenny ! Try leaning the other way."

Penny stirred, sat up suddenly, looked round in surprise and felt her cheek where it was marked by the rough tweed of Jon's jacket. He rumpled her head and grinned before setting off down the hill with David just behind him.

The searchlight on the fire engine was suddenly swung round towards them and the two boys were picked out in its beam. They waved wildly and a man lifted a megaphone and called to them.

" We can't take you back now, but your people know where you are. . . . Are you all O.K. ? Good ! They're coming to fetch you 'fore the tide comes up again. We've brought you some grub and two flasks of cocoa. . . . Can you catch ? Here they come," and with a mighty heave he flung a loaded haversack across the water to their feet.

When they got back to the fire Dickie took one look at their burden and brightened considerably.

" Gosh ! " he said. " That's quick. They've found my bottle," and as everybody was too hungry to answer him, he remained convinced that he alone was responsible for this

workmen again. . . . They only got the motor boats over from Rye by road about an hour ago. . . . Somewhere just here, wasn't it, Vasson ? "

" Yes sir," said the porter. " Back of this bungalow with a red sundial and the high rockery. We got in from the rockery and I'll tie up here again. . . . Now then, out you get."

They splashed through the puddles in the strange back garden and found a cheerful, bald little man in an old car in the front. The road was covered with water, but it was not very deep and before long they reached the foot of Winchelsea Hill. Although it was so early and the sun was only just up there were crowds of people standing about in groups with piles of luggage, and many more coming down the hill to see what had happened. Their driver was paid and thanked and Vasson said :

" If you'll wait here, sir, I'll go and find your car which we parked up the lane somewhere. I'll pick you up here in a few minutes."

While they were waiting for him they strolled up the hill and looked at the amazing scene of the levels covered with water which was shining pink in the sunrise. Under the old cliff where the ground was higher, hundreds of sheep were jostling each other frantically and baaing in panic. But many hundreds of valuable sheep were lost that night.

" I want a bath," Penny said suddenly. " I bet I look a sight."

" You nearly had one," David said, and " You certainly do," Jon added.

Penny punched them both and then said to David :

" Your father seems a bit peevish, doesn't he ? He's over there talking to that old man instead of to us. And where are the twins ? "

Nobody seemed to have realized that the twins were not with them. David looked worried.

" I'll get into another row if they disappear again," he said. " There's a big crowd of people down at the foot of the hill by that Inn—seems as if someone's making a speech or giving out a notice or something."

" I wouldn't be surprised if somebody is making a speech ! " Penny said. " From what I can see that somebody is Dickie or Mary or both of 'em."

David looked even more worried. " Come with me, chaps. I'd better tell Father, I s'pose. Come and soften the blow."

Mr. Morton took one look and set off down the hill with long strides. Penny was panting by the time they reached the fringe of the crowd. It was quite a large crowd with several children in the front and five dogs on the outskirts. A small car was parked close against the wall of the Inn and a young man wearing horn-rimmed spectacles and with a lot of hair was leaning towards Dickie and Mary with a notebook in his hand. The Morton twins, flushed with triumph and bright-eyed with excitement and lack of sleep, were seated on the bonnet of the car facing their large and appreciative audience. Macbeth was also seated on the bonnet next to Mary, who was now tying one of her own bedraggled hair ribbons to his collar.

" When are you going to take the photograph ? " they heard her say in her clear treble and they also heard Mr. Morton groan as he tried to force his way through the crowd.

" Orl right ! Orl right ! " said several indignant voices. " No hurry, is there ? Stay where you are and don't shove ! You'll hear just as well from the back."

Another woman was heard to remark that she " got here first and wasn't going to lose her place for any rude gentleman as ought to have better manners, but had seemingly forgotten them ! "

Dickie was speaking now. One hand was grasping a partially consumed bar of chocolate which had been presented to him by a sympathetic onlooker and the other was being waved carelessly in the air by way of emphasis.

" . . . . and jew know what happened next ? O' course you don't. You weren't there. We were the only people there—'cept some men working, and one or two of our friends we let come with us. . . . We were the only ones in the world that knows what happened. . . . Listen. . . . Mary and me will tell you. . . ."

The crowd hung breathless on his words and Mr. Morton whispered to David : " Slip round the back and grab 'em both off that car ! "

" Well," the orator continued, " Mary and me were just wondering whether we ought to help those men by stoppin' up the hole with our bodies. . . ."

" Like the little Dutch boy in the story," Mary interrupted with a winning smile, looking up from her ribbon-tying.

" . . . But the others who were with us were afraid and wouldn't let us. . . . So I stood in the path and told the lorry men where to go, and then suddenly . . . Gosh ! I'm faintin' with hunger.   Could anyone spare a mite of chocolate or a dry crust or something ? "

Again offerings were made and accepted, and while Dickie was filling his mouth Mary took up the tale.

" . . . All alone, we were !   The wind was howlin' and I was blown over six times. . . . You see this little dog ? Almost drowned, he was, 'cos his legs are so short. . . . Well, suddenly there was a mighty roar and a sort of typhoon came and hit the bank, and it all disappeared, and there we were swimmin' and swimmin' . . . OW !   YOU BEASTS ! LET ME GO ! . . ."

" It's you, David, of course," Dickie yelled.   " It would be.   LET ME GO ! "

And in the confusion Mr. Morton got through to the front, smiled grimly upon the crowd and explained that these brave children were his and that he was taking them home to bed !   Then Vasson sounded the horn and the Mortons and the Warrenders retired amidst the murmured appreciation of the crowd, but the young man with the ready pencil seemed particularly disappointed.

Twice on the way home—and Vasson took them by the inland road over the cliffs—Jon tried to tell Mr. Morton the full story.   But he could barely keep awake now, and the words tumbled into each other.

" Don't worry, old man ! " said Mr. Morton.   " Plenty of time to hear everything when you've had a bath and a sleep. . . . Nobody is mad with you, but your mother will be glad to see you."

Dickie and Mary were strangely subdued, and once or twice Penny noticed David smile quietly at his father without speaking.

As they ran down into Rye they could trace the river by its darker, muddy track, but all the levels were covered with water now, and Camber Castle stood forlorn on a little green island.

Dimly Jon remembered stepping out of the car in the

Dolphin yard and noticing a flash of red as Penny pushed him aside and ran over to hug her aunt. There was a lot of confusion and talking ; his mother's arm round his shoulders, Mrs. Morton surrounded by twins, but smiling at him over their heads ; Penny brushing her hand across her eyes ; a steaming hot bath ; cool sheets and a hot-water bottle ; drawn curtains with the sun shining through ; hot soup and dry toast and then blissful drowsiness through which his mother's voice came soothingly.

" Don't worry, old man. I'm sure you did well. . . . Grandon has gone for good . . . he telephoned me last night to say he was never coming back here and that you were all locked in *Beach View.* . . . But we knew that before he rang up, because the lorry-driver back from the beach told the police ; and Vasson had already warned them, too, when I told him Grandon hadn't returned from Hastings . . ." and her hand smoothed his tousled hair just as it had done ten years ago and he slept at last.

CHAPTER XII

THURSDAY—15-6-10

———————

IT was probably because Jon had kept himself awake
when they were marooned on the hill at Winchelsea
beach that he slept so dreamlessly when his mother
left him in bed in the early morning following the great
adventure. After she had gone he remembered nothing
until his bed began to creak and move as if the house were
being shaken by an earthquake.

He grunted, stirred and turned over, but the movement
continued, and as there was nothing he hated more than
being disturbed when sleeping he muttered something that
sounded like "Gerraway!" and pulled the bed-clothes over
his head.

Slowly his dawning intelligence grasped that a well-known
voice was chanting, "WAKE UP, Jonathan! . . . WAKE
UP, Lazybones! Jonathan . . . WAKE UP!"

He tried in vain to slip back into sleep, but the chanting
persisted, so he turned over and groped, as he always did,
for his spectacles beside the bed. Even before he had them
on he realized that his room was glowing with the gold of
the afternoon sun, and that something even redder was
between the bed and the window!

"Penny," he growled, "why can't you leave me alone?
I suppose I've got to lock myself in to be safe from you.
. . . You know I'm no good in the morning. . . . Go
away!"

"But it isn't morning, darling! It's nearly tea-time, and
I've been awake half an hour and nobody seems to be about,
so I thought we'd have a talk at once—just us two, Jon,
if you see what I mean?"

"I know what you mean when you say just the two of
us! Even I can grasp that. But you will come butting in

at such stupid times, Penny. I'm still unconscious, and I want to go to sleep again."

Penny stopped bouncing on the bed and looked at him seriously with her wide grey eyes.

" Will you be decent if I go and get you a cup of tea ? " she asked. " I promise I won't fool about, Jon ; but we must make up our minds what we're going to tell the grown-ups, and if we go down Auntie or somebody will grab us and we shan't know what to say."

Jon sat up. She looked very nice and clean and fresh, he thought, and not a bit as if she'd spent last night in a gale marooned on the top of a storm-swept hill. Funny how girls managed this sometimes ! He ran his fingers through his hair and yawned.

" You all right, Newpenny ? Not pneumonia or any-thing ? "

She gave him a relieved and radiant smile. He was going to be decent after all !

" I'm fine, Jon. My poor old bones ache a bit, though. Are you stiff ? "

" At the moment my legs are paralysed," he said, " but I expect that's because you're sitting on them. . . . Get off and we'll see if I'm likely to be bedridden."

" We'll pretend you are and I've come to visit you. Poor Jonathan. How awful for you ! " and she got off the bed and went over to the window and drew back the curtains. When she spoke again she had her back to him.

" P'raps I was wrong about not telling the grown-ups," she began. " Maybe we wouldn't have got into that mess yesterday if we'd told your mother about what we had found upstairs and all about the clues and everything."

Jon grunted. " Chuck me that pullover. If I've got to sit up and talk I might as well be comfortable. . . . Thanks. . . . Oh ! I dunno, Penny. I expect the grown-ups will say we did lots of things wrong, but I don't think not telling them was too awful. . . . It was just that I wasn't sure what was the best thing to do. I never mind doing things, but sometimes it's knowing when to do them that's so difficult."

She was sitting now over by the window with her hands clasped in her lap and looking suspiciously demure.

" Sometimes," she said, " I loathe you, but other times,

like now, you're quite nice. . . . Now, let's arrange what
to say. I suppose we must tell them everything. . . . Do
you realize, Jon, that after all that excitement yesterday we
haven't found the treasure and that we forgot all about it ?
. . . Let's tell the others all about Miss B. and Slinky—I
wonder what's really happened to them ?—and then have
another meeting and start all over again to find the treasure
by ourselves. . . . Do you know, Jon, I'd give anything to
find that for Auntie. . . . And if those other beasts have
run away, and I bet they have, we shall be able to hunt
properly without interruptions. I'm sure there must be a
treasure or the Ballinger wouldn't have been so keen to get
the map and an answer to the clue."

" Go away and leave me in peace," Jon groaned. " You're
always worrying me to do something you've thought of.
. . . Go and cool your red head somewhere, ducky. Go and
hold it in a draught while I dress. . . . When I come down
I'll get Mother to ask the Mortons to come and have whatever
meal is due next, and then we must tell them all what we
know. . . ."

" You said just now it didn't matter about not telling
them, Jon ! Now we're so near let's go on by ourselves."

" We're not near, you chump ! We're no nearer than we
were when we got to earthen vessels. . . . Now get out,
or I'll throw things at you."

Sadly Penny departed. Over her shoulder she gave him a
soulful and reproachful look and then slipped out hurriedly
when he bent under the bed for a slipper.

When Jon came downstairs she was sitting on the arm
of one of the big leather chairs in the lounge talking to her
aunt. A log was smouldering on the iron dogs and the
sun slanted in through the windows, set Penny's red curls
aflame, and then settled in a golden pool on the floor. Jon
walked over and kissed his mother, and before he could
change his mind, said :

" We've got such a lot to tell you, Mother, but, if you
don't mind, the Mortons have been such sports—and I'm
sure Mr. Morton will be able to help us now—that I wondered
if we could all have tea together in here and talk it over. . . .
Did I dream it or did you tell me that Grandon has gone for
good ? "

" Yes, he's gone. . . . I expect we've got a lot to tell each other, and Penny wouldn't say a word until you came. . . . I don't mind about the Mortons, Jon, but do you really think they want to be bothered with our business ? "

" What's that about the Mortons ? " said a cheerful voice from the door. " Or is this a family council, Mrs. War-render ?   You know, I'm losing count of meals and I shudder to think what a state Richard will be in when he wakes up. . . . I couldn't help overhearing what you said just now, and I do hope you will let us help you in any way we can. We'd like to feel we're friends now besides being the *Dolphin's* first guests."

And so it was arranged, for it was difficult to reject such friendliness ; and Vasson wheeled in two big trolleys piled with toast and tea and jam and crumpets and cakes.   The twins, with flushed and shining faces and neatly parted hair, and David still smothering a yawn, came in with their mother and they all sat round the fire.   Just before they started Jon whispered to David that he was going to tell the grown-ups everything.

David nodded.   " You know best.   It's your show, any-way, and not ours. . . . I've just had a letter I want to show you as soon as I can."

When the trolleys had been pushed aside and the grown-ups had lit their cigarettes, Jon told the story from the beginning.   Once, when he got to the secret passage, his mother interrupted, and twice Penny helped him, but he told everything that had happened to them clearly and well. Mrs. Morton had some difficulty in keeping the twins quiet, but they both struggled gallantly not to spoil Jon's story by adding their own unique contribution.

" And so, you see, sir," Jon finished, turning to Mr. Morton, " that although we are sure that they stole the actual clue we are just as certain that they never got as far as ' earthen vessels.' "

" The solving of that clue was very clever work." Mr. Morton replied.   " You were smarter than they were.   Can you remember what the parchment was like, Jon ?   I mean, how big was it ? "

Jon frowned.   " Oh, quite small, really. 'Bout four inches wide and the writing was very spidery and old-fashioned, but it was clear enough. If you'll lend me a pencil, sir, I'll try and draw it."

When he had passed it over, Mr. Morton looked at Mrs. Warrender.

" I believe these children are really on the track of something," he said, " but do please say if you'd rather we didn't investigate this any further. It is, after all, entirely your business, and I wouldn't have you think . . ."

But Mrs. Warrender made it clear that she would be grateful for any help he could give them. So Jon fetched the map, which he spread out on the floor so that they could all see it.

They all examined it again for a long time until finally Mr. Morton got up from his knees and lit his pipe.

" There are too many coincidences," he said at last, " for this to be a fake, and I really do believe there is treasure hidden round here somewhere. Jon may be right in this theory about it being hidden in an old Roman vase. A smuggler on the Marsh is likely to have unearthed Roman remains and I dare say you all noticed that the map showed a route across the Marsh to this place—and I think they must mean the *Dolphin*, because it's specially emphasized on the map."

" We're sure this is a smugglers' inn, Mr. Morton," Penny broke in excitedly. " And when you see our room upstairs and the passage you'll be sure, too. . . . We think smugglers hid from the King's men in our room."

" That's something we've never done," Dickie said. " Smugglin', I mean. Wish we had ! "

Mr. Morton drew at his pipe and picked up the map again.

" And there seems to be a link between the *Dolphin* and Camber, and then the track goes on to the hill on which you sheltered last night and then goes on a little way further towards Cliff End. I believe there was once an old inn on the edge of the beach there, but it was destroyed by the sea some time ago. Anyway, if it wasn't destroyed, then it will have gone last night. We'll ask Vasson, but I think I read somewhere that it was once used by smugglers. . . . I believe there's an extra clue somewhere that you haven't yet found. Do you remember, Jonathan, if the parchment looked as if it had been torn or cut ? "

Jon shook his head. " I can't remember. I don't think so . . . but I tell you what, sir, I believe the message was written at the bottom of the paper."

" I was thinking that perhaps you'd only got hold of half the message. . . . Does Mrs. Warrender mind if we explore the secret passage now ? I think we ought to do that at once. I must admit that I'm as excited as any of you."

Mrs. Warrender smiled. " I don't mind. I haven't seen it yet, you know. Let's go at once. Shall we want candles and torches, Penny ? "

" What I want to know," Dickie said loudly, " is what's happened to the storm and the sea ? Will someone tell me if we are utterly surrounded with water in this place and if the sea is still coming through that hole, and if they've been able to stop it and if *Beach View* is still burning and whether Slinky has been caught and . . ."

Penny grabbed the twins, took them into a corner and told them what she knew and that Vasson had already said that the wind had dropped and that the gap in the bank was being filled.

" We're meeting in your secret room in five minutes," David called, and Penny then excused herself and ran up to her bedroom for a jersey.

There she leaned from her window and sniffed at the breeze coming in from the sea. The storm had long since blown itself out and the sky above the chimney-pots was a delicate egg-shell blue, across which a few white, woolly clouds sailed serenely. For some reason she couldn't explain, Penny felt disappointed and rather sad. She had expected to do so much for her aunt, and although they had certainly all had an amazing adventure, she had really done very little. It was nice of Mr. Morton to be so friendly and helpful, but she did wonder whether he was only pretending that there might be a treasure so that they shouldn't be disappointed.

Yesterday had been fun—specially up on that hill in he night round their camp fire—but now they had got to the explaining part of an adventure and Penny always hated that.

She glanced round into the little walled garden now glowing in the evening sunshine, and noticed at once that the old wall through which the withy tree had been growing had collapsed in the storm and lay now across the flower-bed in a pile of dusty rubble ; and the tree, round which some kindly mason, many years ago, had built the wall, now lay amongst the ruins.

Penny ran down the little stairs to the main corridor, hoping that she would find Jon before the others came. She leaned over the banisters and saw her cousin rather moodily kicking the smouldering logs in the lounge fire.

" Oy ! " she called vulgarly.   " Where are the others ? "

Jon looked up.   " I think they're all changing into clothes suitable for exploration !   What do you want ? "

" I've got something to tell you."

He strolled up and they sat together on the top stair.

" What's up, Penny ?   You look glum. . . . I feel a bit flat, too. . . . Everything seems to have fizzled out, doesn't it ? "

Penny was rather surprised that he felt the same, but she told him quickly of the fallen wall and what it might mean.

" Don't you see, Jon, that the passage may have been filled up ?   We'd better be ready for it.   What do you think Mr. Morton is going to discover ?   I don't really want him to find anything, Jon.   I want *us* to find it."

But before he could answer the others came into the lounge, and they all trooped upstairs together.

Jon unlocked the door of their room and stood aside for the grown-ups to enter first.   Then the twins showed their father the diamond-scratched window-pane, and would have opened the panel immediately if David had not pulled them back.

" Would you like to see the other papers now, sir ? " Jon said.   " Or shall we do the passage first ? "

" I want to see the passage," Mr. Morton replied. " Nothing else really interests me because I've never been in a secret passage before !   We've all got torches. . . . May I suggest that Jon and Penny should lead and Mrs. Warrender go next, because after all the *Dolphin* is hers.   The

Morton parents will guard the rear and the twins and David look after the centre. Agreed ? "

The twins looked as if they wished to disagree very strongly, but an ugly look from David and a nudge from their mother silenced them just as Penny went down on her knees before the panel and cried :

" The trap threads ! I'd forgotten them, Jon. I set these yesterday morning just to see if Slinky came up here. . . . This one hasn't been broken, but I forgot to look at the other one on the landing, although, of course, we shall all have broken it coming in."

" Never mind that now," Jon said. " Press the catch, Penny, and show the ladies and gentlemen ! "

Mrs. Warrender looked at him in surprise, because he sounded a little peevish, but before she could speak the door swung open and they were greeted with the usual stale smell. The twins were twittering with excitement and Jon made amends by smiling at his mother, saying :

" You gave us a grand surprise when you gave us this room, didn't you ? Come and see what we've found."

So with Jon and Penny in the lead, Mrs. Warrender close behind, they stepped into the passage. Their torches gave plenty of light and Jon led them down easily and quickly past the entrance to Slinky's room, where he had to admit that they had not yet discovered a way of opening the panel from this side.

" Are you going to take us as far as the passage goes, Jon ? " Mr. Morton called, " or shall we search the walls and steps for a hiding-place as we go ? "

" Let's do the passage first," Penny pleaded. " You'll all be jolly surprised to know where this comes out. When we've got to the end perhaps Mr. Morton will have an idea about the best way to search for some earthen vessels."

This was agreed, and Jon continued down to the cellars and then into Trader's Passage proper. Penny had turned to explain to her aunt that they were now underneath the steps by the side of the *Dolphin* which led down to the river when Jon stopped suddenly and she bumped into him.

" You clumsy idiot . . ." she began and then saw where his torch was pointing.

" You were right about the roots of the tree, Penny," he was saying. " Look. Shine your torch. Half the roof and the side of the wall is down. . . . Just a sec. . . . There's something odd here. . . . Come here, Newpenny."

Penny caught the excitement in his voice and squeezed up beside him. The twins in the rear set up a querulous duet that " they couldn't get on," but she heard none of this, for she was staring at the spot of light from Jon's torch which was focused on a pile of fallen earth and rubbish almost at his feet.

And so Penny found the treasure after all and Jon stepped quietly back so that the honour should be hers. In the dust of broken masonry and mortar something gleamed and sparkled in the light of the torch and she bent slowly and picked up a string of shimmering diamonds that trickled like fire through her trembling fingers.

The others pressed forward, but Penny was thinking only of her aunt and she turned and flung her arms round her.

" I've found it for you, darling. I wanted it as a surprise for you and we've got it after all. . . . Look, darling ! It's the *Dolphin's* treasure and it belongs to you and we've beaten the Ballingers in the end."

Mrs. Warrender's voice was rather shaky when she managed to disengage herself and then pandemonium broke out as the others tried to see what was happening. Eventually Mr. Morton restored order by leading the way back to the cellars, where there was more room.

" We'd better see if the diamonds are real before we celebrate," he said. " Shall we go back upstairs to the light and see ? "

" I'd like you to see where Penny found them first, sir, if you don't mind," Jon said. " The others might go up with mother and we'll join them in a minute."

So while Penny led the way upstairs again Mr. Morton went back to the broken wall with Jon who went down on his knees in the rubble.

" Look, sir ! Don't you think these bits of clay are the remains of an old vase. I think the necklace was in the vase which must have fallen from somewhere and broken."

" I think you're right, Jon. Let's pick up all the pieces and examine them in the light," but before they went up after the others they found a niche which had been hollowed out of the earth wall behind the roots of the withy tree. It was obvious that as the wall had crashed in the gale it had brought

AND SO PENNY FOUND THE TREASURE AFTER ALL . . . A STRING OF
SHIMMERING DIAMONDS TRICKLED LIKE FIRE THROUGH HER TREMBLING
FINGERS

down the old tree and part of the roof and side of the passage with it. It seemed as if the roots had hidden the cavity holding the clay vase, but Jon had to admit that they had never really searched there and it might have been possible to have found it if they had known where to look.

When they joined the others Mrs. Warrender was putting a match to the dry sticks in the fire-place and Mrs. Morton was fixing the diamonds round Penny's neck.

" Penny says you won't mind if we all stay up here and talk, Jon ? " his mother said from her knees. " She says you can show us all the papers now. . . . Have you found any more treasure ? I don't think I could bear it if you have."

Mr. Morton laughed and shook his head as he emptied the pieces of broken clay from his handkerchief on to the table. And then Penny, with the diamonds blazing round her neck, dashed over to Jon, who was closing the panel.

" You really found the treasure, Jon. You stood out of the way and let me pick them up and then I got so excited I swanked a bit as if I'd found them and it's you as much as me and I'm going to tell everybody . . ."

" Don't be a silly little girl," was all he said as he gave her a push back towards the centre of the room.

Next they showed Mrs. Warrender and the Mortons the other papers and Uncle Charles' letter, and it was while his mother was reading this that Jon turned to Mr. Morton.

" But the clue isn't fair, sir," he said. " That earthen vessel we found might have been hidden anywhere within a hundred miles. How could the holder of the clue possibly know where to look ? "

" I told you before that I believe you've only got half the clue. Where did you find it ? "

" In the Bible. Pinned to the letter Mother is reading now. The letter written to me by Great Uncle Charles."

" Then let's look in the Bible again. Mary, my lass, bring it over to the window if you can lift it ! . . . And may I look at the letter or is it too private ? "

Mrs. Warrender came over with the letter in her hand.

" I heard what you were saying, Mr. Morton. Jon, did you realize that old Uncle Charles says that *clues*, not a clue were attached to his letter. Are you sure there was only one piece of paper ? "

Jon was sure of that and then Mary took the big Bible by the edges of the two covers, turned it upside down and with great difficulty shook the pages. Several things fell out—a pressed flower, an old envelope which contained a baby's curl of hair and a small piece of parchment.

" Got it ! " Jon said triumphantly as he pounced on the latter. " Well done, Mother and Mr. Morton."

" And what about me ? " Mary said. " I acksherley found it," but nobody took any notice of her.

" Penny ! David ! " Jon called. " Look what we've found. I bet this paper would fit the one the others took."

The message on the parchment was very brief :

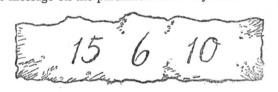

Jon polished his glasses.

" Gosh," he said. " What does this mean ? The other, which I s'pose was written above this before it was torn, said ' nt 8 April 7.' "

" And it was the ' nt ' which set us off on the right track," Penny said. " It's only because we're being properly brought up that we guessed ' nt ' meant New Testament. I was sure Slinky wouldn't know what that was. . . . Try it again, Jon ! It might work. Find the fifteenth book of the New Testament."

Jon took the great book on his knee and turned the pages.

" Timothy I," he said after a lot of turning of pages and counting. . . . " Now Chapter 6. . . . I see what you mean. What an intelligent child you are sometimes, New-penny. . . . I've got it. . . . I've got it ! This must be it. Verse 10 starts : ' *For the love of money is the root of all evil.*' . . . *Root* is the clue I suppose ? Don't you think so, sir ? "

Mr. Morton laughed. " Very ingenious ! I suppose everyone who used the *Dolphin* much would know the withy tree and all the smugglers who used the secret passage would know about the roots, of course. *Earthen vessels.* . . . and then *the root of all evil* is possible."

Mrs. Warrender laughed shakily and held up the diamonds

which Penny had just handed to her, to the fading light from the window.

" If these are real and I think they are," she said, " I'm going to see that the money is properly used and not the root of all evil. . . .! This means lots of extra things for the *Dolphin* and the most important things for Jon and Penny, too . . ." but Penny saw tears in her eyes and changed the subject quickly by asking about Miss Ballinger and Slinky.

Mr. Morton signed to the children to sit on the floor round the fire and then explained as well as he could what the police had told them this morning.

" As far as we could make out from the detective who came over from Hastings. . . ."

" A real detective ? " Dickie interrupted. " A real detective came and you let us stay in bed ? Seems to me we don't even dare to stay asleep now, twin, else something happens."

Mr. Morton ignored the interruption.

" It seems that Miss Ballinger has been watched for some time, because she appears to have had some dubious dealings with antiques and pictures. They had not anything definite against her, but there is no doubt that she was a suspicious character. Grandon was her assistant and accomplice and between them they must have heard of this treasure. It may be that Grandon came to the *Dolphin*—and we haven't found out just exactly when he did come to old Mr. Charles—in order to discover if there really was a treasure. Anyway, the police believe that Miss Ballinger forged the letter recommending Mrs. Warrender to keep Slinky, as you call him so aptly, on at the *Dolphin* and forgery is a serious crime in itself. How and when the passage was discovered we don't know, but almost certainly through the entrance into Grandon's room and this was very lucky for him. . . . But, of course, Ballinger was the brains and the police are very keen to find her and her pretty niece as soon as possible."

" Have they got anything against that girl ? " Jon asked.

" We didn't ask and we don't know whether she really is a niece or just an accomplice. What was she like, Jon ? Did she try to tempt you ? "

" Jon's blushing ! " Mary announced brutally, and was then pushed into the background by her mother.

David came to th rescue of his friend. " Whatever she

may have done wrong she did come back after Ballinger had locked us in. She smashed the window and threw in the key of the front room where the twins were, and I'm sure she was against leaving us there, anyway, and that's something in her favour."

" I still don't know everything you've been doing these last few days," Mrs. Warrender said to her two, " but I s'pose you will tell the old people some time, won't you ? Meanwhile I think Mrs. Morton will agree that it should be early bed for everybody to-night."

" But we've only just got up," Dickie protested.

" Might as well have stayed in our pyjamas," Mary added.

" I'm not going to bed *again*," said Penny, and " You don't really mean that, do you Mother ? " Jon asked.

" Anyway, I'm jolly hungry," Dickie went on, " and it's bad to go to bed on an empty stummick."

But it was David, the only one to remain silent, who had the bright idea.

" It's rather a special occasion," he pleaded, " and I don't think any of us could sleep—not even the twins—if we did go to bed. I'm going to ask Dad to help us finish off the day in style and drive us down to the beach so that we can watch them mending the bank and climb up our hill again. . . . It's not cold and the moon will be up later and I don't suppose any of us will ever see such a sight again. Acksherley, as Dickie would say, I think we ought to go because it's so very educational ! "

Protests from Mrs. Morton and Mrs. Warrender were swept aside in the enthusiasm which followed this argument and the twins dashed down for coats and rugs. Mrs. Warrender produced two thermos flasks and filled pockets with cake and then stood under the archway with Mrs. Morton to see them off.

Penny sat in front with Mary and Mr. Morton and watched the sun sink down behind Winchelsea Hill as the car splashed along the straight road that crossed the levels. To their left the grass was still covered with water and Camber Castle was surrounded by the widest moat its walls had ever seen. On the other side the marsh was higher and although in some places the dikes had overflowed, the flooding was not so severe. In a few places the roadway was under a few inches of water and everywhere else the surface was treacherous with slime and mud, but they ran along steadily enough until they turned into the narrower road leading to the beach. In many places here the road was completely under water still and there had been so much heavy traffic on it that the surface was badly broken up.

" Lucky we had the sense to bring rubber boots," Jon said from the back. " We'll all have to walk soon," and in another few minutes Mr. Morton turned the car off the flooded road into the garage entrance of a deserted bungalow.

" Wouldn't like to go back now, I suppose ? " he said as he opened the door. " It's not going to be an easy walk ! "

This remark was greeted with howls of derision and so they splashed along the track which led directly to the beach until they were stopped by a large policeman.

" Sorry, zur, but my orders is no sightzeers. You'll have to go back."

Mary edged to the front and looked up at him appealingly.

Dickie began, " But you can't say that to *us*. You don't know who we are. Why, we're the people who . . ."

The policeman regarded the small boy without much interest and Mr. Morton intervened hurriedly and explained that these were the children who had been marooned all night on the hill and of their connection with Miss Ballinger of *Beach View*. Then there was a crackle of paper and something passed between Mr. Morton and the constable, who was heard to say :

" Strickly irregular, o' course, zur. Thank you kindly, zur. I'll be here when you come back. Better not let those youngsters get too near those cranes."

The track which they knew so well was now a mass of churned-up mud and shingle. In some places bundles of faggots had been laid down in an attempt to make a surface fit for traffic, but so much of it had slipped down into the water that the lorries would never be able to get back until the floods had subsided. They scrambled along the top of the shingle bank on the right of the track until they reached their hill and climbed up to the old hut. From here they could see an army of men filling the great gap. A huge mechanical excavator was at work and fire engines were pumping water from the pits which the incoming sea had torn in the soft earth. As the light faded the strange scene was lit by searchlights from the fire engines and even on the bank, fires, made by the workmen, flickered weirdly in the dusk.

" I want to see that digger machine working," Dickie said. " Will you take me, Daddy ? Or shall we have the cake first ? "

" I'll come, too," Mary said. " An' I can't see why we can't eat cake as we go."

The others watched them go down the hill, pick their way through some pools, and climb the great bank.

" Funny," said David, " but we've hardly had a chance to say a word to each other since last night—or this morning, wasn't it ? . . . I never told you, Penny, how glad I was you found the treasure after all. . . . But last night was the best fun, wasn't it ? . . . I've got a letter I want to talk to you about."

Jon and Penny were leaning against the hut looking out over the burned-out ruin of *Beach View* to the sea. It was a good idea to have come back here, because it was always fun to live an adventure over again in the same place, and they were both thinking that nothing that could ever happen to them would be as exciting as the adventure of the *Gay Dolphin's* treasure. Jon was thinking, although he did not say so, how plucky Penny must have been with the twins in that locked room in the dark and how splendid it had been of her not to write the note to him. And Penny was thinking —and she was too shy to say so—how calm and steady Jon had been when he rescued them and how certain she had been that he would come in the end just because he had never let her down. And so although they both liked David very much, they were not really listening to what he was saying, but just enjoying their thoughts and each other's company as good friends always can.

" Wake up, you two. I want to tell you about this letter I've had from Peter."

Penny grinned and stretched her arms over her head. " Sorry ! I was dreaming. Tell us about Peter. . . . Wake up, Jon ! It's too cold to sit down, I s'pose, but I don't mind telling you two I'm too tired to walk about."

David took a crumpled letter from his pocket.

" I think I told you that we've a secret club," he began. " We started it up at Witchend in Shropshire, and it was really Peter's idea."

" Who's in it ? " Penny asked.   " I love secret societies."

" Peter and the twins and me, of course, and a grand chap called Tom Ingles, and a jolly girl called Jenny. She hasn't done much yet, but she's good fun and had a big adventure with us. . . . I think I told you that Peter couldn't come to the *Dolphin* with us this time, but I wrote and told her a bit about you both, and how we were going to help you find the treasure. Of course, she doesn't know what a marvellous adventure we have had, but in the letter I had from her this morning she says that if I agree we'd like you to be members of the Lone Pine Club as well. . . . Here. . . . I'll read it to you. Got a torch, Jon ? Thanks. Here it is. . . ."

" ' You don't know how sick I am at missing a hunt for treasure and you must write and tell me everything that happens. I met Tom yesterday in Onnybrook and told him about you, and he said it was just like the pictures but he always says that. Then we had two ices and got talking and we think you had better ask Jon and Penny if they would like to be members, too, because they sound like good chaps. It's no good them joining if we can't all meet and perhaps they could come up here somewhere next hols. Christmas hols. are never the most fun after Christmas is over. Ask them, David, and report back, and give my love to the twins. I do wish I could have come, but I know I was right to stay with Daddy. . . .' "

David stuffed the letter back in his pocket and switched off the torch.

" That's about all," he said. " Will you ? I'd like you to."

Penny squeezed Jon's arm. " I'd love it," she said, " and thank you for asking us."

" Of course we will," Jon said. " Grand ! And that's a good idea about next hols."

Before David could answer, there came from below them the mournful whistle of a peewit. " Peeee-wit. Peeee-wit ! "

" What's that ? " Penny asked.

" I'll teach you that," David laughed. " That's the signal of the Lone Piners. . . . Here we are, Dickie. We'll flash the torch."

In a few minutes the twins came toiling up the hill.

" Daddy can't make it," Mary panted. " He's miles behind."

Dickie flung himself down beside her.

" Jew know what that man in the big shovel thing said to me ? He said if I didn't clear out of the way he'd drive the beastly thing at me and dump me in the sea. . . . I wondered whether I'd let him."

He turned round and faced the sea and for a minute they all stood, waiting for Mr. Morton and watching the line of the sea, the flooded levels and the light of Dungeness winking its warning and an answer to the faint flash of distant Gris Nez on the coast of France.

" It's most peculiar," Dickie went on, " But it's Thursday still and we only came on Monday. Things do happen to us chaps. I wonder what we shall do to-morrow ? "

Westend Farmhouse,
    Wheathampstead.
January–May, 1945.

The other books
about the Lone Pine Club
are
MYSTERY AT WITCHEND
SEVEN WHITE GATES
and
THE SECRET OF GREY WALLS

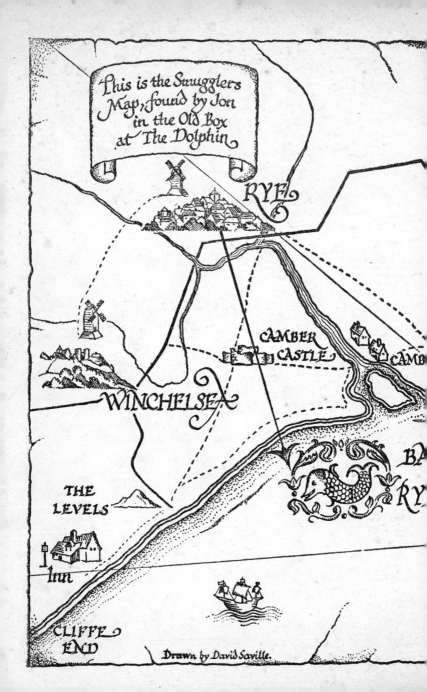